RIPPED OFF

ALSO BY JEANNE GLIDEWELL

A Lexie Starr Mystery Series

Leave No Stone Unturned

The Extinguished Guest

Haunted

With This Ring

Just Ducky

Cozy Camping

Marriage and Mayhem

The Spirit of the Season

A Ripple Effect Cozy Mystery Series

A Rip Roaring Good Time

Rip Tide

Ripped To Shreds

Rip Your Heart Out

Ripped Apart

Ripped Off

No Big Rip

Soul Survivor

RIPPED OFF

A RIPPLE EFFECT COZY MYSTERY, BOOK 6

JEANNE GLIDEWELL

Judy —
Thanks for
your editing
skills. Hope you are
doing well!
Huss! ☺

Jeanne Glidewell

ePublishingWorks!
love what you read.

Book and cover design by eBook Prep
www.ebookprep.com

May, 2021
ISBN: 978-1-64457-181-1

ePublishing Works!
644 Shrewsbury Commons Ave
Ste 249
Shrewsbury PA 17361
United States of America

www.epublishingworks.com
Phone: 866-846-5123

DEDICATION

Like most of the world, I was pretty much under "house arrest" throughout the Covid-19 Pandemic of 2020, and wrote Ripped Off in record time. Early on during the pandemic, a member of our extended family, Eric Goodman, was lucky to survive the coronavirus. He spent nearly a month in the hospital and was on a respirator much of that time. Thankfully, he pulled through and has made a remarkable recovery. Later in 2020, one of our dearest friends, Kathleen Smith, died from complications of the virus, as did several other friends and acquaintances.

I'm dedicating this book not only to them, but to all of the victims of Covid-19 and their families. We've lost way too many people to this horrific virus. Practically every single person in the world has been impacted by the pandemic: through job loss, financial issues, contraction of the virus, sickness and/or death of a loved one due to the virus, social distancing, depression and/or loneliness, rigid stay-at-home orders, toilet paper, disinfectant, and other product shortages, and many other factors. (What was the deal with the toilet paper hoarding, anyway?)

I'd like to believe we learned something from this pandemic, whether it be the stockpiling of personal protective equipment for our front-line medical employees, personal hygiene, or simply the most efficient and effective way to fight a rogue virus such as Covid-19. If, and when, it happens again, we'll hopefully be more prepared. We now have a new normal—neither better nor worse—just different. If arrested, I can no longer provide finger-prints, as the creases in my fingertips have been scrubbed off. But I will continue to wash my hands religiously, and I hope you do too! I encourage everyone to get the vaccine, if not for their own protection, then for those nearest and dearest to them. We have to band together to defeat this adversary.

Stay safe, healthy, and happy!

Jeanne Glidewell

FROM THE DESK OF JEANNE GLIDEWELL

I'd like to thank you for giving this cozy mystery a chance, whether this is your first time reading a *Ripple Effect* (or *Lexie Starr)* mystery, or you've faithfully read every one of them. Your patronage means more to me than I can say. I can guarantee I'll never write the all-American Classic, like Harper Lee's *To Kill a Mockingbird*, or an edge-of-your-seat, gripping thriller like Stephen King writes. But I do hope you find my stories entertaining. If so, I'd appreciate you taking the time to post an online review. Along with other eRetailer sites, posting a book review on Amazon, Barnes & Noble, and Goodreads is beneficial to both authors and readers. I love hearing from readers and I respond to every message I get. Please contact me at glide1022@att.net.

Happy reading,

Jeanne

CHARACTER LIST

Rapella Ripple - this woman is a nosy, interfering, opinionated, and blunt seventy-year-old. But she's also persevering, gutsy, and committed to seeing that justice is served.

Clyde "Rip" Ripple - Rapella's husband is a patient man who tries to help Rapella discover the truth behind Trey Monroe's death while keeping her alive and on the right side of the law.

Tiffany Carpenter - Rip and Rapella's granddaughter, who is celebrating her thirtieth birthday, unwittingly finds herself being her "Gram's" partner in crime-solving.

Chase Carpenter - Tiffany's husband has invested every dime of his and his wife's savings with an investment firm that isn't as trustworthy as he'd expected. Chase's lack of research lands him in the doghouse.

Trey Monroe - as the owner of Monroe Investments, this investment manager is a close friend of the Carpenters. Whether or not the Clean Sweep IPO fund he promotes to his clients turns out to be a profitable investment for them remains to be seen.

Sandy Monroe - Trey's wife has found herself a good-looking house manager to lean on when the unexpected happens.

Manuel de la Cruz - this physician's assistant finds himself with a new profession that offers more appealing fringe benefits than his previous one.

Howard Hancock III - this elderly neighbor of the Monroes, a retired real estate broker of luxury homes and Trey's largest investor, becomes incensed when his money goes missing.

Babs Hancock - Howard's wife tries to be helpful, but it's hard to trust her "observations." Sadly, she's in the early stages of dementia, or Alzheimer's.

Chen Ho - this bail bondsman is Trey's second-largest investor. He's been fighting prostate cancer, but it's his cronies who scare Rapella.

Harlei Rycoff - Trey Monroe's personal assistant at Monroe Investments is stunned by her boss's immoral actions. She supplies Rapella with useful information, which helps Rapella get to the truth behind Trey's death.

Detective Carlos Gutierrez - the lead detective on the case becomes a friend of Rip's. He agrees to let the Ripples look into the case, as long as they promise to never tell another living soul he did so.

ONE

"Surprise!" I exclaimed as I threw my arms around my granddaughter in a long-awaited hug. We hadn't seen Tiffany and her husband, Chase Carpenter, in two years. My husband, Clyde "Rip" Ripple, and I had traveled from Rockport, Texas, to the foothills of the Sandia Mountains in Albuquerque, New Mexico, to surprise Tiffany for her thirtieth birthday. As full-time RVers, we'd spent the last couple of months in Rockport helping our daughter and son-in-law, Regina and Milo Moore, recover from Hurricane Harvey.

"Oh, Grams and Gramps!" Tiffany began to sob as I embraced her at the entrance to her home. Afterward, she leaned down to give Rip a warm hug. At five-feet-ten inches, Tiffany was several inches taller than her grandfather. She briefly rubbed his protruding paunch as she released him, having always said it was for good luck because his bald head and beer belly reminded her of Buddha. "I'm so glad to see you both. Grams, your hair has gone from salt-and-pepper to beautiful silver, and the new short style looks great. You look a lot like Jamie Lee Curtis now."

"Thanks, sweetheart." I grinned at the compliment from

Tiffany, who smiled back through her tears. I soon realized those tears were not ones of happiness like mine were. Her tall, thin frame—which she'd inherited from her father—looked hunched over, as if she was suffering from the beginning stages of osteoporosis. Her eyes, which were the exact same shade of blue as mine, were bloodshot and swollen. She seemed genuinely distraught. I'd hoped we'd make her day, not make her weep. "What's wrong, sweetheart?"

"Chase just got home from running an errand of some kind and told me Trey is dead."

"Oh, dear, I'm so sorry." I enveloped her in my arms again, stroking her back as she shed tears on my shoulder. "Who's Trey?"

"Trey Monroe and his wife, Sandy, are two of our best friends. Trey *was* one of our best friends, I should say." At the thought of having to use Trey's name in the past tense, Tiffany's crying began anew.

"What happened to him?" Rip asked gently.

"We don't know yet. All Chase heard was that Trey had gone to the Double Eagle II Airport to catch a flight and suddenly dropped dead in the airport's parking garage."

"Oh, my! How awful," I said in commiseration.

"I know." Tiffany sniffed. "Chase is so upset."

"Where is Chase now, Tiff?" Rip asked.

"He was in the garage when you rang the doorbell."

"I'll go talk to him for a few minutes." Rip kissed Tiffany's cheek before heading to the garage.

"Thank you, Gramps!" Tiffany said as he walked off. "Seeing you will certainly help."

A new round of weeping commenced, and I waited for Tiffany to rein in her emotions. When her sobbing abated, I asked, "How did the four of you meet?"

"I was hired to photograph their wedding through an ad I'd

placed online. The four of us quickly became fast friends, and Trey acted as our investment manager, as well. He convinced Chase to invest in an IPO, and hopefully, we stand to make tons of money from our investment."

I didn't know what an IPO was, but I would Google it later. I didn't want Tiffany to think Grams was behind the times. "That's wonderful. How nice to have a venture pay off so splendidly."

"Yeah. It was a tech company that soared after it went public. Trey was going to sell it for us today." For a brief second, I saw Tiffany smile; it was that of the rich kitty who'd eaten the solid gold canary. Had I blinked, I would've missed it. "I sure hope he completed the transaction before he…well, you know."

"Yes, I know. But that's neither here nor there right now. The most important thing is your dear friend lost his life."

"That's true. But I'm worried about our finances, too. I don't know exactly how much money Chase invested, but I know it was quite a bit. We wanted to sell our portion of the Clean Sweep IPO fund before everyone starts cashing out now that its six-month lockout period is over."

"I'm sure your money is safe and that Trey took care of all his obligations before heading to the airport for a trip out of town." I wasn't familiar with IPO funds, tech stocks, and lockout periods, but I did think it was a little shallow of Tiffany to be so stressed out about the financial aspect of the tragedy. It seemed to me she should limit her focus to Trey's sudden death. "I think it'd be better for you to just concentrate on the loss of your friend for now."

"You're right, Grams. The financial part of it will work itself out. As you said, I'm sure Trey made the sale before he decided to leave town." With a smile, she reached out to give me another hug. "I'm so glad you two are here. Thanks for the wonderful surprise."

"We are thrilled to be here, sweetheart. We've been looking forward to spending time with our favorite granddaughter."

Tiffany laughed. Knowing she was our only granddaughter, it was a quip that always tickled her funny bone. "I look forward to spending time with you and Gramps, too. After finding out about Trey's death, Chase told me he'd planned a surprise party for tomorrow night to celebrate my birthday. We didn't know how we could celebrate anything after this horrible news, so we've decided to cancel it and just have a quiet dinner here at home."

Tiffany had a point. To host any kind of party the day after one of your best friends suffered an untimely death sounded cold and heartless.

"I'm so sorry, honey."

"Thanks. I'm not overly upset about having to call off the party. Considering what's happened, it was necessary."

"We'll make sure to celebrate your birthday in style, even if it's just the four of us. But for now, I'm sure you have a lot of phone calls to make," I said, "so we won't keep you. After Rip chats with Chase, Gramps and I will go back to the RV park and get settled into our site."

"All right. After you rest up from your trip, can you come back around seven for supper? I'm sure we'll have found out more about Trey's death by then, and perhaps more about the investment money, as well. And I actually *do* have a lot of calls to make. Bruiser's Barbecue, who Chase had hired to cater the event, raised a fuss but finally decided to let us cancel without paying a stiff penalty for the last-minute cancellation. There's still five or six people who were invited to the party we've been unable to reach, including Sandy. I've called a dozen times, but my calls always go to her mailbox, which is now full. She's probably being bombarded with calls or has just turned her phone off while she grieves. And it's not like she'd still be planning to attend a birthday party after the unexpected loss of her husband."

"I think I'd turn the phone off if I were in her shoes. The emotional support would be appreciated, but it'd be awfully tough to answer a lot of questions this soon after Trey's death." I gave Tiffany another hug. "Would you like me to fix something for supper tonight?"

"No, but thanks for the offer. Why don't we just have a couple of pizzas delivered? Would that be okay?"

"That's more than okay. We love pizza." *Not so much the agonizing heartburn that comes with it*, I could've added. Naturally, I didn't. Both seventy years old, Rip and I suffered from acid reflux. His heartburn was so severe I often wondered if he was having another heart attack. Rip had recently undergone a triple bypass following an attack that occurred while we were on our golden wedding anniversary cruise to Alaska. That was not an experience either one of us wanted to repeat. "We'll pick up the tab for dinner. Order some breadsticks too, if you'd like."

Tiffany looked truly touched. "But, you and Gramps are our guests."

"Regardless, we'd like to pay for supper." I gave Tiffany a quick final hug before walking back to our truck. "See you in a couple of hours, honey. Again, I'm sorry for the loss of your friend."

We'd reserved a site at the Route 66 RV Resort, a park only a short drive from the Carpenters' middle-class housing development. We didn't want to be underfoot during our stay. Plus, traveling with Dolly, our tubby grey and white tabby, it was always best if we stayed in the Chartreuse Caboose. The unusual name of our thirty-foot travel trailer was based on the color I'd painted the exterior to make it stand out in a crowded campground or Wal-Mart parking lot. The colorful sunflowers I'd added just enhanced its uniqueness. According to our daughter, it also greatly elevated the level of the trailer's eyesoreness.

As Rip and I drove back to the campground, I relayed my conversation with Tiffany.

"Chase was very upset about his buddy's death," Rip replied before cocking his head to the side. "Rapella, honey, what's an IPO?"

"An IPO is an initial public offering." I'm sure I sounded as if I was patronizing him, despite the fact I'd only known what an IPO was for about fifteen minutes. "It's when a company launches into the stock market and sells shares of their company to institutional and retail investors."

"Yeah, okay." Clearly unimpressed with my knowledge, Rip asked, "Just Googled that, didn't you?"

I nodded with a laugh.

Rip grinned. "What's for supper tonight?"

"Pizza and garlic breadsticks at Tiffany and Chase's house."

"Oh, good grief. I can taste the acid reflux already." Rip clutched his chest in mock anguish. "Don't forget to bring the Tums."

"I won't. Oh, and we're paying for the meal, too."

"In more ways than one, I'm sure."

That evening, we discussed Trey's death as we sat around the Carpenters' kitchen table dining on the Chicago-style, deep-dish pizza they'd had delivered. Our conversation stopped when Chase's phone rang. Looking devastated, he listened to the caller for only a few minutes before ending the call. His expression was like that of a man whose favorite football team had just lost the Super Bowl by missing a twenty-four-yard field goal attempt with one second left on the clock.

"What's wrong, son?" Rip asked.

"I've got good news and bad news. It seems Trey was

murdered. Someone apparently injected him with a large dose of fentanyl shortly before he collapsed at the airport." Chase now looked angry rather than upset, which baffled me.

"Oh, no!" Tiffany sniffled. "I can't imagine anyone who might want to kill one of the nicest, sweetest guys we've ever met."

"Right now, I can think of a few who might." Chase shoved his phone into his back pocket as he spoke.

"What?" A befuddled Tiffany, Rip and I asked in unison.

"Never mind." Chase was growing more upset with each second that passed. He pushed his Coors Lite bottle away so roughly, it tilted, and a big dollop of beer splashed out on the wooden table. I quickly wiped the spillage away with my napkin.

"So, what's the good news?" Tiffany asked.

"That *was* the good news." Chase had all three of us putting our pizza down with that remark. "The bad news is he cleaned out all of his clients' accounts yesterday, including ours, according to Harry Rouse, a friend of ours who is also one of Trey's clients. That was Harry on the phone just now. He told me his wife, Gloria, had just gotten off the phone with Trey's personal assistant."

"What?" Tiffany repeated, taking the one-word question right out of my mouth, and probably Rip's as well. "Are you saying Trey stole *all* of our money?"

"That's exactly what I'm saying."

"He can't do that, can he?" Tiffany's expression was one of pure disbelief. I could almost visualize their plans to move to a nicer house going up in smoke in her mind as she spoke.

"Apparently, he can, and he did. After we learn more about Trey's death, I'll place a call to his personal assistant, Harlei Rycoff. Harry said Harlei told Gloria she has no idea what happened to the proceeds from the sale of the IPO fund or the rest of Trey's clients' portfolios. The money hasn't been deposited into any of our accounts, as if it disappeared into thin air. The flight Trey was about to board was scheduled to land at the Owen Roberts International Airport in Grand Cayman. Although she told Gloria she had no way of knowing for sure at this point, Harlei believes Trey might've been skipping town when he was killed, and all of his clients' money could possibly have been deposited into an offshore account in the Cayman Islands."

"Perhaps he was just taking a much-needed vacation," I suggested.

"By himself?" Chase asked. "His wife, Sandy, knew nothing about the trip. Not to mention, he was found with a one-way ticket to Grand Cayman in his possession."

We all sat suspended in a state of shock.

"I don't get it." Tiffany was the first to speak. "What does that mean?"

"It means it appears as if we've been ripped off!" Now Chase was furious, to the point his cheeks were more crimson than the dab of marinara sauce clinging to his moustache. "It also means we're almost broke. I invested every dollar I could scrape up with Trey."

"Every dollar?" Following her husband's nod, Tiffany replied angrily. "What a no good, slimy rat bastard!"

Wow! Tiffany went from describing Trey as "one of the nicest, sweetest men they'd ever met" to a "no good, slimy rat bastard" in less than thirty seconds. I'd have to check the *Guinness Book of World Records* to see if she'd broken the record for the quickest 180-degree turn-around of all time. Of course, that's assuming she was referring to the man who'd ripped them off, and not her husband who'd invested all their money in such a risky gamble to begin with.

I was setting a new personal record myself; my heartburn was already intense, and I'd only taken two bites of pizza. Or maybe that was just my gut telling me Rip and I were in for another bumpy ride. We couldn't just sit back when our only granddaughter and her husband were in such dire straits. We'd have to do our best to find out if the funds Trey had stolen from his clients had truly been deposited in an offshore account, as his personal assistant suspected. And if not, where were the funds now? Folks like Chase and Tiffany, as well as Harry and Gloria Rouse, deserved their money back.

In the process of doing that, we might find out who killed Trey Monroe. Even if the man was a con artist and a thief, he deserved justice for his death. Whoever killed him should pay for their crime. My mind whirled with questions. Had one of his investors taken getting ripped off just a little too personally and exacted revenge? Only time would tell.

TWO

D inner that night was a subdued affair. It was a far cry from the joyous occasion I'd envisioned when we'd first planned to surprise our granddaughter for her thirtieth birthday. Tiffany's mood waffled back and forth from sorrow to indignation. Chase seethed internally while outwardly defending his decision to invest every dime of his and Tiffany's money he could scrounge up.

"I knew Clean Sweep stock would come out of the gate pumping on all cylinders and shoot right up in value," he claimed. "And I was right, wasn't I?"

I glanced at Tiffany, who remained tight-lipped. I started to speak but caught Rip's warning glance. "Stay out of it," was his unspoken message.

When Tiffany failed to respond, Chase repeated his inquiry, "Well, wasn't I right?"

"I suppose," Tiffany finally replied. "Even so, it doesn't make us any less broke."

"I realize that, Tiffany. I guess it's a damned good thing I backed out of the negotiations on that new house in Sandia

Heights today after I checked our account several times and the money from the IPO fund sale had yet to show up."

"Yeah." The tone of Tiffany's one-word response spoke volumes. She was clearly upset about losing out on a home she'd dreamed of owning. She appeared to be silently fuming at Chase as he continued.

"How was I to know we were being conned by a guy we thought was such a good friend? If you had any clue he was setting us up to rob us blind, you should have said something!" Chase's voice had shot up a couple of notches. He was too angry to care that he was making his guests feel uncomfortable. At least now I understood why Tiffany was so concerned about their finances earlier that day. She'd probably had her heart set on a fancier house in a more upscale neighborhood. Their current home was nice, and certainly comfortable, but it wasn't spacious enough to accommodate a growing family if and when they decided to have children.

Tiffany threw Rip and me an apologetic smile, before responding to her husband. "Perhaps you should have said something to me before cleaning out our savings account to invest with a guy you hadn't known all that long. At least it sounds as if Trey got our shares in the fund sold for us."

"He didn't sell it for us, Tiffany," Chase said. "He never invested our money in the IPO to begin with. It was a scam from the beginning. I should've known it was too good to be true."

"You know what they say about things that sound too good to be true," Tiffany began. "It's because—"

"—they are," Chase finished in an aggravated tone. "I don't need you rubbing salt in my wounds right now. I'm torn up enough already, knowing I foolishly invested in Trey's Clean Sweep Ponzi scheme."

"You got that part right, at least," Tiffany said with bitterness in her voice. Her voice had risen too. "It looks like Trey cleaned us out in one clean sweep."

I thought Tiffany's play on words was clever. But, Chase? Not so much. Glaring at his spouse, he spat out, "Yeah. Real cute, Tiffany. I get it! I'm a total screw-up! You should have known that when you agreed to marry me."

"I believe this is the best crust I've ever tasted!" I exclaimed.

"It is good, isn't it?" Rip chimed in, aware that I was trying to change the subject to something less confrontational. But my attempt was in vain. My words went over both of Tiffany's and Chase's heads like a clay pigeon about to be reduced to shards by a twelve-gauge shotgun.

"I wonder what kind of cheese is baked inside of it," I continued. "I'd guess provolone, but it could be——"

"Screw you, Chase!" Tiffany shouted, clearly not caring whether the crust contained provolone or ricin mixed with arsenic. Ignoring me completely, she jumped to her feet as her eyes welled up with tears. The abrupt motion caused her chair to tilt and fall backward to the tile floor. The resounding thud resonated around the small dining room. Chase pushed back from the table immediately afterward. His chair slammed into the dining room wall so hard it left a permanent crease in the sheetrock. Rip and I could've been flies on the wood-slate blinds for all the attention the couple gave us as they stormed out of the room in different directions.

"I think it's mozzarella, dear," Rip said. He shook his head and rolled his eyes simultaneously. I gave him a dumbfounded look, stunned by his lack of concern. "Don't fret, Rapella. Young couples can have volatile spats like this one minute and be steaming up the sheets the next. Don't you remember the old days when we were young and our emotions swung back and forth like a pendulum?"

"Honey, I don't remember what happened last week, much

less back in the old days. However, I doubt we were ever that disrespectful toward each other. I just hope their marriage can withstand such a shocking turn of events."

"Don't worry," he said, as he winked at me from across the table. "I promise you they'll be having hot make-up sex tonight. In fact, as soon as we finish eating, we should get out of here so they can talk it out and get their feathers all unruffled. This house is just too small for a private conversation. And, speaking of hot sex, I might be in the mood for some luke-warm canoodling myself tonight."

"Well, it'll have to be by yourself, because I'm beginning to get a headache already." I laughed at Rip's comical expression following my response and threw a breadstick at him.

"Bummer," he mumbled.

As Rip ate, I leaned back in my seat and nibbled on a piece of pizza crust. Rip was right. It *was* mozzarella, and very tasty. But after witnessing the nasty quarrel between Tiffany and Chase, I'd lost my appetite. Rip, however, polished off three slices of pizza, topped generously with several kinds of meat, extra cheese, mushrooms, and gobs of marinara sauce, along with two breadsticks, including the one I'd thrown at him. It'd take a good deal more than a suppertime disagreement to ruin his appetite. He could probably witness a sewer rat leave a calling card on the pizza and still eat from the part of the pie without the extra "toppings."

I left the rest of the pizza and breadsticks on the table, but carried our plates to the kitchen and placed them in the dishwasher before we headed back to the Chartreuse Caboose. We'd signed up for a week's stay at the RV resort, which offered a ten-percent discount for Good Sam members, but I had a sneaking suspicion our reservation would be extended before all was said and done.

It was October twenty-first, but still a comfortable evening in the campground, which was an extremely nice facility along I-40, a few miles west of downtown Albuquerque. It'd been cooler at the Carpenters' house, where their two-bedroom brick ranch was located in a small neighborhood nestled into the foothills of the Sandia mountain range. And, unfortunately, it'd been downright chilly at their dinner table earlier that evening, which had nothing to do with the thermostat.

I had greatly admired the view from Tiffany and Chase's back patio. You could see the Sandia Peak tramway. When I inquired about the tram, Tiffany promised to take us up to the top of the mountain on it one day while we were in town. I looked forward to it and knew I'd definitely need to wear my warmest jacket on that adventure.

"What in the world would possess a man to do something like Trey Monroe did to his best friends and clients?" I asked Rip later that evening as we sipped on our once-a-day cocktails.

"I ask myself a dozen times a day what would possess a person to do something they've done. I haven't come up with an answer to that question yet, and I'm not apt to this time around either. One word probably sums it up in many instances, including this one. Greed."

"You're probably right. Money truly is the root of all evil. My guess is that one of his clients didn't react well when he discovered Monroe had stolen their money and was attempting to flee the country with it. It seems like the obvious conclusion."

"I agree it *seems* that way. But it's a little early to make assumptions at this point." Rip sat his Crown and Coke down on the little wrought-iron table I'd set up between our sling-back chairs. We kept the lawn furniture stored in an undercarriage compartment of the trailer when we were on the road. Our chairs had drink holders in one of the arm rests, but the openings weren't large enough for the quart canning jars I served our drinks in. Dr. Herron, our primary physician, whose office was located in our hometown of Rockport, Texas, had told us we should allow ourselves no more than one alcoholic drink per day, but she hadn't specified what size that one drink should be. I erred on the side of liking my tequila a bit too much to serve that single beverage in an eight-ounce wine glass. Rip picked up his drink again to take another long swallow, and said, "Actually, dear, assumptions should never be made when it comes to murder."

"I agree, but he paid the ultimate price for his gluttony. I don't condone murder under any circumstance, but it sounds as if Trey had it coming. How did they know he'd been injected with fentanyl?"

"That, too, was probably an assumption made from the medical examiner's initial findings. I doubt there'd been time for him to complete an autopsy or get back the results of a tox screen." Rip sat his drink on the table and wiped his mouth with his shirt sleeve. "But, as I just said about assumptions, the cause of death probably isn't carved in stone yet."

"It will be interesting to see what the official cause turns out to be, and if they've already got a suspect in custody."

"Let's not call Tiffany and ask about it. Okay, Rapella? I'm sure she'll call us as soon as she's given any updates. Best if we don't get involved in the kids' personal squabbles. I'm certain they'll work things out on their own. The money will be located eventually, and they'll be made whole again. They should be happy with the return of their investment and not be concerned about the healthy profit on that dicey investment Chase was crowing about."

"Oh," I said, picking up on the adjective Rip had used to

describe the venture. I turned to Rip and asked, "So, you agree with Tiffany that it was too risky a chance to take?"

"Don't you?" Tiffany always had been the apple of Rip's eye, so I wasn't surprised he'd taken her side. If Chase said he thought having two children was the best idea and Tiffany contended that striving for an even dozen would be a much better goal, Rip would no doubt agree his granddaughter was correct.

"Absolutely! I can't imagine someone investing the family's entire savings without running it by his or her spouse and doing some serious research first. But I have to wonder. If their investment manager *had* deposited a huge chunk of money into their savings account, would Tiffany feel differently? Would she still be livid at Trey for investing the money without getting her approval in advance?" I asked.

"Guess we'll never know."

I merely shrugged in response. I picked up my Tequila Sunrise and leaned back in my chair in deep thought, as Rip checked for a sports report on our iPhone. He'd said that eventually, the kids would get their money back. What if they didn't, or it took a long time to set things right? Would their relationship be damaged beyond repair by the time they were "made whole again"? Was there anything I could do to rectify the situation? Could Rip and I somehow assist in the matter? I knew Rip didn't think we should get involved, but could we really just sit back and let Tiffany's marriage implode as she and her husband's financial security crumbled around them?

As I pondered these questions, I noticed what felt like an inappropriate smirk on Rip's face. I thought he should be more restrained, given the circumstances. Just then he turned to me and said, "Remember that kid named Patrick Mahomes we used to watch when he quarterbacked for Texas Tech?"

"Of course. Great arm and very crafty player, if I remember right. Had an adorable smile too," I said.

"Yes, well, he was picked up by the Kansas City Chiefs in the tenth round of the draft this year. I was just reading an article about him. Something tells me this kid might make something of himself one of these days. I can see him being a Super Bowl MVP in the not-so-distant future."

"Didn't you say the exact same thing about David Carr when the Houston Texans drafted him in the first round of the 2002 draft?"

"Yeah, I guess I did," Rip said with a sheepish grin. "And if memory serves me right, he accumulated more sacks during his five years with the Texans than Wal-Mart hands out on a typical day."

We shared a chuckle before retreating inside the Caboose and settling in for a night of watching our favorite shows on CBS. We didn't need Netflix, Hula Hoop, or whatever it's called, or any of those other new-fangled ways to watch television. Give us the three main network stations, an old set of rabbit ears to tune them in, and a bowl of salt-free, reduced-fat popcorn, and we were content as a couple of moths in a closet full of cashmere sweaters. Not that I wouldn't have rather been sitting in the Carpenters' living room, reminiscing about times past, laughing at humorous anecdotes, and catching up with two people I held dear.

When I said as much to Rip, he shook his head. "It is what it is, dear. I'm sure we'll have plenty of time to visit with them before we head to Missouri."

THREE

W hen Tiffany called early the next morning, she was sobbing and it was difficult to make out what she was saying. "Please aim to the blouse (sob) and hayed cheese go to tee hazing to (sniff) live a—" At this point, she was crying so hard she stopped speaking because she was having difficulty catching her breath. She sounded as if she was having an asthmatic attack, even though as far as I knew, she'd never been diagnosed with asthma.

I had the phone on "speaker", and Rip motioned for me to hand it to him. He cupped his hand over the front of it as if he were holding the handset of an old rotary dial telephone, and said, "Tiff says she did something to her blouse while she made cheese—"

"No," I interrupted because his interpretation of Tiffany's words was beyond bizarre. "I'm sure she said they'd advised Chase to report to the police station to give a statement."

"Really? How'd you get that out of the gobbledygook she just said?" Rip listened to Tiffany for a while longer, then looked at me and shrugged as if he had no clue what she was carrying on about. Frustrated, he ran his free hand through what few strands of hair he had left on his head as he shook it back and forth. Finally, after asking her to repeat herself three times, he said, "It's standard protocol, honey. I'm sure all of the investment manager's clients are being asked to give a statement, as well. It's not just Chase. They are trying to gather as much information as they can to build a case while they search for the perpetrator in Mr. Morley's death."

"Mr. Monroe," I corrected him, but he just waved me off and continued trying to comfort his beloved granddaughter. Apparently, she'd corrected him, as well. "Okay. Mr. Monroe...all right...Trey, then. My point is, being asked to give a statement doesn't mean Chase is a suspect in Trey's death. Not yet, at least."

Tiffany's sobbing intensified after Rip's last comment. So much for comforting her. I shook my head at Rip and whispered, "Tell her everything will be fine and she has nothing to worry about."

Rip nodded before digging himself an even deeper hole. "Sweetheart, calm down. There's nothing to get upset about. As long as Chase is innocent, he has nothing to worry about, and neither do you. Unless, of course, they have reason to believe Chase needs to be interrogated further, and then they might hold him for up to forty-eight hours."

My jaw dropped open wide enough to insert Rip's size eleven foot, which is exactly what Rip should have done when I handed him the phone. I could hear Tiffany's hysterical voice coming over the speaker and snatched it out of Rip's hand before he said something to upset Tiffany even more.

"Relax, honey. Your grandpa didn't mean he thought they'd detain Chase. He just meant that at this point in the investigation, everyone who was adversely affected by Trey's fraudulent actions might have a motive for murder, and will be considered a suspect until their alibis can be verified. I'm sure Chase will have no trouble getting his whereabouts at the time of Trey's death confirmed."

All I heard after that was a muffled scream and Tiffany's voice saying, "Oh my God! I can't believe this is happen——" Then the line went dead. I looked at the phone as if it had just sprouted wings and a scorpion's tail. I looked up at Rip, who rolled his eyes and sighed deeply as he said, "Good job calming her down, Rapella."

Moments later, we were in the Chevy truck headed to the Carpenters' house, which was about fifteen minutes away. I was afraid something, or someone, of the nefarious variety had forced Tiffany to hang up the phone. I wanted to call 9-1-1 immediately. Had Trey's killer struck again? Now I was as hysterical as my granddaughter had been.

"She's fine, dear. She hung up the phone because you convinced her something terrible was about to happen. That wasn't the scream of a woman being attacked by a knife-wielding serial killer. It was the scream of someone who's freaking out because she's afraid her husband will be viewed as a murder suspect. Trust me; I've heard both types of screams numerous times in my career in law enforcement."

Rip had started out his career as a beat cop before being promoted to detective. He eventually retired as the sheriff of Aransas County, Texas, after nearly a decade serving in that capacity. I trusted his judgment completely, but would still be relieved to find Tiffany alive and well when we arrived at her home on Comanche Road.

I glanced over at my husband, wondering how he could remain so calm. "You don't think she has any doubt about

Chase's innocence, do you? Maybe she has reason to think he might have had a hand in Trey's death. Perhaps she knows more about Chase's whereabouts during the time of the murder than she's letting on."

"It's possible, but doubtful. You know as well as I do that Tiffany—God love her—has always been a little bit on the dramatic side. I think she's just overreacting, as she is prone to do in situations of this nature. I wouldn't fret about it too much if I were you. No sense having you become hysterical too. I can only slap one of you at a time to bring you back to your senses." I knew Rip was trying to make me laugh so I wouldn't worry myself silly about the predicament Chase and Tiffany had found themselves in. But I was too uptight to chuckle. I punched him in the arm instead.

"What if his alibi is impossible to confirm?" I asked. "I recall when we first arrived, Tiffany told me Chase had just gotten home from "some" errand he'd had to run. Maybe she *does* have some inkling about where he *really* was at that time and is afraid to bring her suspicions to our attention, just in case it leads to Chase's arrest."

"You're borrowing trouble, dear. Do you know how many security cameras must be strung out from one end to the other at the Double Eagle II Airport? I'm guessing there are cameras in the parking garage, as well. I'm sure the authorities are examining the footage from those cameras as we speak. In fact, I'll bet they have the perpetrator in custody in the next day or two, if not within hours."

"I hope that's true, Rip," I replied with a sigh of relief. Rip was no doubt right. He was also correct that there was no sense borrowing trouble. "And then with the perpetrator behind bars, the kids can get their lives back on track and Tiffany can enjoy her thirtieth birthday today."

"Oh, yeah. I'd forgotten that was today. Glad you reminded

me. I want to stop by a flower shop today and buy Tiff thirty red roses for her birthday, and maybe Godiva's biggest box of chocolates. I know those are her favorite sweets."

Rip was adorable. Clearly, he'd never priced Godiva chocolates, much less their largest box of them. It would be as if Tiffany was biting down on a solid gold nugget whenever she popped a chocolate candy in her mouth. Nor did Rip have a clue that thirty roses was going to cost him the better part of his next social security check. As expected, Rip ended up buying an arrangement of chrysanthemums and baby's breath because he thought "it just looked more like Tiffany's style than the overrated roses ."

The chocolate was crossed off the shopping list entirely after I reminded him that Tiffany, although thin as a rail, was nearly always on one kind of diet or another. Last I knew, she was on the South Beach diet. This month, she told me, she was trying out a highly-recommended diet referred to as Keto, and was severely limiting her carbohydrate intake. I doubted Godiva chocolate was on any diet. And, for that matter, I couldn't imagine the Chicago-style pizza and breadsticks we'd indulged in the previous night were on a low-carb diet, either.

Although I had no way of knowing it at the time, my concern that Chase's alibi might prove difficult to confirm ended up being spot-on. It would be the straw that broke the camel's back when it came to my decision to jump into the investigation headfirst with no regard for my own safety or well-being. The fact that my involvement in the case might turn out to be life-threatening never even crossed my mind.

FOUR

I expected to find a distraught granddaughter when we arrived at the Carpenters' house. I even expected to find her husband stressed out and angry. What I didn't expect, however, was to find a trio of police cars in their driveway and Chase spread-eagled, leaning up against the hood of one of them. We couldn't make out what he was saying when we first pulled up to the curb, but we could sense his remarks were heavily laced with four-letter words. We were even more sure of that fact when one of the police officers forced Chase's head down against the hood.

"Oh, my!" I exclaimed. "Isn't that considered police brutality, Rip?"

"It's hard to say what Chase just said to the officer. He might've threatened him in some way. They're investigating a man's murder, and Chase has a motive. He should be cooperating and showing a little respect so he can be eliminated as a possible suspect. The detectives are just doing their jobs to protect and serve the public. They certainly didn't injure Chase in any way. Police officers often get a bad rap, as you know. The foolhardy actions of one bad cop can make the public paint the country's entire police population in a bad light."

"I agree, honey. It often seems like no one appreciates that the officers are putting their lives on the line every single day to protect the citizens of their communities from crime. I don't think most folks would like martial law, or a completely lawless society, as much as they think they would."

"You're preaching to the choir, dear." Rip spoke while watching the scene taking place in front of us. At that point, Chase was having a spirited conversation with several officers, who appeared to be growing more and more aggravated with the unruly young man.

"What in the world's going on?" I asked.

"I don't know, but Chase had better slow his roll before he ends up in cuffs." Just as Rip stopped talking, an officer slapped a pair of handcuffs on him.

"Too late," I said. I looked over at Tiffany, standing in the middle of their front lawn. She was in tears and speaking to one of the other officers. As I got out of the truck in order to go console her, I asked Rip, "Don't you think you ought to intervene?"

"Intervene? I'm in no position—or mood—to get in the middle of this confrontation."

"But you were a law enforcement officer! A county sheriff, no less."

"You're right. I *was* a law enforcement officer. I'm retired, Rapella, and have been for eight years." Rip appeared disappointed I'd ask him to step in and try to set things straight. "Even if I was still on the police force, it'd be in Rockport, Texas, not Albuquerque, New Mexico. I'd have absolutely no authority here, and I'd likely wind up handcuffed myself and in the back of a paddy wagon sitting next to Chase."

"Can't you at least try to talk to Chase? Get him to calm down before he makes matters even worse for himself?"

With a look of impatience and a heavy sigh, Rip replied, "I'll try. But don't hold your breath. If the officers ask me to back off, I will do so without hesitation. It was people like me who drove people like them crazy in situations like this."

"Thank you, dear." I headed toward Tiffany as Rip reluctantly made his way over to where the five responding officers were swarming around their cuffed captive.

After I gave Tiffany a quick hug, I asked, "What's going on?"

"Two cops came to the door to speak to Chase, upset that he hadn't reported to the station to give a statement. They asked him where he was at eleven-fifteen yesterday morning, which was the estimated time of Trey's death, and if he had any idea who might have targeted the murder victim. He told them he knew of a lot of people who probably wanted to kill the lying S.O.B. who robbed them blind."

"Probably not the smartest thing to say," I replied.

"Gee, you think?" Tiffany replied sarcastically. "And it gets worse. When the officers asked Chase if he was one of those people he was referring to, he said, 'you're damn right I am, but unfortunately, someone beat me to it!' You and I both know he was just spouting off like that because he was not only angry at what Trey had done, but also hurt that his friend would betray him like that. Chase clammed up after that and refused to respond to their questions."

"Which might have been a good thing."

"No doubt," Tiffany said. "The next thing I knew, they were calling for backup."

"Why wouldn't Chase just answer the questions? Doesn't he want to help the officers find out what happened to your so-called friend and investment manager?"

Tiffany shrugged. I waited a few moments for a response, and when none came, I spoke again.

"He should have realized his refusal to cooperate would not go over well."

"Well, to be fair, they were being very rude and treating him like a murder suspect."

"It sounds as though he gave them reason to treat him that way." I was disgusted with Chase's behavior. He was acting like he didn't have the sense God gave a bathtub ring. "Where *was* Chase at the time of Trey's death?"

Tiffany shrugged again.

"You don't know?"

"Not really."

"Yesterday, when we first arrived, you told me he'd just returned from running an errand. Did he never mention what kind of errand he ran, or where he went?"

"No," Tiffany responded. After I gave her an incredulous look, she added, "Today's my birthday, Grams! I assume he'd gone somewhere to pick up a present for me or something he needed for the party he was planning on throwing for me tonight."

"So you knew he was planning a surprise party?"

"No. It wasn't until shortly before you and Gramps arrived that I found out what he had planned. When we heard Trey had died, Chase told me about the party and said he felt as though we should cancel it out of respect, as I told you yesterday. I can't honestly say I was terribly disappointed. I hate being surprised like that!"

"I've never been thrown a surprise party, but I don't think I'd like it much either. And, I hadn't thought about it being your birthday, but that's undoubtedly the kind of errand Chase was running. Happy birthday, by the way." I gave her another hug.

"Yeah," Tiffany replied sarcastically. "Real happy start to my thirtieth birthday. Watching my husband being cuffed and stuffed into the back of a cop car is not exactly what I'd wished for."

"Well, sweetheart, he hasn't actually been stuffed into the police car, and hopefully, he won't be. You need to calm down, Tiffany. Getting totally bent out of shape certainly won't help matters any."

With an apologetic expression, Tiffany said, "I'm sorry if I'm acting like a drama queen or being rude. I don't mean to be, Grams. I'm just feeling overwhelmed by the entire situation."

"I understand, honey. I probably would be too. However, it will be better all the way around if you remain calm and collected. Your grandfather is going to try to reason with the officers, and——"

As if on cue, one of the officers opened the back door of his cruiser and, while placing his hand on the top of Chase's head to protect it from banging into the frame of the car door, he stuffed Chase into the back seat. It seemed to me like the officer could have completed the task a little less roughly. Chase, at average height and weight, was half the officer's size. There was no call for slamming the car door closed in Chase's face the way he did, either. They were treating Chase like he was their prime suspect in Trey's death, which was preposterous. Although we hadn't been able to get to know Chase all that well, the three times we'd been around him in the past, he'd always treated us with the utmost respect and courtesy. He was friendly and thoughtful and clearly thought the sun rose and set on his bride of three years. Tiffany was deliriously happy, and Rip and I were glad she'd found the man she called the love of her life.

The love of Tiffany's life was currently gazing up at her from the back seat of a patrol car, as if hoping she could do something to get him out of the mess he'd so stupidly gotten himself into. Tiffany stood beside me, feeling helpless and emotionally drained. There was nothing any of us could do for Chase at that point.

I watched Rip shake his head as he said something to the officer who appeared to be in charge. The officer, who had the same shorter-than-average stature as Rip, but with incredible posture, responded, and the two men laughed before shaking hands and walking away from each other. *What could Rip possibly find amusing about this whole ordeal?* I wondered. I didn't find it funny at all. I felt bad that Tiffany's special day was quickly becoming one of the worst days of her life.

"Don't worry Tiff," Rip said soothingly to his granddaughter after the patrol cars, including the one hauling Chase to the police station, had pulled away from the curb. "Chase will be home shortly. Providing, that is, he cooperates a little better than he did earlier."

"I hope so," she said between sniffles. She'd been doing a respectable job of keeping her cool the last few minutes, but that was about to change.

"That's assuming he has nothing to hide, of course. Refusing to answer their questions makes him look as if he does. It was kind of a bone-headed thing to do."

After Rip spoke, Tiffany gasped and covered her face with her hands. I was perturbed at Chase for playing such a big part in making Tiffany so distressed on her milestone birthday. Finally, Tiffany looked up and wiped tears from her eyes with a tissue I'd handed her several minutes earlier. She verbalized exactly what I was thinking about her husband. "Chase is acting like a damn fool. I don't know why he was being so stubborn. If he was out picking up a present or something for the birthday party, he should have just told them so. I want him (sniffle) here on my birthday, not locked up in the county jail."

"Don't worry, Tiff. It'll all work out.." Rip spoke calmly to Tiffany again to calm her down. As he patted her back, he said, "If he's not home in an hour, or two, I'll run down to your local police station and see if I can find out what's going on. Okay? Just try to relax in the meantime. Maybe you can chat with your grandmother while she bakes a birthday cake in your kitchen."

"Okay. That'd be (sniffle) great. I'll join you after I call Mom. Chase told me she and Dad had talked about coming for the surprise party, but Chase told them it would be better if they stayed in Rockport to get things back in order following Hurricane Harvey. Chase promised we'd travel to Rockport before Christmas to spend the holidays with them."

"That will be nice, sweetheart. Your folks will love that. We'll be spending the holidays with our friends, Lexie and Stone, in the great state of Missouri. There's rarely a dull moment at the Alexandria Inn. While we're there, we hope to catch a Kansas City Chiefs game. Your grandpa just loves their head coach, Andy Reid."

I pulled the Mississippi Mud chocolate cake, Tiffany's favorite, out of her oven an hour and a half later and stuck a toothpick in it to make sure it was done. As I did, Rip stuck his head in the kitchen doorway.

"I called and found out that Chase is being held at the Albuquerque Police Foothills substation on Lomas Boulevard. I'll drive over there. I'm not sure my presence will be welcomed by the officers at the station, but I'll do what I can to at least find out why they're holding him. Chase should have been home by now if they just wanted him to write and sign a statement."

"Okay, good. Tiffany said his phone was going straight to voicemail."

"I'm sure they had him turn it off so he wasn't distracted by incoming texts and calls."

"No doubt," Tiffany replied, as she sat glumly at the kitchen table doodling on the back of an envelope from a birthday card her mother-in-law had sent. "His phone was blowing up earlier this morning."

"Oh my!" I exclaimed. "What would cause it to malfunction like that? Was there actually smoke coming from it?"

Tiffany laughed loudly. I didn't know what had amused her but was glad to see her mood lighten. After another hearty round of laughter, she explained. "Grams, 'blowing up' a phone just means bombarding it with texts and calls. Everyone was contacting him about Trey Monroe's death, in case Chase hadn't already heard about it."

"Well, that's a relief. I was a little worried about carrying around a device that could blow up at any moment."

"Well, a few models *have* been known to burst into flames spontaneously," Tiffany said.

"Seriously?" I asked. Rip didn't say anything, but I noticed him remove the phone from his rear pocket.

Tiffany nodded before asking Rip, "Gramps, can I go with you? I have a right to know why my husband is being detained."

Rip was clearly tentative, but eventually he nodded. "I guess so. It *would* be nice to have someone with me who knows the area. You can guide me to the substation. But let me do the talking. All right, Tiff?"

"Of course."

I decided to ride along with Rip and Tiffany. The toothpick had come out clean, so I left the cake to cool down on top of the kitchen counter while we were away. Rip didn't exactly look delighted that I'd decided to join them, and repeated his earlier remark. "Like I said, Rapella. I'll do the talking!"

I noticed it wasn't a question or a request, as it had been with Tiffany. It was an outright order for me to remain silent. I didn't want to be left behind, so I promised him I'd keep my pie hole firmly shut. It was a vow I tried diligently to keep. I truly did!

FIVE

"Like I told you yesterday, Mr. Ripple, all Mr. Carpenter has to do is explain where he was at the time of the victim's death yesterday. Once we've verified his alibi, we'll release him." Rip nodded at the same Hispanic police officer he'd spoken to and shared a laugh with the previous day. The badge on his shirt indicated his name was Detective Carlos Gutierrez. "He said he's under no obligation to answer our questions, and if we don't have proof he killed the man, we need to release him immediately. As you know, we can hold him up to forty-eight hours while we look for evidence that he's guilty of a crime."

"I understand that." Rip nodded at the detective.

Rip might have understood, but neither Tiffany nor I did. She looked at me in an obvious plea for me to do something to resolve the situation. She clearly did not want to celebrate her birthday while her husband was locked up in an interrogation room for two days. I shook my head and remained silent, as I'd promised Rip I'd do if allowed to tag along.

Detective Gutierrez then looked directly at Tiffany. "Can you verify your husband's whereabouts yesterday at eleven-fifteen?"

"Yes." Tiffany sounded defiant, but confident. My head swiveled toward her like a startled barn owl. She'd told me she'd had no clue where he was at that time. Her next remark made it clear her affirmative response to the officer had been ambiguous. "He was out running an errand."

"He was out running an errand?" The detective repeated her words in a mocking tone. "Could you possibly be any vaguer?" When she failed to respond, he glared at her and rephrased the question, "Can you be more specific, please?"

"Um, no. Not exactly."

"You have no idea where he went to, um, 'run the errand'?" The fact the detective used air quotes told me his suspicions regarding Chase's innocence had just ratcheted up another notch. "Did this 'errand' have anything to do with injecting potassium chloride in another man's arm?"

"I don't even know what that is, and I doubt Chase does either. Besides, he had no reason to kill Trey. We thought he was our friend and investment advisor who was making us a ton of money. Chase didn't even know we'd been ripped off until later."

"Then can you explain why he's refusing to explain exactly what yesterday's errand entailed?" Carlos Gutierrez asked.

Tiffany shook her head, looking defeated and in deep despair. "No, sorry. But since today is my thirtieth birthday, I'm guessing it had something to do with a present he was buying me or maybe something he was picking up for the party he'd planned to throw for me tonight. At that point, the party was still supposed to be a surprise. I only found out about it when Chase was forced to cancel it because of Trey's death. I'd really like for him to be home tonight to celebrate my birthday with me. Otherwise, my whole day will be ruined."

There's a lot more at stake right now than a birthday party, I thought. *Tiffany doesn't seem to understand how serious the situation is. I hope that's due to the shock of having her husband arrested and not self-absorption.*

43

Following Tiffany's last response, the detective's expression looked contemptuous. His next statement was heavily laced with sarcasm. It was as if he'd read my mind. "Chase could have told me he was picking up a gift for his wife and I'd have pinky-sworn not to tell her about it. I wouldn't have wanted to ruin someone's surprise birthday party just because a man was murdered in cold blood. The loved ones of the deceased are clamoring for answers and will undoubtedly be demanding justice. Like me, they don't consider your birthday a top priority right now!"

Detective Gutierrez was practically shouting at Tiffany by this time, and I was having none of it. As Tiffany began to weep into her hands, I looked at Rip. He read my expression perfectly and shook his head. I'd wanted him to step in, and he'd declined. I might have promised to keep my mouth shut, but I would never promise anyone that I'd remain silent as Tiffany was being raked over the coals for something she was not responsible for. I put my hands on my hips and turned to the detective.

"Now listen to me, young man! You may be the individual in charge of this investigation, and Mr. Carpenter might be acting like a horse's ass, but that doesn't give you the right to talk to my granddaughter that way!" I stopped just long enough to glance at Rip, who was shaking his head at me while simultaneously rolling his eyes so far back into his head he was probably looking at the inside of his own skull. "If she had any idea where Chase was at eleven-fifteen yesterday morning, she'd have told you. My guess is that if you treated Chase with a little more respect, he'd be a lot more open with you, as well. The way your men manhandled him this morning in front of his own home was disgraceful. There was no call for it, and you should all be ashamed of yourselves."

"Manhandled him?" The detective asked. "Seriously, ma'am? We treated Mr. Carpenter with a lot more kindness and respect than he deserved."

Rip put his hand up in front of my face as I opened my mouth to respond. "All right, Rapella. Let me handle this."

I was still fuming when Rip shuffled me behind him so he could speak directly to the detective. "Detective Gutierrez, I apologize for my wife's outburst, but we are all understandably distressed about the situation. As I told you earlier, I spent my entire career in law enforcement, and I've found myself in the same situation with a suspect as you're in now. Is there any way I can have a word with Chase? I'm sure if I had a chance to talk some sense into him, you'll find he'll be much more cooperative."

I glanced at Tiffany after her grandfather had referred to Chase as a suspect. She looked stunned, and then angry. I patted her hand and whispered, "Don't let it get to you. He's just trying to suck up to the detective so he can speak with Chase."

After a moment of deliberation, the detective nodded. He pointed to a couple of chairs for Tiffany and me to sit on while we waited. I held up a hand as if waiting to be called on by a third-grade teacher.

"Yes?" Detective Gutierrez asked.

"We'd heard Monroe was killed with fentanyl, but you just told Tiffany a few minutes ago that he was injected with potassium chloride. Which was it?"

"It turned out to be potassium chloride. The fentanyl was the initial assumption, but potassium chloride is what showed up on the tox screen."

"I see. Has your team viewed all the footage from the airport's security cameras? If so, didn't it show images of the killer injecting Mr. Monroe?"

"Yes, they've watched the camera footage, but the perpetrator was never caught on film."

"How can that be?" I asked.

Detective Gutierrez shrugged. "A security camera caught his vehicle arriving at the check-in kiosk at the parking garage, and he was the car's sole occupant. That was the last time he was caught on security footage."

"Oh? So there's no footage of him *inside* the parking garage?" After the detective shrugged, I continued. "I take it the autopsy has been completed, since you said potassium chloride was found in his system."

"I'm not sure, but I doubt it. I think only the tox screen results have come back at this point."

"So, you're not even certain the toxin was injected. It's basically just another assumption, then?" I knew I was coming across as if I was a prosecuting attorney grilling a defendant on the witness stand. I could sense the detective beginning to squirm under my intense questioning. Rip caught my eye and mouthed, "Stop."

"Yeah, I guess so," the detective replied. "Dr. Wilkens, the medical examiner, said it was probably injected into the victim while he was still in his car in the parking garage, since that's where the body was discovered."

"*Probably*? So, in other words, yes, it's only an assumption." I was building up a head of steam in my efforts to question the detective since my husband seemed reluctant to do so himself. "Do you typically detain suspects based on assumptions?"

Again, the detective shrugged. He looked at Rip for support. Rip merely shook his head in response.

"It's more than that," the detective finally replied. "We had a hunch Mr. Carpenter knew more than he was telling us. We're holding him until he is completely forthcoming with us."

"Oh, good!" I clapped my hands in feigned delight. My sarcastic display made Detective Gutierrez blush. Then using air quotes as the detective had earlier, I said, "So now you're telling us you operate on 'hunches'? Is that what you're saying?"

I was a fine one to belittle the detective for his choice of words. I put a lot of emphasis on my own gut feelings whenever I was looking into a murder case—which, I might add, I had no legal authority to do in the first place.

Without responding to my last question, Detective Gutierrez turned to Rip, and asked, "Do you want to speak to Mr. Carpenter, or not?"

After Rip nodded, he turned to Tiffany and me and motioned us to the chairs Detective Gutierrez had pointed out a minute or so earlier. "I won't be long."

The detective tipped his hat at Tiffany and me and led Rip down a long hallway. I'm sure his respectful gesture was not a genuine reflection of his feelings about me.

"Thanks for butting in, Grams," Tiffany said with a smile after the two men exited the room. She wiped a tear off her cheek as I dug through my purse for a tissue.

"Well, someone had to!" I replied as I handed her another Kleenex. "Here, your mascara is a mess. I noticed a restroom down the hall. Why don't you go clean up while I wait here?"

"Okay."

"And don't fret, sweetheart. I'm sure once your grandpa's had a chance to speak with Chase, he'll be more forthcoming and they'll release him immediately. We'll still have most of the day to celebrate your birthday in style. I promise! It'll be a great day after all."

"That'd be awesome," she said with a relieved smile.

As she walked away, I wondered if I'd regret making such a promise. I sent up a prayer that my encouraging words to Tiffany would turn out to be exactly the way the rest of the day would transpire. I didn't want to be guilty of reneging on a promise I'd made to my only granddaughter.

It seemed like hours but was more likely only about forty-five minutes when Rip returned to the waiting room where Tiffany and I were pacing around. Tiffany ran to her grandfather as if she hadn't seen him in five years. After giving him a warm hug, she asked, "So? Are they going to release Chase?"

"I imagine so. After I spoke with Chase, he agreed to answer the detective's questions. I told him he was being selfish by being so bull-headed. I reminded him his wife was trying to celebrate a special birthday and he was solely responsible for making her so upset."

"So," I said, "you put him on a guilt trip?"

"Exactly." Rip nodded. "Trying to convince him to give the detectives the information they wanted by using other methods was going over like a balloon full of mud."

"Whatever works," I agreed. "Did he tell you where he was yesterday at eleven-fifteen? And why was he being so secretive about his whereabouts?"

"Therein lies the problem."

"What do you mean?" Tiffany cut in. "Where was he?"

"He claims he was parked in front of the Monroes' house at the time of Trey's death and Trey was nowhere around. Apparently, when he'd called the man's office earlier in the morning to inquire if the Clean Sweep stock had been sold, Trey was not in his office," Rip explained. "His assistant told Chase that Monroe routinely reported to the office at ten forty-five every morning. It was only nine-fifty at the time of Chase's call. So Chase asked his assistant to tell him the balance in your account and she said it was zero. Chase argued with her and the assistant finally confessed to him she thought Trey had made off with the money. I doubt she was supposed to say anything because of client confidentiality laws, but she was understandably distraught and overwhelmed. She told Chase that Monroe had not only sold off the bulk of the stock in all of his clients' portfolios, which had her baffled, but also, she assumed, the entire Clean Sweep fund."

"She assumed?" Tiffany asked. "What's that mean?"

"She said she couldn't find any transaction bills for the sale, and when clients began calling in, she dug through the file cabinets and couldn't find any documentation that showed the Clean Sweep fund had ever existed. She made calls and was unable to find any proof Trey had ever even invested in the IPO. His assistant assured Chase she'd look into the matter further and get back with him."

"Are you saying Chase knew the truth about our investment money yesterday morning?" Tiffany asked, sounding as though she was on the edge of hysteria. "Did he know the money was missing before he found out Trey was dead?"

"Yes, I'm afraid so," Rip told Tiffany. "He was worried about how you'd react. He didn't want to upset you, so he didn't say anything to you about it at the time. He still believed it was all just an unfortunate mix-up. He was confident Trey had sold your shares in the IPO fund and the money was still in the process of posting to your account. He had no idea at the time that Trey's body had been found with a one-way plane ticket to the Cayman Islands in his possession. I'm sure he planned to tell you all about it once the money was back in your account."

"I don't know whether to be pissed off at him or appreciate the fact he was trying not to worry me," Tiffany said. She looked as if she had the weight of the world piled upon her shoulders, so I kept my thoughts to myself. Personally, had I been in her shoes and my husband had been fooled by a con artist, I'd have wanted to wear out a cast iron skillet on his noggin.

Luckily, Rip was more diplomatic than I. He patted Tiffany's hand and said, "I'm sure Chase was only trying to protect you. I'd suggest you give him the benefit of the doubt until you have reason to do otherwise."

"All right." Tiffany sounded depressed but resolute as she turned to me. "We'll get our money back one way or another. Right, Grams?"

"Yes, sweetheart, I'm sure you will." *If I have anything to do about it anyway,* were my unspoken words. "So, Rip, go on with what Chase told you."

"Following the phone call to Trey's assistant, Chase went to the Monroes' house hoping to confront him and find out what was going on. He rang the doorbell around ten-thirty, and the door was answered by a guy named Manny, or something like that. I assume he's the Monroes' nanny."

"Manny the nanny?" Tiffany laughed at her grandfather, knowing he had difficulty remembering names. "His name is actually Manuel de la Cruz, and he's their house manager."

"Their house manager?" I asked. "That sounds like a fancy name for a maid."

"He does do the housekeeping, but Manuel takes care of a lot of other things too. He plans social gatherings, medical appointments, and stuff like that, along with handling the grocery shopping and regular maintenance and upkeep of their home. He's been keeping their household running like a well-oiled machine for about two years, I think."

"Does he care for their children, as well?" I asked.

"No. Like us, they don't have any. I don't think either of them had any desire for children. We, on the other hand, plan to—"

"Yes?" I asked excitedly when Tiffany paused.

Rip tapped me on the shoulder, "Don't get side-tracked, Rapella. You two can discuss that later."

I nodded and motioned for Tiffany to continue her discussion about the Monroes. "I don't think Trey and Sandy planned to add to their family. I really enjoyed their company, but I think they were both too selfish to share their attention with children.

Raising kids would interfere with their social lives, their non-stop vacationing, and so forth."

Rip nodded. "Chase said Manuel told him that neither Trey nor Candy were home at the time."

"Mrs. Monroe's name is not Candy," I scolded him. Rip shot me a look that could weld two cast iron pipes together.

"Yeah, it's actually Sandy, Gramps, but please, continue," Tiffany said.

"Okay. As I was saying, before I was so rudely interrupted," Rip began with a wink aimed at Tiffany, "the house manager told Chase he hadn't seen either Monroe or his wife all day, but would leave Trey a note that Chase had stopped by. Incidentally, that note was seized as evidence when the detectives searched the Monroe home yesterday afternoon. It read, 'A Mr. Carpenter stopped by to see you at ten-thirty. He seemed extremely irate.'"

"That doesn't sound very promising. In fact, it could be construed as being incriminating," Tiffany said.

"Perhaps, but it's really just circumstantial evidence. It's certainly not proof Chase assaulted Trey in any way." Rip motioned for Tiffany and me to follow him out to the parking lot. He continued speaking as we walked. "Chase decided to wait around in case Trey or his wife showed up. At about eleven-thirty, he gave up and drove back to your house. As he was pulling into your garage, he got the call about Trey's death. We showed up on your doorstep about half-an-hour later. Not having a confirmable alibi, or even one that doesn't sound incriminating, is what kept Chase from cooperating with the police."

"I still can't believe Chase didn't tell me we'd been ripped off when he first found out about it." Tiffany continued struggling to forgive her husband for keeping her in the dark. "The first I heard about the missing money was when he answered that phone call at dinner last night."

"Like I said earlier, Chase assured me he hadn't wanted to

worry you. He felt sure it was all just a misunderstanding. He hoped to get it all worked out and the money deposited in your account without you ever knowing there'd been a hiccup in the process. But once the news of Trey's death being ruled a homicide broke, Chase knew he had to let you know the status of your investment money was currently up in the air. What he failed to mention was that the funds may have already been spent by Trey and/or Sandy, who Chase claimed both like to flaunt their wealth."

Tiffany nodded at him in agreement. "Yeah, he and Sandy were always going on fancy trips and purchasing expensive automobiles. She's a little show-offish, but he was twice as much of a big-feeler."

"Well, honey, I can understand why Chase wouldn't want to upset you, especially on the eve of your birthday. I might have done the same thing had such a thing happened to me and your grandmother. Regardless, Chase promised he'd spell the story out to the detectives in its entirety. I'll drop you two off at the house and come back to pick up Chase once I get notice he's been released."

"Thanks," Tiffany replied. Her demeanor had improved a lot from when we'd first arrived at the police substation. "Maybe I'll have a happy birthday after all."

"Of course you will," I assured her. "I promised you as much, didn't I? And when has Grams ever let you down?"

Tiffany and I linked elbows and walked arm in arm to the truck. I felt a sense of relief. It sounded as if the situation would rectify itself soon. Rip had indicated the detectives felt certain they'd locate the money and return it to the investors. They'd also indicated they expected a suspect in Trey Monroe's death would be apprehended in short order.

"When we get back to your place, I'm going to frost the cake and bake some cookies. This is the kind of day that calls for comfort food like a batch of Snickerdoodles. So, tell me dear, what kind of icing would you like on your Mississippi Mud birthday cake?" I asked the birthday girl.

"Chocolate, of course!"

"Then chocolate it shall be."

We were all in good spirits by the time we returned to the Carpenters' house. It's a crying shame our good spirits were not destined to last very long.

SIX

While visiting with Tiffany in the kitchen about twenty minutes later, I frosted the cake and then nosed around in the pantry until I found the ingredients needed to whip up a batch of cookies.

"I'm glad you're going to make Snickerdoodles, Grams. I was so excited when you sent me a box of them last month, knowing they're my favorite. That must have been around the time you were baking cookies for the construction workers you told me about."

About a month earlier, I'd been dubbed "the cookie lady" by the crew repairing the house next to Tiffany's parents' home on Key Allegro Island in Rockport, Texas. At that time, I'd used my cookies as an excuse to speak to the subcontractors about the mysterious disappearance of the homeowner's wife. It had been a means to an end. *I guess I'm doing the same thing now*, I thought. *Only this time, I'm using them to try to cheer up my granddaughter.*

"Yes, it was when I was trying to woo the workmen into confiding in me. I had a regular old cookie factory up and running in the Chartreuse Caboose. I decided it was the ideal time to whip up a batch to send to my favorite granddaughter."

I greased a cookie sheet while Tiffany measured out two cups of sugar for me. We worked together in relative silence for several minutes. While the cookies were baking and there was a lull in the conversation, I decided to broach the subject of Chase and his hair-trigger temper. "Honey?"

"Yes?"

"I was just wondering," I began. I then paused, hesitant to say what was on my mind. I didn't want Tiffany to think I had a single doubt that her husband was innocent of any wrongdoing. Although he'd always been extremely hospitable to Rip and me, I'd seen Chase get hot under the collar more than once in the three or four times we'd spent time with him. On one occasion, I'd watched him cuss out the mail carrier because she hadn't brought a check he'd been expecting. She'd rolled her eyes and dismissed him, as if accustomed to his rudeness, but I'd been embarrassed by his behavior.

"Yes? Go ahead. What were you wondering, Grams?" Tiffany asked when she noticed my reluctance to continue.

"I was just curious. Have you ever witnessed Chase exhibit any violent behavior?"

Her loving smile faded and a wounded expression took its place. "Are you wondering if Chase could have been involved in Trey's death? How could you think he'd do something that despicable? He's a kind man, and as gentle as a lamb."

That was a relief to hear, but let's face it, she was his wife. A man might never have contemplated hurting his wife, or any other woman, for that matter, but not think twice about beating another man who'd done him a bad turn into a bloody pulp. "Trust me, sweetheart, I didn't mean to imply I thought he'd abused *you* in any way. I know both of you better than that. You'd have dropped him like a bag of flaming doggy doo-doo if he'd ever harmed you."

"Flaming doggy doo-doo?" Tiffany asked with a chuckle she couldn't restrain. "Thanks for the visual, Grams. And you are absolutely correct. I would kick him to the curb if he ever laid a hand on me."

"I would hope so. Does Chase have a temper by any chance?" I was fully aware he did, as I'd witnessed that temper of his in action, but I wanted to hear what Tiffany had to say about it.

"I suppose. But no more than most people. I've certainly never witnessed him exhibiting violent behavior. He might get a little hot under the collar once in a while, but who doesn't? For instance, a few days ago we drove over to Sandia Office Supply on Singer Boulevard to pick up some drafting paper. There were only two spots, side-by-side, left in the parking lot," Tiffany said. Chase was an architect, so I understood his need for drafting paper. "As Chase aimed toward the parking spot, an old man in a block-long Chrysler sped up, cut Chase off, and pulled into the spot."

I wanted to say, "First come, first serve," but didn't. Instead, I asked, "So did Chase just pull into the spot beside the Chrysler? You said there were two side-by-side spots available."

"That's just it! The old fart parked right in the middle, taking up both spaces. Chase yelled at him out the window and the man paid absolutely no attention. He just got his cane out of the back seat and ambled into Elevate, across the street from the office supply store."

"Elevate? What's that?"

"It's Elevate: Performance, Health, Wellness, a fitness center."

"Oh, I see. Perhaps the gentleman had just had a hip replaced and was going there for a physical therapy session." I was trying to justify the man's desire to find the closest parking spot available.

"Maybe," Tiffany replied with a disinterested shrug. "But that doesn't mean he had to take up both spaces."

"That's true. So, what did Chase do when the man ignored him?"

"Well, naturally, he blew a gasket."

Naturally, I thought. *What perfectly healthy young man wouldn't lose his cool when forced to walk a few extra steps because a much older, disabled man with a cane prevented him from parking in his preferred spot?* I shook my head in dismay and was further appalled when Tiffany continued.

"He yelled at the old man again to move his car. The man just waved back, all friendly-like. That's what irritated Chase the most."

"Incidents like that tend to tick off most folks. I wouldn't really consider that a volatile temper."

"Yeah, I agree." Tiffany had then shrugged once more.

"I'd be more concerned if Chase had assaulted the guy in some way, or vandalized his vehicle. Chase would never do something of that nature, would he?"

"No way. Not Chase! He's just not that kind of guy, Grandma." Tiffany only called me "grandma" when she was annoyed with me. She not only sounded irritated, she now wore an expression of disappointment. She looked at me like a six-year-old would look if she'd been promised a pony and instead unwrapped a toy hobby horse, a stuffed horse head glued to the top of a stick.

"Okay. I'm sure you're right, sweetheart." I studied Tiffany's expression as I spoke. It had not wavered. She still resembled the six-year-old who'd just thrown her stick pony across the living room in a fit of fury. "You know I love you more than life itself, don't you?"

Tiffany nodded sullenly in response.

"All I care about is your happiness and well-being. Gramps and I care deeply for Chase, too, of course, but you will always be our number-one priority. No matter what, we will always have your back. Our love for you is unconditional and always will be."

Tiffany smiled and then embraced me in a warm hug. "I know, Grams. I love you both, too."

I was Grams again. Things were definitely looking up. As I continued to hold Tiffany in my arms, she said, "I'm so glad you came to surprise me for my birthday. I would never have believed you could keep a secret like that."

"Neither could your parents or Rip. They all wagered I'd let the cat out of the bag long before we arrived."

"I'm glad you left that cat in the bag." She stopped for a moment, and then chuckled. "That sounded bad, for the cat's sake, anyway. What I meant was that it was a wonderful surprise to open the door and find you two standing on my doorstep. I don't know what I'd do right now if not for you and Gramps."

As much as I wanted to come to the old man in the Chrysler's defense, I didn't say anything. Not only was he driving a block-long vehicle that I'd have needed two acres to maneuver into a parking spot, but he was also elderly and clearly disabled. Due to his advanced age, he likely had less than stellar vision, and like Rip, probably stored his hearing aids in his toiletry bag for safe-keeping. Rip operated on the theory one might lose one or both hearing aids if he actually wore them in his ears. And good quality hearing aids aren't cheap. Maybe if we'd only paid twenty-nine bucks for a generic pair of sound-enhancing devices instead of the high-quality pair costing five grand, he'd actually wear the damn things.

The point is that the poor Chrysler owner probably never even heard Chase yelling at him from the car window. If he had, I'm sure he'd have gotten back into his vehicle and moved it over to free up the extra parking spot. Or he'd have done what Rip would've done under the same circumstances—flipped Chase off and told him what he could go do to himself. Either way, he undoubtedly would've responded in some fashion if he'd heard Chase yelling at him. It sounded as if it was the fact Chase felt he was deliberately ignored that pissed him off the most.

I watched now as Tiffany pulled the baking sheet out of the oven, and using a spatula, scooped up a hot, gooey cookie. "Wanna sample one, Grams?" Her mood had turned on a dime. I was happy to see her more cheerful.

"You betcha, Sweet Pea! I'm gonna give mine a minute to stop steaming. If you didn't like the visual of a flaming bag of doggy doo-doo, how'd you like to see me spit my false teeth across the room with a smoldering cookie stuck to them?"

We both laughed, and while Tiffany carried two cookies on a saucer through the kitchen door out to the back patio, I grabbed two of the Seagram's "Jamaican Me Happy" wine coolers in the Carpenters' refrigerator and followed her outside. I was praying the fruity alcoholic beverage would live up to its name.

We spent the next forty-five minutes discussing her age, among other topics. I told her my happiest, healthiest decade had been my thirties. Then we talked about shaving after she mentioned if she didn't shave her legs soon, she'd have to use a weed-whacker. I told her that I'd noticed in my sixties that the hair under my arm pits had migrated north to my chin and upper lip. I warned her, "That's a preview of coming attractions, and something you can look forward to in the next three or four decades."

We followed that exchange up with a conversation about the best way to work out a cramp when a calf tightens up like a banjo string in the middle of the night, and where to draw the line when it came to sexual harassment on the job. I said, "Nearly every man I ever worked with would be in prison if the "me too movement" had come about in the sixties instead of now."

During those forty-five minutes, we each downed two wine coolers and talked about anything and everything other than Chase and his possible involvement in the death of Trey Monroe. We avoided that subject like it had a bad cough and runny nose. I'd already upset her once, and I had no desire to repeat the mistake. She'd been in good spirits at the time, and I'd wanted to keep her that way.

We were discussing how we both wanted to see the vivid colors of the foliage on the east coast this time of year when Tiffany's phone rang. Just as those autumn leaves fade in time, I watched the color drain from Tiffany's face as she held the phone to her ear.

"I don't understand," she said to the caller. "But...yes...I know...no...of course not...how can you do that?"

Her short responses were not very informative, but I watched her high spirits sink like an anchor that'd been pitched overboard before being tied to the boat. I'd been there and done that and, believe me, it's not a good feeling when you realize your over-sight. I listened to a dozen or so more one- or two-word replies before she finally said something that helped explain her sudden mood change.

"No, that can't be!" she exclaimed. "Why would you arrest him? There's no way Chase would do something like that! No frigging way. He's just not a violent person. He wouldn't harm a flea, much less someone he considered a close friend."

I patted her back, hoping to soothe her. I didn't want to tell her that Trey Monroe was no longer someone either of them would call a close friend. In fact, I'd heard both Tiffany and Chase call him several much less complimentary things while eating pizza the previous night. Tiffany's remarks to the caller were meant to convey the message her husband wasn't a brutal person. I had to admit I couldn't see Chase killing another human being. He didn't appear to have that kind of total disregard for others.

"All right," Tiffany said in a tone of resignation before ending the call.

"What is it, sweetheart?" I asked, but she was too choked up to answer. I waited a few moments before repeating my inquiry. "What's going on?"

"They are planning to arrest Chase on first-degree murder charges."

"Why in the world would they do that?"

"That's what I asked the detective," she said. "All he would tell me is they had reason to believe he'd been involved in Trey's death. He wouldn't explain what had made them think that, though."

"But you're his wife! I'd think you'd have a right to know."

"I'd think so too."

So far, I hadn't learned much from Tiffany, so I gently asked, "Did he say anything that would make you think they aren't telling you because they want to question you as well? In that case, I'd expect they don't want to give you any information because they want to see if your story matches Chase's."

"Oh, God! I hadn't thought of that, but I bet you're right. I'm not sure what story he told them. What if I say something that gets him convicted for a murder he didn't commit?"

"Let's not get ahead of ourselves. They haven't asked you to come in and give a statement yet. If they do, just tell them exactly what you know. The whole truth and nothing but the truth, as they say. That's all you can do, sweetheart. You can't possibly be held responsible for what happens to Chase if his story to them doesn't match what he told you. That's all on him, not you. Chances are, it's a moot point."

The point didn't stay moot for long, however. An hour later,

Detective Gutierrez called and demanded Tiffany come to the police station to give a statement. Rip offered to go along for support, but for some reason, insisted I stay behind. I can't imagine why he'd think I'd say something to stir the already murky pot, but I got the distinct impression he did.

I was as nervous as a mole with a grub allergy while pacing around the Carpenters' house for the next two hours. *Why is it taking so long?* I wondered. *It's not like it'd take more than two minutes for Tiffany to tell the detectives everything she knows. Did they order her to come to the police station, only to make her sit on her thumbs for two hours waiting for them to question her? Was it a ploy to get her to divulge incriminating information about her husband?*

I hoped that wasn't the case. I was glad Rip had accompanied Tiffany to the police station, although Rip wasn't the most patient person in the world. His impatience often raised its ugly head when he was forced to wait on someone else. That was especially true when it came to sitting in a physician's waiting room. I've seen him get up and leave his cardiologist's office at two-thirty because he hadn't been called back for a two-fifteen follow-up appointment. I'd wanted to thump Rip on the lengthy incision running down his chest with the seven-year-old *Popular Mechanics* magazine I'd been thumbing through. Instead, I'd forced him to return to the waiting room and he was called back to a room two minutes later.

Fifteen minutes was nothing, as far as I was concerned. I'd once waited over two hours in a long line at a local gas station just to get a free car wash my Ford Taurus didn't even particularly need. To help pass the time, I'd cleaned the crumbs out of the cup holders, a melted milk dud off the carpet, and ten-year-old insurance cards out of the glove compartment. I figured it was not wasted time as long as I used it productively. Not to mention saving ten bucks on the drive-thru car wash.

The memory made me determined to find something productive to do to pass the time as I waited for Rip and Tiffany to return. I almost wished Tiffany wasn't such a meticulous housekeeper. I couldn't find a single dust mite to wipe off the shiny wood furniture, or a speck of lint to vacuum off the carpeted floor. So I gave up. Instead of being useful, I snatched my third wine cooler of the day out of the fridge, grabbed two Snickerdoodles, and returned to the back patio to chill out and relax.

SEVEN

"**G**rams? Wake up."

I heard Tiffany's voice as if it was coming from the opposite end of a tunnel and felt a tap on my shoulder. I slowly worked my way through the haze and opened my eyes. When I did, Tiffany's light blue eyes were peering back at me in concern.

"Are you all right?" Her voice sounded uneasy as she glanced at the three empty wine cooler bottles lined up like dead soldiers on the wrought-iron table next to me.

I chuckled. "Don't worry, sweetie. I didn't black out in a drunken haze. I was just tired from not having slept very well last night."

"Yeah, tell me about it!"

"I can imagine you didn't sleep a wink, considering what's going on," I said. "So, tell me. What happened at the police station? Did they question you?"

"You could call it that. It felt more like I was being interrogated as a suspect. Like you said, I think they were trying to determine if my story matched Chase's."

I nodded. "You can bet your behind that's exactly what they were doing."

"But I remembered your advice. I told them everything I knew, the whole truth and nothing but the truth."

"Good girl! I'm sure that pleased the investigators."

"On the contrary, they seemed disappointed with my responses. I think they'd been hoping I'd say something that would incriminate my husband."

"Well, dear," I began, "I don't think they actually *wanted* you to say something that would implicate Chase, but I'm sure they are anxious to find out who's behind Trey's murder."

"Maybe," she responded. I could tell she wasn't convinced they hadn't had high hopes of pinning the crime on Chase. His belligerent attitude toward them the previous afternoon had probably not endeared him to them very much. "They asked me if Chase or I had any potassium chloride in our possession. That really ticked me off. I wanted to tell them we kept a gallon of it on hand at all times, just in case one of us had a sudden hankering to knock someone off."

"But you thought better of it, right?" I asked. I knew Tiffany had a tendency to say things off the cuff like her Grams often did. Inheriting a number of my traits wasn't necessarily an advantageous thing for my granddaughter. Having eyes the color of a French hydrangea was one thing. Being recklessly impulsive was quite another.

"Of course, I thought better of it!" Tiffany giggled. "Do you think I'd be standing here talking to you now if I'd said that to the investigators? While I was being grilled by two homicide detectives, Gramps talked to Detective Gutierrez."

"I'm surprised the detective would talk to him, with you being asked to give a statement and your husband potentially being charged with murder."

"Yeah, I was surprised too. But he did. In fact, even though they've threatened to charge Chase, they promised Gramps they wouldn't report the arrest to the media, as he's really just a person of interest at this point. I think Gramps has formed some kind of coppish connection with Gutierrez."

"'Coppish' connection?"

"Yeah, you know, a brothers-in-blue type of bond between police officers."

"Oh, I see. You're undoubtedly correct." I wasn't surprised. Rip had a way of worming his way into the confidence of other law enforcement officers, even though he no longer carried a badge. He's the type of guy who gives the impression you could trust him with your secrets, your money, and even your life. It was just a God-given gift he had. Kind of like my God-given gift of being able to get people to open up to me whether they want to or not. I also was gifted with the ability to tie a cherry stem into a knot with my tongue—an entirely different type of skill, but still impressive. Truth be known, that's one of the reasons tequila sunrise was my drink of choice. They were usually served with a maraschino cherry and it offered the opportunity to impress others with my stem-tying talent. I came out of my reverie when I noticed how tired Tiffany looked. "Are you all right, honey?"

"I don't know why, but I feel drained," Tiffany said. "I think I'll go shower and change into a t-shirt and shorts. I feel icky because this jumpsuit makes me perspire."

Are you sure it wasn't the grilling you just endured, and not the jump suit, that's made you sweat? I wanted to ask in a joking manner, but I decided Tiffany was in no mood to be teased. "Good idea. In about three or four hours, we're going to celebrate your birthday in grand style, whether Chase is here or not. Okay?"

"I guess." Tiffany appeared glum, and her tone was completely joyless. I didn't know how Rip and I would be able to brighten her spirits with a three-person birthday party. There was no way it could ever match up to the surprise party Chase had planned, with fifteen to twenty of her closest friends attending. I was going to try my damnedest to make her smile, however.

I was beginning to think there had to be something I could do, with or without Rip's assistance, to exonerate Chase and help find the true perpetrator of the murder. The cherry-stem-tying gift might not be of any help, but I hoped my ability to get people to talk would.

As soon as Tiffany left to freshen up, I went looking for Rip. I was anxious to find out what Detective Gutierrez had told him. I hit pay dirt, too. Rip shared a bit of information that inspired me on how to go about getting Chase released.

"As it turns out, the medical examiner found so many injection sites on Trey's body that he couldn't determine if any one of them was a result of the lethal injection of potassium chloride that showed up on the tox screen," Rip said.

"How strange," I replied.

"Not really. Dr. Dan Wilkens, the medical examiner, told me that—"

"You talked to the medical examiner who performed the autopsy?" I interrupted in astonishment.

"Yes, Carlos introduced me to Dan."

"Okay." I don't know why I was shocked that Rip was already on a first-name basis with the Albuquerque detective as well as the medical examiner. It was just an aspect of his God-given gift I mentioned earlier. "Go on, dear."

"Dan told us Trey was a type II diabetic who'd recently become insulin-dependent. He took several insulin shots a day, resulting in numerous injection sites on his arms, legs, and abdomen. Apparently, he liked to spread them around so that no one particular area would become scarred or sore."

"That makes sense."

"Dan also explained that potassium chloride is used to prevent or treat low potassium levels, a condition he referred to as hypokalemia, and it's needed for several bodily functions, including the beating of our hearts. He said that people with kidney failure often have the opposite problem called hyper-kalemia, or high levels of potassium due to decreased urine output. Nonetheless, according to Trey's wife, um…"

"Sandy," I said, supplying the name for him. I couldn't fault him for not remembering a name he'd probably only heard Tiffany say a few times. I had no trouble remembering it because I'd had an aunt named Sandy on my mother's side. Sadly, Aunt Sandy had died in a bizarre hunting accident. Uncle Titus had mistaken his wife for a feral hog late one night. At least that was his story, and he stuck to it until his death from alcohol poisoning two years later. His drinking had escalated dramatically after Aunt Sandy's passing, for some reason. *But that's murky water under the bridge*, I thought, as I turned my attention back to Rip.

"According to Sandy," Rip continued, "Trey was on several medications: the insulin I already mentioned, an antidepressant, a statin for high cholesterol, and a fiber supplement for his chronic constipation. Sandy said her husband had never met a vegetable he couldn't refuse. Refuse to eat, that is."

"Hmmm, he sounds like someone I know." I looked at Rip pointedly. "Fortunately for that person, his wife does not give up easily and forces greens down his throat whenever possible."

"Yeah, lucky for him," Rip muttered. His tone was cynical, but his expression was one of good humor.

"Speaking of Trey's wife, how is Sandy doing? Did Carlos mention her?" I asked. "Trey's death had to have come as a huge shock to her."

"I would imagine. Carlos said she seems to be holding up fairly well but hadn't been very cooperative in supplying the investigating team with any information she thinks might help track down his killer or in writing out a statement for the detectives. Carlos is hoping that once the shock has worn off, she'll be more accommodating."

"I'm sure giving a statement to the police is the last thing on her mind right now. You said potassium chloride was a mineral, a supplement used to maintain a healthy potassium level in humans. Couldn't he have accidentally ingested it himself?"

"Not likely," Rip replied. "It would take a lot higher dose than typically found in supplements or pill form. For a man Trey's size, Dan said he'd have had to have swallowed nearly seven ounces of the mineral for it to be lethal, whereas an injection of only seventy-five, or more, milligrams can cause cardiac arrest and rapid death. They still think an injection was the most probable way the lethal dose was introduced into his system. On another front, the detectives spoke to the house manager to confirm Chase's alibi."

"What did Manuel de la Cruz say?" I asked. It was probably obvious I was showing off, knowing Rip couldn't have come up with the man's name under threat of having his toenails ripped off.

"He confirmed Chase came to the Monroes' front door around ten-thirty."

"That's good. So, why won't they release him?"

"Because he then added that he saw Chase drive away from the curb in front of the house a few minutes after he returned to his car. He said Chase's vehicle was nowhere in sight when he left the house at around eleven."

"Which would give Chase the time to track down Trey and inject him with a lethal dose of potassium chloride before the victim arrived at the airport a short while later," I said, as I was thinking out loud.

"Exactly."

"Could Manuel have been mistaken about the time?" I asked. "How many people look at their watch and note the time whenever someone knocks on their front door?"

"That's true, but according to Carlos, the house manager seemed positive about the time. He indicated he was keeping track because he had an appointment to keep and didn't want to be late." Rip shrugged and added, "I hate to say this, honey, but Chase is starting to look like he might have gotten his ass in a jam. I don't want to think he could ever do such a thing as commit murder, but he's looking better and better for it all the time."

"Oh, wow! I don't want to even consider that possibility. Could de la Cruz have lied to cast suspicion away from himself, or because he hadn't appreciated Chase's attitude, which he'd mentioned on a post-it note was extremely enraged?"

"Anything's possible, dear."

"Did you repeat any of what Carlos and Dan told you to Tiffany?" I asked. I didn't think so, or she'd have acted a lot more agitated when we'd spoken on the back patio.

Rip confirmed my suspicions. "No. I didn't want to upset her any more than necessary. I wish there was some way we could help confirm his alibi."

"There might be." My mind had begun whirring with ideas. "Do you know if Sandy has a Ring doorbell?"

"What other kind is there than a doorbell that rings?"

"Do you remember that bit on *Inside Edition* about a month ago that showed porch pirates being caught red-handed on video stealing packages off people's front porches?" I asked.

"Vaguely."

"Well, it's a very popular device that has a video camera inside the doorbell. It's called a 'Ring' doorbell, and you can access it through an app on your phone. If someone walks up to ring your doorbell, you can be visiting Machu Picchu, Peru, and your phone will go off and let you know someone is on your front porch. You can speak to them right through your phone with its BlueTooth capability. It picks up motion too, and records it on your phone."

Clearly, from his expression, I'd lost Rip after I'd mentioned accessing the Ring through an app on the phone. I only knew about it because I'd researched the device after watching the episode about porch pirates on *Inside Edition*. I'd quickly decided the Chartreuse Caboose would have to suffice with its "knock" doorbell. I'm too cheap to invest a hundred bucks in something we'd have so little opportunity to use. When Rip continued to stare at me silently, I said, "The Monroes employ a guy to manage their lives for them, for goodness sake, so they clearly weren't hurting for money. I'd guess a house as fancy as theirs is apt to have a fancy doorbell, as well."

"So?" Rip asked.

"So?" I repeated in annoyance, wondering if he'd heard a word I'd just said. "Tiffany and Chase were good friends with the Monroes before the crap hit the fan. Tiffany might know if they have a Ring doorbell. If not, she knows where they live. We can go over to offer our condolences to Sandy and check it out. If they do have one, there should be a record of Chase's arrival and departure, and it could possibly show if his car was in front of their house when Manuel left. I'm sure each video clip is time-stamped. It's possible Manuel could have been distracted and not noticed Chase's car."

"I'm not real comfortable with this ruse of yours." Rip shook his head and grimaced. After a long moment of deliberation, he added, "But I don't have any better ideas, other than to not inter-fere in the case to begin with. Something tells me that suggestion isn't going to fly with you, however." At my smile and nod, he shook his head again. "Oh, all right. Let's go talk to Tiffany, but tell her as little as possible about what Dan and Carlos said. Okay?"

"Of course," I replied in agreement. I would've never imagined I'd be asking God for someone I'd never met before to own some fancy new doorbell. But there I was, saying a silent prayer, asking God to deliver a means by which we could prove Chase could not have killed his former friend and investment manager.

EIGHT

It was three o'clock in the afternoon and Rip, Tiffany and I were on our way to one of the most exclusive areas in Sandia Heights where million-dollar homes were the norm. Tiffany had been nearly certain the Monroes had a Ring doorbell. She was clearly a little hesitant to show up on Sandy's doorstep, despite the fact they'd been the best of friends. I'm sure she wondered if Sandy was in on the hoax, considering she hadn't returned any of Tiffany's text or phone messages following Trey's death.

"Won't she think it's suspicious if I show up to console her on the loss of the man who just stole our life savings?" Tiffany asked. "Not to mention that my husband is in lockup waiting to be charged with her husband's murder?"

"Don't let that stop you," I said. "Remember why we're going there in the first place—to prove Chase's innocence. She may not even know Chase is in jail. Act as if you are oblivious to what Trey did as far as stealing all of his clients' money. Let her think that Chase didn't tell you all the sordid details in order to keep from ruining your thirtieth birthday."

"Yeah. I guess I could play dumb."

"That's my girl! The dumber you act, the better." Rip shot me a look of skepticism after my remark. I directed my attention to him and said, "It'll work. Trust me."

I don't think Rip trusted me for one hot second, but it was the only plan we could come up with as we pulled into the Monroes' driveway. Tiffany and I walked to the Monroes' front porch with purpose; we both felt an overwhelming sense of being on a mission. Rip shuffled along behind us. It was obvious he felt an equally overwhelming sense of dread.

After several rings, a voice came from the Monroes' Ring doorbell. "Can I help you?" It was a sharp reminder that the home's occupants could see and hear everything. I was glad we'd remained silent while we'd waited on the front porch.

"Oh, hello, Manuel. Is Sandy home?" Tiffany spoke directly into the doorbell.

"No, Mrs. Carpenter, I'm afraid she's away from the house right now. Can I give her a message?"

"Um…" Tiffany turned around and looked at me for help in responding. I shook my head and whispered, "We can try again later. Tell him you just wanted to offer your condolences in person and ask when she'll be home."

Before Tiffany could repeat what I'd suggested, the door flew open and a blond-haired, distressed-looking woman about Tiffany's age stepped across the threshold and enfolded her friend in her arms. "Oh, Tiffany. It's so good to see you. I guess you've heard about Trey. Isn't it just awful?"

Tiffany agreed that Trey's death was terrible and incredibly shocking. She introduced Sandy to Rip and me, and then said, "I'm so sorry, Sandy. I can't imagine why anyone would murder Trey."

"Murder?" Sandy looked truly taken aback. "Did you say murder? I was told Trey died of a heart attack. Oh, my. Please, come in and tell me what you've heard."

Now who's acting dumb? I thought. *Or is she truly in the dark about the truth behind Trey's death?*

"No one told me that Trey's death was due to foul play. Are you sure?" I had to admit Sandy appeared genuinely shocked as she spoke.

"Yes, and I'm so sorry to be the one to tell you," Tiffany said before stopping abruptly. I sensed she was uncertain about telling her friend what was really going on. Eventually, she came to the conclusion she had to if she was going to be of any help to Chase in his current predicament. "We were told Trey was given a lethal dose of potassium chloride shortly before his death. That's what prompted the heart attack."

"Potassium chloride?" Sandy had a very puzzled expression. "What's that?"

"It's a mineral often used for certain health conditions."

When Tiffany's response did not seem to satisfy Sandy's curiosity, I decided to further explain the uses of potassium chloride, thanks once again to information I'd read on the Internet.

"Potassium chloride is widely used for making a fertilizer called potash. It can also be used as a salt substitute in food. Ironically, it's one of three drugs used in executions by lethal injection. Although it is often used to regulate the potassium level in the human body, too much of it can cause cardiac arrest, as occurred in your husband's case." During a short pause, it occurred to me I might sound cold and callous to the victim's spouse, so I added, "God rest his soul. I'm so sorry for your loss, Mrs. Monroe."

My last two remarks hadn't sounded sincere in my own ears, and I'm sure they sounded even less so in Sandy's. Rip's expression when he glanced at me made it clear he thought I should keep my disingenuous sentiments to myself. But I couldn't bring myself to believe this was the first time the victim's wife had heard her husband had been a victim of foul play. Why else would the detectives ask her to come give a statement at the police station? In the same vein, why would she not cooperate with that request? Detective Gutierrez had mentioned searching the Monroes' home, seizing the post-it note regarding Chase's visit there just minutes before Trey's death. Did Sandy think it was common practice for homicide detectives to scour through a residence, collecting evidence, following the homeowner's natural death by cardiac arrest? She couldn't possibly be that naïve, could she? Granted, Sandy was a blonde. But the woman's dark brown eyebrows suggested it was the kind of blond hair she'd gotten from out of a box, not a Swedish gene pool.

"By the way," I began, "were you aware that all of your husband's clients' portfolios were sold off and the money from those sales appears to be missing? His personal assistant can't locate any of it and thinks Trey might have been running off with the funds. I assume you were told his body was found in the airport's parking garage, and he had a one-way ticket to Grand Cayman in his possession."

Rip and Tiffany both turned to me in unison. They wore matching expressions of disapproval. I knew I shouldn't be saying anything that could land Harlei Rycoff in hot water. Discussing any of Trey's clients' business matters with Chase had been a definite breach of confidentiality and I shouldn't be sharing anything with the victim's spouse that could be exposing Harlei's lack of ethics.

When I returned my attention to Sandy, I noticed her complexion had paled dramatically. She'd looked woozy earlier, but she looked downright disoriented now. Suddenly, her face dropped into her hands and she began to weep. Although there were no actual tears welling up in her eyes when she looked up at the three of us, she did appear to be truly distraught. *Could those be crocodile tears?* I wondered. *Or, as I should say, a lack of them? Carlos had indicated Sandy had been unaware that her husband was planning to leave the country to fly to the Cayman Islands. How could he have known of her obliviousness without bringing the subject up with Sandy?*

When she finally spoke, Sandy reached her hands out and clutched Tiffany's. "I had no idea about any of that. I'm sorry. I'm just completely shocked the authorities believe Trey's death was not due to natural causes. Trey had heart issues in the past. In fact, he was born with a heart murmur."

As was I, and something like seventy percent of other babies, I wanted to say. *Most often the murmur goes away as the child ages. And something tells me you already know that, lady.*

"I'm sorry to break it to you like this," Tiffany said. "I guess we just assumed you knew. The police are actually holding Chase at the police station and threatening to charge him with Trey's death. Can you believe that? We both know Chase would never hurt anyone, especially Trey, one of his very best friends."

"I wonder if the police consider me a suspect, too?" Sandy asked, clearly not giving a rat's behind about the situation Chase was in. "After all, I was probably the last person to see him alive. Yet, I've not been asked to give a statement."

"Really? The spouse is always a prime suspect in a murder case," Rip told Sandy. His voice made it clear he didn't believe her. "I'm sure you'll be questioned in due time. The investigating team is probably giving you a little time to grieve before asking you to come down to the station and give a statement."

We watched *Dateline* regularly and I knew there was never any consideration given to grieving time for the victim's spouse. As did Rip, who was only trying to offer a little comfort to Sandy. She was obviously upset by all of the details we'd just shared with her about her husband.

"Yes, I suppose you're right." Sandy sniffed before continuing. "A Detective Gutierrez came to the house to inform me of Trey's death yesterday. He never mentioned anything about murder or me needing to give a statement. Instead, he asked a couple of questions about Trey's morning, which seemed odd at the time."

I knew we had likely caught her in a lie, but didn't know if it pointed to anything incriminating. It could just be because she was a scatterbrained blonde with big silicone boobs, a lot of money to toss around, and only a spattering of good sense. Carlos had commented on her lack of cooperation in giving a statement, and I was pretty certain he wouldn't have made that up. Granted, in her understandably shocked state of mind at the time, she might have not assimilated much of what the detective had said to her.

"What type of information did Detective Gutierrez ask about?" Rip asked Sandy.

"Things like what time Trey left the house and what he'd eaten for breakfast. I told him Trey hadn't eaten anything, but he'd downed half a pot of coffee before leaving for work. Then the detective asked me if I knew of anyone who might want to hurt Trey, which kind of threw me for a loop. But I was hysterical at the time, so I didn't give it any more thought."

Of course, you didn't. The thought of Trey downing half a pot of coffee made me realize my own bladder was starting to protest. All three of the Jamaican Me Happy wine coolers I'd consumed earlier were now Jamaican me have to wet my panties if I didn't find a restroom soon.

Sandy pointed the way to the ladies' room after I told her I was in desperate need of relieving myself. I didn't want to mention the three wine coolers I drank earlier in case she was a teetotaler, even though she looked a little unsteady, as if she'd just polished off a bottle of Dom Perignon.

I walked down the hallway to a restroom that had more square footage than in the entire travel trailer we call home. The fixtures were opulent, the counters were a classy marble design, and the ample cabinets could store enough bath towels to dry off the Monroes and several hundred of their closest friends. The blue and white tiled shower was large enough to accommodate the Jackson Five and the Four Tops all at the same time. I was both impressed and disgusted. It was a beautiful room, I'll give you that, but it was entirely too large and garish for my taste. Of course, that could be the green-eyed monster coming out in me, as it was wont to do in situations like this.

As I sat on the fanciest commode I'd ever seen, I studied the contraption next to it. I knew it was called a bidet and had been created by some French guy long ago to help keep Europeans' keisters clean, especially those who were flush with money. Pardon the pun. I'd never actually seen one in person and was uncertain how it operated. It seemed to me it'd make for a real mess. The bidet also seemed to me to be more of a social status statement than something useful. I doubt it'd been utilized a dozen times since it'd been installed.

The Monroes' restroom was the total opposite of the outhouse I was intimately familiar with for the first fifteen years of my life. That outhouse had been a stark, dimly lit and some-what smelly wooden box with no frills or decorations. *But it got the job done,* I thought. *For one heck of a lot less money!*

I looked up just then and noticed three medicine bottles on the bathroom counter. They were all prescribed to Sandy, but I didn't have time to study them any further. For some reason, I felt compelled to snap a photo of the labels with my phone. I don't know why, but I wanted to find out what kind of diseases or disorders they treated. It was pure nosiness, to be honest. *Later,* I thought, *when we get back home to the Chartreuse Caboose, I'll look the medications up online, just to satisfy my curiosity.*

I finished my business and hesitated before drying my hands on a fancy hand-painted towel that looked like it'd been hung in the towel ring solely for decorative purposes. I had to dry my hands, however, and decided if Sandy didn't want anyone to use the snazzy towel, she shouldn't have hung it up next to the sink in the first place. I dried my hands and exited the restroom to rejoin the others in the kitchen. As I was walking down the hallway, I heard Sandy and Tiffany reminiscing about a Bruno Mars concert the two couples had recently attended together. I smiled because even I couldn't help but to bust a move to the catchy tune of the singer's *Uptown Funk* song when it played on the radio. I just had to be careful I didn't bust a hip in the process.

"Thanks for the use of your facilities," I said as I joined the others. As I spoke, I noticed a cell phone in Sandy's back pocket and thought it was about time we got down to the business of trying to exonerate Chase. "Sandy, do you have the Ring doorbell app on your phone, by any chance?"

"Yes, I do. Why do you ask?"

I couldn't be sure, but her voice seemed to have a wary tone to it when she responded. It could have been due to my abrupt change of subject, or the fact that it was none of my dang business what she had on her phone. Either way, I was relieved when she pulled the phone out of her pocket.

"Do you mind going to the app? Chase stopped by to chat with Trey yesterday morning, and——"

"He did?" Now her tone sounded more than just wary as she cut in. It sounded distrustful and suspicious. "What time did he stop by?"

"That's just it," I replied, wondering why Sandy's house manager hadn't told her of Chase's visit. Had the detectives seized the post-it note before she'd had an opportunity to read it? "He said he arrived around ten-thirty and was greeted at the door by Manuel. After Chase was told neither of you were home, he waited a while in his car. He gave up and left at about eleven-thirty. Problem is, there's no way to prove the timing to the authorities unless you have a video of his arrival and departure. I'm guessing it will show the time on the video clip of Chase ringing your doorbell. Do you mind pulling that video up on your phone?"

Sandy gave me an odd look, and then glanced at Tiffany for support. Tiffany nodded and said, "It might answer a couple of questions for both of us. We're hoping there's something on those videos to prove Chase couldn't possibly have been anywhere near Trey at the time of his death."

Sandy reluctantly pulled up the app on her phone. I noticed she had the very latest version of the Apple device——the iPhone 8 Plus——which I knew had just recently been released by Apple. That fact didn't surprise me in the least. She did a lot of scrolling and switching between screens within the app until she finally proclaimed, "I guess I accidentally deleted all the videos prior to this morning. The only one here is of you all from a few minutes ago."

When the three of us stared at her in disbelief, she became visibly uncomfortable. She went back to the phone and pulled up the most recent video of Tiffany, Rip, and me. We watched ourselves on the screen, fidgeting on her front porch as we spoke to Manuel via the Ring doorbell. I was embarrassed that you could hear me whisper to Tiffany that Sandy might have told Manuel she didn't want to see her. Sandy pointed to the screen. "See? This is the only video on my phone. I don't recall deleting any, but I might have done it without thinking. They start piling up after awhile if I don't delete them *en masse* on occasion."

"So, you're saying you don't recall erasing them, even though it had to have been done quite recently?" I asked.

"No, I don't remember doing so, but I've been under a great deal of stress."

"Yes, of course. Does your house manager have access to your phone?" I asked. "Might he have deleted them?"

"Nah, I don't think so," she replied. "I've never known Manuel to mess with my phone. He carries around an old-fashioned flip phone and I doubt he'd have a clue how to even find the Ring app, much less delete the videos."

"I see. Well, that takes care of that, I guess." I sounded perturbed only because I was. I found it difficult to believe the woman would take the time to delete a "mass" of video clips on her phone in the midst of grieving the untimely death of her husband. And, more unbelievable yet, not recall doing so? *Bull hockey,* I thought. Did she not have more important things to be taking care of right now? If it had been so important a task to take care of during this difficult time, wouldn't she remember doing so? As Rip had told Sandy earlier, the spouse was always considered a suspect in the mysterious death of their husband or wife. Sandy was quickly becoming my number one suspect in Trey Monroe's death.

On the other hand, there was also the house manager. Sandy had introduced us to Manuel shortly after we'd entered her home. I'd found the polished gentleman had the personality of a very uppity-up statesman. Excuse my French, but to be perfectly frank, the dude acted as though his poop didn't stink. *Perhaps I'd been wrong,* I thought, *and Manuel uses the bidet religiously.*

I found it unfathomable that Manuel ran the Monroe household like a "well-oiled machine" and managed all of their social engagements and medical appointments, along with all the other intricacies of managing the lives of Trey and Sandy, while using a flip phone rather than a smartphone.

Is it reasonable to believe the house manager doesn't have enough sense to delete videos from the Ring app on his employer's phone? I asked myself. *That sounds patently ridiculous. Even I could figure out how to delete videos from the doorbell app, and I'm about as dinosaur-ish as it gets when it comes to high-tech devices.*

Which is why directly under Sandy's name on my own personal suspect list went her house manager's name, Manuel de la Cruz. *Good grief! Even the man's name sounds pretentious!*

NINE

W e piled into Rip's truck and backed out of the Monroes'
driveway, which was made of colored, hand-stamped
concrete. I figured they'd invested more money in their driveway
than we had in our home on wheels and truck combined.

Once we were parallel with the street, I studied the beautiful
home across the street. It had a similar Mediterranean-style
architectural design as the Monroes' house. Suddenly, I yelled,
"Stop!"

Rip hit the brakes instinctively, as if afraid he was about to
run over a two-year-old on a big-wheel bike. He scanned the area
quickly and asked, "What is it? Why'd you holler for me to stop?"

"Look at that house!" I pointed excitedly at the mansion. I
was practically hyperventilating as I spoke. I was glad to see Rip
remove his hand from his chest, which he'd been clutching since
I'd scared the bejesus out of him by hollering for him to hit the
brakes. I needed to be more careful since he had experienced
serious heart issues in the recent past.

"Yeah. So?" Rip replied, obviously on edge.

"It has an identical doorbell as the Monroes'. Maybe we can

get them to look through their videos from around ten-thirty yesterday morning. Their doorbell might have picked up Chase's car arriving at the Monroe house, and it might also show him driving off. If we can notate the times, we might be able to prove it was impossible for him to have been anywhere near Trey shortly before his death."

"That's a great idea, Grams!" Tiffany exclaimed.

"I don't know." Rip was more hesitant, which came as no surprise. "I'm not sure approaching the Monroes' neighbors to look at their doorbell videos is such a smart idea."

"Why not, Gramps?" Tiffany asked. "I don't know them well, but I have met the lady of the house before. I believe her name is Babs. She'd walked over to sort through the castoffs at Sandy's garage sale at the same time as I had. If I remember right, she bought an old Tupperware pitcher and a couple of books. She seemed very nice."

"You not only remember her name, but you remember what she bought at Sandy's garage sale?" I asked, totally blown away. "Why didn't Regina ever tell me my granddaughter had a photo-graphic memory?"

"I think it's actually called an eidetic memory, as there's no proof that photographic memories really exist." Tiffany's response was ambiguous, and a bit condescending.

"Okay, now you're just showing off." I laughed, and she chuckled along before responding.

"Trust me; I have neither a photographic nor an eidetic memory. I only remember being shocked that someone who lived in the house they do would want a piece of crap like the scarred-up plastic pitcher she'd purchased and two Harlequin romances. I mean the lady's got to be close to eighty."

"Hey! I'm only a few years younger than her, and I'm not too old to enjoy a good romance. Frankly, though, I'm surprised someone who lives in a house like Sandy's would stoop to having a garage sale in a neighborhood like this to begin with." I glanced around at all the highfalutin homes on the block. "You'd think she'd prefer to donate it all to charity or to the local dump. Selling your worthless junk to your neighbors for a dime or a quarter is a little humiliating, even for me."

"Even for you? Seriously?" Tiffany exchanged a knowing look with Rip and they both chuckled.

I wasn't sure how to take Tiffany's remark, so I ignored it and motioned for Rip to pull into Babs's driveway. To be honest, I'd held a huge garage sale when we'd sold off most of our stuff to become full-time RVers. I'd felt a bit embarrassed at first but got over it quickly when someone paid me ten bucks for a lamp I'd purchased at someone else's garage sale for half that much.

Tiffany opened the truck door. "I'll see if Babs is home and motion for you to join me if she's willing to let us look through her doorbell videos."

I crossed my fingers as Tiffany walked up to the front door. An older woman came to the door and conversed briefly with her before Tiffany turned and waved at us. Rip cut the engine and we joined Tiffany on the front porch.

After we exchanged introductions, Babs led the three of us to a comfortable sitting area beyond the living room. We sat around a small mahogany table and sipped on glasses of iced tea she'd poured from a sun-tea pitcher. I thanked our gracious host for the much-appreciated beverage because I *was* extremely thirsty. I quickly set it back down when Babs proudly said, "I bought this tea at the World's Fair in Seattle. Howard and I were there for our honeymoon."

I knew the World's Fair in Seattle, Washington took place in 1962, which would make the tea well over a half-century old.

Suddenly, I wasn't as parched as I thought. Instead of gulping antiquated tea as though I was dehydrated, I listened in as Tiffany explained our situation to Babs in more detail.

I'd only seen the entryway, sitting room and living room of the Hancock home, but noticed a drastic difference in motif from the house across the street. Where the Monroes' home had felt staged and ostentatious—and had a disturbing lack of personal photos and knick-knacks—the Hancocks' house felt homey and well-lived-in. You can be damned sure there was no bidet to be found in the Hancock home. The walls had framed family photos of all sizes, a fire burned in the huge rock fireplace, and a half-finished afghan Babs was in the process of crocheting was draped over a well-worn leather recliner.

Scanning the room, I noticed a collection of carved wood birds filled a curio cabinet in the corner of the living room. When I commented on their beauty, Babs told me carving was a hobby of her husband's. "He carves while I crochet."

The furniture, although classy and obviously expensive, appeared comfortable, and I could imagine myself curled up on their oversized couch in front of the crackling fire with a cup of coffee and a good book. In contrast to the Monroe home, I wouldn't feel guilty using a hand towel in the restroom here.

Tiffany sat sipping on her tea. Clearly, the age of the beverage hadn't registered with her. As she told Babs that their investments with Trey's company had disappeared and that her husband was being held as a person of interest in Trey's death until his alibi could be confirmed, Babs' lips formed a tight line.

At Tiffany's request to check out her Ring doorbell videos, Mrs. Hancock looked confused. When Tiffany pointed to Babs's phone on the kitchen table, the woman picked it up and handed it to her. Tiffany smiled, no doubt used to us older folks being technologically-challenged. Babs might even make my tech skills look accomplished, which were akin to a cave woman from the

Paleolithic Age trying to FaceTime her mate on a smartphone while he was out slaying a woolly mammoth for supper.

Tiffany quickly brought up the Ring app on the phone. She located several of the videos that included Chase's image. The first video showed Chase pulling up to the curb and exiting his vehicle at ten twenty-eight the previous morning. The video shut off as Chase waited at the Monroes' front porch for someone to open the door. The second video showed Chase standing at the front door conversing with Manuel. It'd been triggered by a van driving down Zinfandel Avenue. It shut off shortly after the house manager had closed the front door.

It was the third video that caught our attention. It was time-stamped at eleven-thirty-six on the morning of October twenty-first. It clearly showed Chase sitting in the front seat of his white muscle car, a Dodge Charger with blue accent stripes up its hood. You could see him glance at his watch, turn the key in the car's ignition, and pull away from the curb. He pulled away very slowly, as if hoping one of the Monroes would return home at the last moment. You could even make out his license tag number as he drove off. The videos proved Chase had correctly stated his whereabouts during the time in question.

"That ought to be enough to get Chase released from police custody. Thank you, Mrs. Hancock," Rip said. He looked at me and said, "Good thinking, Rapella."

"Thanks."

Then Rip turned his attention to Babs. "Would you be willing to drive down to the Foothills substation so the detectives can view a couple of these video clips on your phone?"

"Um, well…" Babs seemed reluctant.

"We don't want to impose on you any more than we have to," I told her. "You've been more than gracious already. But it's critical the authorities view these videos."

"Maybe you could just share them to my phone," Tiffany suggested.

"Share them to your phone?" Babs repeated in the form of a question. By her expression, you'd have thought Tiffany had asked her to video herself doing the "floss" dance and post it on TikTok, which would have left me flamboozled too.

"It might be better if one of the Hancocks could meet us at the police station so Detective Gutierrez can view the videos directly from their phone," Rip advised. He then turned to Babs. "As long it's not an imposition, of course."

"It's no imposition whatsoever, folks," Babs replied after a lengthy pause. "I understand how important it is to have your son-in-law cleared of any wrongdoing. My husband, Howard, and I would really like to see Trey's murder solved, too. We'll do whatever it takes to help make sure it is."

"Thank you, Babs," I said. "After all, the Monroes are not only your neighbors, but also your friends, I'd imagine."

The expression on Babs's face was unreadable. I wasn't sure if she looked sad, angry, or a mixture of both. It was the latter, I realized, when she next spoke.

"We *were* very close to them. That is, until Trey unloaded our entire stock portfolio without our consent or knowledge a couple of days ago. Like you, Tiffany, Trey has stolen nearly every dime we have. He managed to gain Howard's complete trust and talked him into putting all of our investments in his hands. Trey even made us believe he was getting us in on a special deal involving the IPO fund of a tech stock he guaranteed would skyrocket in value. And it did. Now, that money is nowhere to be found, according to his personal assistant, whose name I can't recall. I've never seen Howard so hurt, or so livid. I'm afraid for his health if he doesn't calm down. That's why I'd like to see the police get to the bottom of this situation as soon as possible."

"I'm so sorry, Mrs. Hancock," Tiffany said. "I know exactly how you feel. I feel exactly the same way."

It went without saying that the Hancocks had lost a considerable amount of money, probably much more than the Carpenters.

"Please call me Babs, dear. And I'm sorry, too. It appears that you and I are in the same boat," Babs said. Then with a rueful smile, she added, "And it looks like our boat's up Shit Creek without a paddle."

We all chuckled at her remark, which seemed in stark contrast to her gentle, ladylike demeanor. I then asked, "Babs, did you happen to notice if the Monroes' house manager ever left their house in his car yesterday?"

"Manuel doesn't own a car," she replied. Babs went on to say the house manager used Sandy's Lincoln Navigator whenever he went to the grocery store, or somewhere of that nature. "I don't recall whether he left their place yesterday or not. I was busy planting petunias in my underwear drawer."

"Say what?" Tiffany asked. The expression on her face was priceless. It was as if the elderly woman had just ripped off her blouse and was twirling tassels attached to her sagging breasts.

"That's all right, Babs." I smiled at Babs and then Tiffany as I spoke. Unless the woman actually did have two types of "bloomers" in her underwear drawer, something wasn't quite up to snuff with Babs's mental condition. I didn't want to fluster her any further. "It's not important."

"Are you sure?" Babs asked, looking puzzled.

"Yes, everything's fine," Tiffany replied, catching on to the issue with Babs's mental state. She patted the top of Babs's hand. "I didn't notice any vehicles leaving their property on any of the doorbell videos we viewed."

"The Monroes have several vehicles. Along with the two-car garage in front, there's a single-car garage in the rear of their home, as well. There's a driveway back there that exits onto Beringer Avenue." Babs sounded perfectly coherent once again. As suspected, her lucidness didn't last long.

An elderly gentleman walked into the sitting room just then. He glanced around anxiously. "What's going on?"

Babs looked up and said, "Howard, these nice people stopped by to chat about the World's Fair where we went on our honeymoon. I'm going to drive to Seattle to meet them."

"Babs can't drive anywhere," Howard said, looking at Rip.

Without a doubt, I knew then that his wife was suffering from what was probably the early- to mid-stages of age-related dementia or Alzheimer's. She was of sound mind one moment and in a world of her own the next. I was saddened by the idea the poor woman and her husband had such an awful issue to deal with. I knew the condition would worsen and get increasingly more difficult to manage as time went on. At least I now felt safe drinking the iced tea, because I really was beginning to feel dehydrated.

"That's all right, Mr. Hancock. We'll figure out something." I listened as Rip went on to describe the conversation that had been taking place before Howard had entered the room. I could sense the longer Rip spoke, the angrier Howard got. He was internally seething while trying to maintain his composure in front of their uninvited guests.

Howard nodded frequently, but the only comment he made, other than agreeing to meet Rip at the police station in half an hour with the phone, was, "At least the thieving S.O.B. got what was coming to him."

I decided it was time we left. No sense getting Howard riled up any more than he already was. I thanked Babs and Howard and we bade them farewell.

Had Manuel been truthful about leaving his employers' home at eleven? Where did he go at that time? Did he use the driveway on the opposite side of the Monroes' house to follow Trey to the airport? I wondered. *Maybe I should move him to the top of my suspect list. And perhaps Howard Hancock had earned a spot on the list, as well.*

As we exited through the Hancocks' front door, I promised Babs and Howard we'd do our best to find out what had become of their money. We'd intentionally not mentioned the lack of evidence any funds they'd given Trey had ever been invested in the IPO fund. If they weren't aware already, we knew they'd find out they'd been played like a fiddle soon enough.

Babs thanked us, and as we were leaving said, "Thanks for coming to visit. It's been so long, I was beginning to think you were mad at me."

Excuse me? I thought. *We've never met before.* Babs then enveloped me in a warm hug and said, "I love you, Henrietta."

I smiled and nodded. I didn't know what to think, but I didn't want to hurt her feelings, so I said, "I love you, too."

Rip looked at me and raised his eyebrows. I shrugged in response. I heard Tiffany trying to suppress a giggle. After we got farther down the driveway, she said, "Wow! That came out of nowhere. She seemed so sharp there for awhile."

"Dementia and Alzheimer's are like that, I'm afraid." My mother had suffered from memory loss. "Your great-grand-mother, Nana, was the same way until she got to where she didn't recognize anyone. Ever. It's a terrible disease, more for the victim's family than the victim. As Nancy Reagan titled her book about her husband, it's a 'long goodbye' for the family of the affected."

Paddle or no paddle, by the time we pulled away from the Hancocks' home, I was damned and determined to do whatever I could to help both the Carpenters and the Hancocks find their way down Shit Creek to wherever their money was now located.

TEN

"Look who's shown up for dinner!" Rip hollered cheerfully when he walked into the Carpenters house with Chase in tow. It was nearly ten hours after Chase had been hauled off in the back seat of a patrol car. Rip had dropped Tiffany and me off at the house before meeting Howard Hancock at the police station. Rip presented the phone to Detective Gutierrez so he or their tech experts could retrieve the pertinent videos off the Hancocks' Ring app in order to verify Chase's alibi.

Rip had thanked Howard for his cooperation and time. About an hour later, he drove his newly released grandson-in-law home. Chase was quickly enveloped in a warm hug from Tiffany, who squealed in delight. I gave Rip a hug, too, for putting in such an effort to get Chase released from custody.

"Oh, thank God!" Tiffany exclaimed. "I'm so glad you're home, and you got here just in time for my birthday celebration. It would have been really disheartening to have to celebrate it all by myself."

All by yourself? I wanted to ask. *What are Rip and I? Chopped liver?*

Chopped liver that traveled here from south Texas to surprise you on this special day, no less. Naturally, I merely smiled and stayed silent. I knew Tiffany had a dramatic side to her personality. It was a trait she'd inherited from her mother. Rip and I weren't sure who Regina had inherited it from, but it certainly wasn't from either one of us.

"Well, now you won't have to celebrate it alone." Chase kissed his wife on the lips after speaking, but failed to mention the reason she wouldn't have to celebrate "alone" was because Chopped Liver had intervened and got him released. "I'm sorry we couldn't have the surprise party I'd planned for you. Happy Birthday, by the way!"

"Thanks, babe. Don't worry about it. I'm just glad you're home."

"So, what are we having for supper?" Chase asked.

"Gramps is going to grill rib-eye steaks and corn-on-the-cob. Grams mixed up a tossed salad to go with it, and we have baked potatoes in the oven."

"That sounds like a Thanksgiving feast, considering what they fed me for lunch: a bologna sandwich and an apple."

"But you love bologna!" Tiffany said.

"Not when it's one thin slice on two stale pieces of bread with no mustard or mayo to enhance its flavor. It was like eating cardboard."

"Well, you'll eat like a king tonight, Chase," I assured him. "I also made Tiffany's favorite dessert."

"Your world-famous Mississippi Mud chocolate cake?" Chase asked with a glimmer in his eyes, and probably a little extra saliva in his mouth. He licked his lips and added, "I love that scrumptious cake of yours, too. I remember you made it for us the last time you visited."

"Yep! Only this time it will have candles on it."

Chase, who was two years younger than his wife, teased,

"Won't thirty candles put off enough smoke that the neighbors might call the fire department?"

Tiffany gave him a good-natured whack on the back of the head with the palm of her hand. "Actually, it's only two candles: a 'three' candle and a 'zero' candle."

Joining in on the playful banter, I said, "You didn't think I was going to waste money on thirty individual candles, did you? For one thing, I'd have had to make a larger cake."

"Yeah," Tiffany began with a chuckle, "I can hardly imagine the size of cake you needed for seventy candles on your last birthday, Grams."

I gave my granddaughter an equally good-natured whack on the back of *her* head with *my* hand. "You two get ready for supper before I change my mind and devour the entire birthday cake myself."

We'd finished our meal and the four of us were sitting around an outdoor table on the covered back patio. Rip was drinking his daily Crown and Coke, and I was sipping on my tequila sunrise. The three wine coolers I'd polished off earlier in the day were a rare splurge for me, and I figured what my primary doctor didn't know wouldn't hurt me. Tiffany and Chase were enjoying long-necked Miller Lites.

I'd strung up several colored light strands, the party kind with LED bulbs inside plastic red chili peppers. I'd also purchased several helium balloons the previous day. One was in the shape of a roadrunner, New Mexico's state bird, and had the words "Happy BEEP, BEEP Birthday!" printed on one side. The balloons were now attached to the wrought iron side table that held the chocolate birthday cake. I'd also hung a "Happy 30th Birthday, Tiffany!" banner on the stucco siding that I'd had created at a local *Kinkos*. In my mind, this was going overboard for a grown woman's birthday. But, considering the circumstances, I felt it was necessary.

The patio had a definite New Mexican flair to it, and the party decorations only enhanced the celebratory vibe. I'd wanted Tiffany's birthday celebration to have a festive feel to it. For chopped liver, I thought I'd done a pretty fair job of decorating for the special occasion. Not that I was still irked about Tiffany's earlier remark, mind you. And, to be fair, that "irkedness" began to fade after Tiffany thanked her Grams and Gramps for going to such an effort to make her birthday really special. It disappeared completely when she added, "Having you two here means more to me than an entire room full of friends that I get to see and interact with all of the time anyway. Grams and Gramps, you guys are the best!"

I was feeling warm and fuzzy as I took another sip of my cocktail. After a brief exchange between Tiffany and Chase about how delicious her birthday dinner had been, Tiffany asked her husband about his short stint in jail.

"It was insane!" Chase said.

He might have a flair for the dramatic too, I thought. I listened silently as Chase described what he'd been through during the previous ten hours. You'd have thought the guy had just spent the last decade in the San Quentin State Prison in California. After Chase elaborated on what could only be called a near-death experience during his incarceration——according to his description, at least——I changed the subject to what had gotten him sprung from his hellish purgatory in lockdown. I'd bitten my lip not to bring up the fact it was his own stupid fault he'd been placed behind bars in the first place.

"I can only imagine how relieved you are that we thought to review the video clips on the Hancocks' doorbell app." I was proud of myself for sharing the glory with Rip and Tiffany. I was also a bit irritated that Chase had shown no appreciation for my clever idea, or for Rip's intervention on his behalf, even though I knew the young man had a lot on his mind at the time.

"I absolutely am, Rapella. I can't tell you how grateful I am for your involvement in this nightmare. And Rip's too, of course. I apologize for so stupidly making the entire situation worse by not cooperating fully with the police from the beginning. I guess I was angry they thought I could do something so evil."

"They didn't know you from Adam, Chase," I began, "so it's not like they were judging your character."

"I realize that now. And, after all, every one of us who lost money on the deal had a motive to kill the shyster responsible for our loss. That includes Mr. Hancock. Did Rip tell you that after Carlos Gutierrez reviewed the Ring doorbell videos, the detective asked Hancock where he and his wife were at eleven-fifteen yesterday?" Chase asked Tiffany and me. "Hancock went ballistic! In fact, he grabbed his phone out of the detective's hands and stormed out. It was unbelievable."

"I'll say," Rip replied. "I had to calm Howard down and talk him into going back inside the station, assuring him that anyone who'd been victimized by Trey Monroe's deceitful scheme would undoubtedly be asked to come to the station and give a statement. After all, they have the exact same motive to exact revenge against the man as Chase had."

"That's true. So, did Howard give one?" I asked.

"Of course," Rip said. "Apparently, he's a retired real estate broker dealing in luxury properties. From the looks of their home, he's been very successful in the realty business."

"What about Babs? Will she be required to give a written statement?" I had doubts she could give a factual, competent account of where she was at the time of the murder.

"I doubt it," Rip said. "Howard explained her mental issues and assured them that nothing she said in a statement would be reliable, as she probably wouldn't be able to recall the detail of where she was then, or at any other time."

"Yeah, that's for sure. Unless they happened to catch Babs in a clear state of mind. So, where *were* Babs and Howard at eleven-fifteen yesterday morning?" I asked Rip out of curiosity.

"She was home watching the QVC network on television. Howard said he could prove his wife ordered a full set of 1993 major league baseball cards off the shopping network yesterday morning, for which they had no need or desire. He remarked they were neither baseball fans nor collectors of sports memorabilia."

"And Howard?" I asked Rip. I was both amused and saddened by Howard's comments about his wife's recent purchase.

"Howard was taking some photos of a large ranch outside San Antonio he's preparing to list for a client."

"He's listing a property in Texas?"

"No, Rapella. The ranch is in the unincorporated town of San Antonio, New Mexico, which is located on the Rio Grande River. Howard said the client was not on site at the time, or even aware of his visit, and their live-in maid was in Santa Fe visiting her elderly mother."

"I thought he was retired," I said. "He's, like, eighty years old or better."

"He told the detective he still dabbles in real estate once in a while as an independent broker. Unfortunately, his dabbling is going to make his alibi hard to confirm with no witnesses or a paper trail of his trip to San Antonio. He didn't stop for fuel or anything else, either going or returning from the ranch property, which is only about ninety miles south of here."

"Maybe I could come up with a way to help confirm his alibi," I said. *And then again, maybe I'm a little too full of myself.*

"No!" Rip spoke vehemently. "We are not going to get caught

up in Mr. Hancock's involvement, or lack thereof, in Monroe's death. We have enough to do to try and track down where the kids' money is stashed."

My head pivoted so quickly I was afraid I might have to wear a whiplash collar the following day. I was too stunned to even respond. Rip had actually said we should commit ourselves to digging into the situation to track down Chase and Tiffany's money. It was usually me who got us immersed up to our eyebrows in a case like this.

"Absolutely!" I agreed. I knew before my lips stopped flapping that I was pushing my luck. "You are right. We'll be busy just tracking down leads on the money's whereabouts and trying to identify the perp——"

"Whoa!" Rip said, looking at me as if I'd just admitted licking the soles of my shoes before putting them on my feet. "Back up the bus, missy! I didn't say anything about getting involved in the murder investigation. We've done that before, and where'd it get us?"

"At an awards ceremony in Buffalo, Wyoming, receiving an accommodations plaque?" I asked timidly. Then in a bolder tone, I added, "And at a police station in Rockdale, Missouri getting our friend, Lexie Starr, released from jail after our efforts exonerated her. Plus, we——"

"Okay, okay," Rip said. "That's not what I meant, and you know it. It also about got us both killed."

"Well, sure, but——"

"There's no 'buts' about it. We are not sticking our noses in another murder case." Rip's voice had raised several notches in volume. "That's what law enforcement officers get paid to do."

Rip was adamant, and there was nothing I could do or say to change his mind. However, the pretty young lady who'd blessed our lives thirty years ago this very day, and who'd been the apple of Rip's eye ever since, was a different story altogether.

"Oh, Gramps!" Tiffany said, fluttering her long eyelashes at him. "It sure would be nice if we could help find out who killed Trey. He might have suckered us into befriending him, and then into investing all of our money with him, but he was still a big part of our lives for several years. And I still consider Sandy a close friend. None of this is her fault. I know if I were in her shoes, I'd want justice to be served. For closure, if nothing else."

"Like I said, Tiff, that's what law enforcement is for. They'll have this case wrapped up in no time. Trust me!" Rip said, before leaning over and kissing his granddaughter on the cheek. When the dejected expression on Tiffany's face made him feel guilty, Rip made a rash promise to her. "Okay, look, sweetheart. If they haven't made an arrest or located the money by the first of November, I assure you we'll begin looking into it ourselves. At that point, I'll be willing to get involved as long as we don't inter- fere in any way with the investigating team's efforts to solve the case."

The last remark was aimed directly at me, I'm certain. The fact he stared into my eyes as he said it left little doubt. His right index finger pointing straight at my face made the confirmation airtight.

"Oh, thank you, Gramps! I love you so much." Rip smiled at Tiffany and then rolled his eyes at me as she draped her arms around his neck. "It's no wonder you're my favorite grandpa."

Just as Tiffany was Rip's only granddaughter, he was her only living grandfather. Her father, Milo Moore, had lost both of his parents before Tiffany was born. It kind of made their chances of being the favorite in each other's opinion a no-brainer.

I, on the other hand, wasn't opposed to getting involved in the case right away. I'd been involved in a number of murder cases in recent years, sometimes with a lot of assistance from Rip, and sometimes not. But for Tiffany and Chase's sake, and even for the sake of Harlei Rycoff, and the rest of Trey's clients whom he'd swindled, I prayed the case would be resolved as quickly as possible.

Two wrongs don't make a right, I thought, *so the fact the victim perpetrated unforgivable transgressions against his clients doesn't make it all right for one of those people he'd wronged to murder him.*

Waiting until November first to get involved in a personal investigation of the case would not be easy for me. Patience was hardly one of my virtues. I wanted the money back in its rightful owners' accounts, and the killer nailed to the wall by his or her thumbs by sunrise the following morning. I also wanted world peace, a cure for cancer, and calorie-free cheesecake. None of those were apt to happen anytime soon, either.

ELEVEN

W e had spent the last week and a half seeing the local sights and enjoying some southwestern cuisine at several of Tiffany and Chase's favorite restaurants. At the time, the four of us were at the top of Sandia Peak Tramway. We'd ridden the 10,378 feet up in the swinging tram and enjoyed the view overlooking all of Albuquerque before grabbing a drink at the bar. We'd been given our drinks in plastic cups and had taken them to a picnic table outside. It was cold, even with the warm jackets we'd been advised to bring along.

As the other three chatted about the weather, I thought about the fact it was now November first and Rip had promised Tiffany we'd begin investigating the situation if the case had not been solved by today. He had checked in periodically with Detective Gutierrez, who seemed to have formed quite an affinity for Rip. Rip had grown fond of the detective, as well. So much so that he'd invited Carlos over for supper later that evening.

Carlos had not formed any kind of bond with Chase, however. In fact, it was quite the contrary, so Rip had decided we'd have supper in the Caboose, and he'd use the grill that slides out from an undercarriage compartment in the travel trailer to prepare a meal for just the three of us. Rip fancied himself a world-class grill master, and I encouraged the fantasy. If nothing else, it frequently spared me from having to prepare the meal myself inside the trailer. When I didn't feel inclined to cook, I only had to say, "Man, am I craving your incredible garlic-crusted grilled prawns!"

In the same vein, when I wanted to go out to eat, I merely had to make a production of sniffing the package I'd removed from the freezer earlier in the day and ask Rip, "Does this smell all right to you?" Rip would offer to take me out to eat without getting within ten feet of the package. I'd put the pork chops back into the fridge and prepare the meat, which was still fresh as could be, for supper the following evening. I was never really certain if Rip was gullible, or if he just went along with me because he also liked to eat out on occasion.

Speaking of Rip's scrumptious garlic shrimp specialty, that's what I recommended he fix for the detective. Carlos had assured him he loved all seafood and had no shellfish allergy. I love shrimp any way you can fix it, even though my personal favorite is scampi.

As if reading my mind while we relaxed atop the mountain, Tiffany reminded Rip of his promise as we stood in line to ride the tram back down the mountain. Since no perpetrator had been arrested in Trey Monroe's death and the missing money had not been located yet, she inquired if we were ready to begin a personal investigation into the case. Rip was cagey in his response but promised to speak to the lead detective on the case that evening. Although I didn't say so out loud, if Rip didn't bring it up with Carlos, I would.

Rip told Tiffany, "Honey, I just wouldn't feel right not running it past Detective Gutierrez first. If he gives us his blessing to do a little non-intrusive nosing around, then we'll be all over it like a wet blanket. Okay, Tiff?"

She was less than enthused by his remarks but agreed nonetheless. I understood her reaction because I felt as though it'd be a cold day in you-know-where before the lead detective in any murder case would agree to have citizens get involved. The only thing we had going for us was that Carlos knew of Rip's career in law enforcement and seemed to treat him like a father figure.

"That shrimp was delicious, Rip! And, Rapella, I believe that was the best potato salad I've ever tasted. If I could cook anything more complicated than a TV dinner, I'd ask you for the recipe." Detective Gutierrez praised the supper we'd prepared profusely as the three of us retreated to the living room for an after-dinner drink. Moving from our kitchen to the living room takes all of about three steps. But then, nothing in the thirty-foot travel trailer was more than a dozen steps away, no matter where you were in the RV at the time.

Rip scooted Dolly away from his seat on the couch and a few minutes later, he and Carlos were discussing a story about a domestic disturbance call that had gone south when Rip was a beat cop in Texas. He'd responded to a neighbor's call about a couple engaging in a vicious brawl in the couple's front yard. When Rip and his partner arrived, the woman, who was sporting a busted lip and a swollen right eye, cussed at the officers for interfering with the dispute. She then cussed at her husband, calling him every nasty thing she could come up with. Although she was loud and belligerent, the man still had no right to assault the woman, Rip said. After he and his partner cuffed the man and placed him in the back of their patrol car, she turned on them, calling them even more vile things than she'd called the man who'd just beaten her up. The man wasn't in jail for a full hour before she'd shown up to bail him out.

"That's why I hate domestic disturbance calls," Carlos said.

Rip nodded. He turned to me and said, "That's also why they are probably the most dangerous call for police officers to respond to. It's not uncommon for the battered individual to defend their abuser, even after that individual just assaulted them."

"Isn't that something?" I responded absentmindedly. We were drinking our evening highballs and I took a sip of my tequila sunrise. Carlos was drinking a Modelo Rip had purchased that morning, knowing it was the detective's favorite beer. "Speaking of physical abuse, is there any news on the Monroe murder case?"

Rip glanced at me with a scowl, but it didn't look to me as if he was ever going to broach the subject, and that was the first time I'd had an opportunity to segue into the topic of the murder case. Surprisingly, Carlos appeared anxious to discuss the matter.

"Not really. It's been a hard case to solve. It's being treated as a homicide even though suicide has not officially been ruled out. There are so many people who were victimized by Monroe that we've been busy taking statements. Even his personal assistant, his right-hand woman so to speak, lost most of her life savings. They all have the same motive but very different alibis. Most have been confirmed. The few exceptions would be a couple who are neighbors of the Monroes, and—"

"Babs and Howard Hancock?" I asked.

With a surprised look, he nodded. "Well, yes, and there are several others like them who live alone and have no one who can verify they were home at the time of Monroe's death. As you know, Howard Hancock showed us the videos on his phone from their Ring app, which cleared Chase. But Hancock's own alibi has yet to be confirmed. Not one of the remaining suspects really seems capable of murder. For example, one client, named Chen Ho, is frail, about sixty years old, and weighs no more than a hundred pounds. He'd have trouble beating a cockroach to death, much less injecting a thirty-six-year-old man with a syringe. But he undoubtedly has some powerful friends and acquaintances."

"How about Monroe's wife, Sandy, and their house manager, Manuel de la Cruz?" I asked. "Have they been cleared?"

"Pretty much. They basically backed up each other's alibis and neither really fit the profile of a killer. It's been a challenging case, for sure."

"And Monroe's personal assistant?" I asked Carlos. "I think Tiffany said her name was Harley, like in Harley Davidson."

"Actually, it's Harlei, spelled H-A-R-L-E-I, and her last name is Rycoff. She's a single lady in her upper thirties; told me she'd never been married. She said she spent the entire day in the Monroe Investment office alone, answering one call after another about why clients' accounts were showing a zero balance. She didn't know what to tell them, which according to her, put her in a very bad spot. She doesn't remember every single client who called or when, but every client we talked to confirmed they spoke with her the morning of his death, which pretty much confirms her alibi. She said she's the only one who works in the office other than Trey, who came to the office for a brief time, then left suddenly and never returned. He usually reported at exactly ten-forty-five, and stayed at the office until six in the evening, she noted, although he'd often take a two-hour mid-day break to treat clients to lunch. There really wasn't any evidence she'd been involved in either Monroe's fraudulent activities or his death. She seemed to be stunned by the entire situation, but then, she'd just lost all of her investment like the rest of his clients. Speaking with her, I could tell she was still in disbelief her boss was gone."

"No doubt Harlei was in a state of shock," I replied.

Rip seemed reluctant to join in the conversation, so I told the detective a little about other murder cases we'd been involved in, leaving out details featuring one or both of us almost getting killed on a few occasions, or anything with an illegal tone to it, such as breaking and entering. He seemed impressed with our success.

Carlos turned to Rip. "I guess it's hard to get the old detective mindset out of your system. Isn't it?"

Without responding to Carlos, Rip looked pointedly at me.

"Absolutely!" I said. "It's something he did most of his life and he's darned good at it. This makes us kind of want to look into this deal with Monroe ourselves. We wouldn't want to interfere in any way with your team's investigation, but we'd kind of like to snoop around a bit. Our granddaughter is beside herself, as you can imagine. They lost their entire life savings to that scoundrel."

"Um, I don't think that's necessary. It'd be best if you left it up to——" Carlos began.

"Like I said, we wouldn't cross any legal lines," I cut in, "or get in the way of your official investigation in any way. However, if we do come across anything that seems off and might lead to an arrest, we'd bring it to your attention immediately."

Carlos remained silent for a few seconds, obviously deliberating my suggestion. He glanced at Rip, who merely shrugged. After some more thought, Carlos asked, "You wouldn't put yourselves in any kind of danger, would you?"

"Oh, heavens no! We'd never do anything like that." The detective nodded, while Rip looked at me in disbelief. When he opened his mouth to contradict my remark, I quickly cut him off. "We're too old to do anything that might put us at risk of injury. Rip has had both a hip replacement and a triple bypass in the last couple of years. We'd basically just be doing some background research, certainly nothing that'd put us in a precarious predicament."

I heard Rip groan—probably recalling the bullet he'd intercepted with his hip during an investigation I'd gotten us involved in. That was the injury that had prompted the hip replacement he'd been putting off for some time.

Luckily, Carlos seemed oblivious to Rip's reaction. He mulled my proposal over for a few more moments and said, "Hey, why not? We haven't had much luck. I guess a couple fresh sets of eyes on the case couldn't hurt. Rip's one of us, and with his many years of experience, you two might just stumble onto something we've overlooked."

I wanted to tell the detective it was usually I who stumbled on to something that led to the truth, but I kept quiet. Patting myself on the back would serve no purpose at this point, other than conceivably causing Detective Gutierrez to change his mind and Rip to groan again, louder this time.

"Okay, good," I began, "we'll let you know if we find out anything significant or at least worth a second look."

"All right. Just promise me you won't tell my boss I agreed to this."

"It's a promise!" I agreed, a little too enthusiastically. "We'd never do anything that might put your neck or your job on the line. Now how about another bottle of beer?"

"No, I better not. Thank you for the offer," he replied, "but it'd be embarrassing to be pulled over for drinking and driving when I frequently arrest people for doing the exact same thing."

"Good point," I said.

While I checked our email, Rip and Carlos chatted about a number of subjects, like golfing, Cuban cigars, and the shock of Donald Trump's triumphant win in the 2016 Presidential race. The two men had similar golf handicaps and political opinions, which only seemed to strengthen the bond they'd established in such a short time.

After responding to messages from my daughter and an old friend, Gracie Parker, I began musing about how to begin our personal investigation into Trey's death. I still couldn't bring myself to eliminate Sandy Monroe or the house manager, Manuel de la Cruz, from my suspect list. *How does corroborating each other's alibis provide iron-clad confirmation that neither one had anything to do with Trey's death?* I wondered. *What if it was a dual effort on their part to eliminate him? I'd like to visit with both of them. I'd also like to speak to Trey's personal assistant, Harlei Rycoff.*

I reasoned Harlei might be able to give us a more in-depth look at what kind of scheme Trey had carried out to swindle his clients. She also might have some insight into what had made him pull such an unethical stunt and where he might've stashed the money. I truly anticipated a conversation with her might set us on the right path to solve the case. What I hadn't expected, however, was that she'd share a wealth of information with Rip and me, and that information would help steer us down a path that'd put both of our lives on the line.

TWELVE

Rip and I decided to visit Ms. Rycoff the following morning. We thought it best if only the two of us went. Tiffany was too emotional, and Chase too volatile, when it came to the subject of their missing investment money.

The GPS function of our iPhone led us to Trey's office in one of the tallest high-rise buildings in the business area referred to as EDo, or East Downtown. His office was on the tenth floor of the twelve-story New Mexico Bank & Trust Building on Gold Avenue. On the door of his office was an understated placard which read "Monroe Investments." I was surprised the door actually opened when I pushed on it.

A slim, dark-haired woman about my height of five-foot-eight inches, and wearing a cute shoulder-length haircut, appeared to be the only person in the wide-open but small office. The one-room office was not at all what I expected. It held two desks with desktop computers, each with multiple screens; a Xerox machine; a medium-sized rack of hanging file folders; several chairs and a wooden corner table with a single-serving coffee maker and coffee paraphernalia atop it. There were also a number of medium-sized cardboard boxes scattered about the room.

"Good morning." I smiled as I introduced ourselves. "My name is Rapella Ripple. This is my husband Clyde, but he goes by Rip."

"Good morning Mr. and Mrs. Ripple," she replied cordially. "I'm Harlei. Harlei Rycoff. I'm Mr. Monroe's personal assistant. I'm sorry, but we're closed. I can't help you, unfortunately. The SEC shut us down about ten days ago."

"SEC?" I asked.

"Yes, the U.S. Securities and Exchange Commission. I only happen to be here this morning to box up my personal belongings."

"Oh? Why did the SEC shut you down?" I asked. We'd decided we'd approach Harlei as if interested in hiring her boss as our investment manager. "We were hoping to be taken on as new clients of Mr. Monroe."

"Oh?" Harlei seemed surprised. "You haven't heard?"

"Heard what?"

"Mr. Monroe suffered an untimely death about ten days ago." I noticed Harlei didn't mention her boss's "untimely death" was the result of a lethal injection given to him by an unknown perpetrator. "I do have a couple of local RIAs I can recommend, however."

"RIAs?"

"Yes, ma'am. It stands for registered investment advisors, such as Mr. Monroe was."

"I guess a couple of suggestions wouldn't hurt. Thank you." I agreed with her offer in order to go along with our excuse for dropping in. "What happened to Mr. Monroe? His death is such a crying shame. He was apparently a successful young man in his prime who came highly recommended. Cancer, I suppose."

I hoped to prompt the personal assistant to go into more

detail about Trey's death, but she simply shook her head and replied, "Murder, they suspect."

"Did you say murder?" I gasped appropriately and then acted like I'd just had a recollection. "Oh! Hey, I did hear something on the news about an investment advisor who'd been killed while trying to abscond with all of his clients' money. Oh, my!" I put my hands to my mouth in feigned astonishment as if I'd just made the connection in my mind. "That wasn't your boss, was it?"

"Yes, unfortunately it was."

"I'm so sorry." I walked over and put an arm around her shoulder in a show of sympathy. "His death must be especially hard on you, being the victim's personal assistant and all. I imagine the two of you were close."

"Yeah, we were."

"He must have depended on your efficiency and expertise in such a competitive business." I was buttering Harlei up, hoping to make her more prone to want to be open with me.

"Trey depended on me entirely. He often told me so. I don't know how he could've kept this business afloat without me."

"I have no doubt he owed much of his success to you. I just can't imagine what he might have done with his clients' money, or why he would've defrauded them in the first place," I said, as if musing out loud from pure curiosity, hoping she'd explain what was behind the fraud.

"Me neither. To thank me for all I did for him, he put me in the poorhouse." Harlei glanced down at her hands, which appeared to be trembling.

"How did that happen?" I asked. The green-eyed assistant looked as if she instantly regretted having made the admission.

"Oh, no! I'm so sorry, Harlei," I said to gain her trust when she didn't respond to my question. I then repeated it. "How did that happen?"

Harlei hesitated a few moments, but went on to explain. "He talked me into investing almost all of my savings into an IPO fund he was promoting. I'd been sending out monthly statements to all of his clients, having no idea he'd cooked the books, and the figures on the statements were complete hogwash. The profits the IPO appeared to be earning for his clients made me want to jump on the bandwagon. So I emptied out my savings account and jumped in feet first." Now the woman appeared totally ticked off. She looked as if someone had poured sugar into the gas tank of her new luxury automobile and blown up its engine.

I nodded in commiseration, but stayed quiet so she'd keep ranting. The more Harlei talked, the more information we gathered about the situation.

"The entire IPO fund was sold off, along with some other stocks, and I can't find any of the proceeds from those sales. I'm afraid Trey pulled off a Ponzi scheme. Now, I not only look like a fool, but I also look like I might have been involved in the blasted scam. After all, I handled nearly all of the paperwork for Trey and even signed most of the documentation, not knowing what kind of swindle he was perpetuating. Well, 'forged' is probably a more accurate term than 'signed'. It worries me I might be held responsible for a portion of the clients' losses. Is forgery still illegal?"

"Um, yeah," Rip said dryly. "And it's likely to remain so. But as long as you knew nothing about him stealing the money, you have nothing to worry about."

"Thanks. That takes a load off my mind. The detectives were here questioning me again earlier this morning. They asked about my whereabouts on the morning of Trey's death, but I don't know what I can do to have my alibi verified."

"Oh?" I asked. "Why not?"

"I was here in the office alone all morning that day, except for the few minutes he was in the office. I'd only found out about the missing money when clients started calling and asking questions. The same call over and over. Everyone was so worried, and I just kept telling them it must be a computer error. I tried repeatedly to get in touch with Trey, who wasn't answering my calls."

"I wouldn't worry about the detectives. They're just doing their job, I'm sure," Rip said. Detective Gutierrez had already told us they didn't consider Harlei a suspect, having verified her phone records showed she was taking clients' calls all morning, including around the time of Trey's death. But as far as she knew, this was the first we were hearing about his passing. I knew Rip hoped to ease her mind. In Harlei's shoes, I'd have been concerned too. "I can't imagine the detectives were looking at you as a suspect."

"Well, I would hope not!" Harlei almost appeared insulted by his comment. "Mr. Ripple, I had as much, or more, to lose as anyone with his death. Not only are all of my savings gone, but I'm unemployed now, too. I don't know where to go from here. Should I sell my house and move? Should I look for another job here? If so, in the same field, or should I branch out and try something entirely different?"

"I'm so sorry, dear." I squeezed Harlei's shoulders, which I'd draped my arm across again. "Did you care for Trey as a person?"

"Of course." I noticed her eyes begin to water. "He was one of the nicest guys I'd ever met. I was paid very well, twice what most folks in my position make, and he was very lenient as a boss. If I showed up late for work, which I rarely did, he never even questioned me about it. Losing him is like losing a brother. Even though he stole my money, I can't help but mourn his death."

"They say when you lose a loved one—usually a spouse, but a boss and close friend is comparable—you should not make any major decisions for a year. Maybe that's the advice you should take." I didn't want her to sell her home and then regret making such a rash move without giving the decision a lot of consideration first.

"I wish I could," Harlei replied. "I can't afford the luxury of taking a year, or even a few months, to make crucial decisions."

"I suppose that's right." After one more squeeze of her fragile-feeling shoulders, I stepped back and stood next to Rip. "Just think carefully before making a drastic move."

"I will, Mrs. Ripple."

"Please call me Rapella, and my husband prefers to be called Rip."

"All right. Thank you, Rapella."

"I know very little about Ponzi schemes." I was interested in what kind of scam Monroe had pulled off. "Can you explain how Trey managed to dupe his clients?"

"And me, as well?" Harlei asked with a huff. "Basically, Trey talked many of his clients into investing in a fund to purchase shares of a new company who'd developed a highly rated virus protection program called Clean Sweep when it was first introduced as an IPO, or initial public offering. He told everyone he was making them a special offer and only if they banded together could they make this great deal. The only stipulation was it had to be held through the standard "lock-out" period of six months. All the while, without anyone's knowledge, he was cooking the books to satisfy the investors. I can't be one-hundred percent certain this is what happened, but the evidence looks extremely damning. Trey was so cunning; I had no idea I was being deceived right along with the rest of his clients."

"He obviously didn't think as highly of you as you did of him." When I finished my comment, Rip gave me a scathing look. Harlei began to weep. I wished I'd thought my remark through before I'd let it out.

Harlei was able to regain control of her emotions fairly rapidly, and went on with her story. "Trey had some high-dollar investors, many who lived in his own neighborhood in Sandia Heights. It was nothing for him to have one-hundred-and-twenty-million dollars under management. He was riding high on the hog, let me tell you."

We had pulled Harlei's chain and she was on a roll now. Rip settled down into a chair, rubbing the hip that had recently been replaced. I decided to sit down in the chair next to him. I was trying to retain everything Harlei was telling us and being comfortable could only make that goal easier. I thought taking notes might look odd, so I tried to commit everything to memory, which at my age is a monumental undertaking. To keep her talking, I said, "It sounds like he was walking in tall cotton."

"Walking in what?" Apparently, Harlei had never heard that well-worn adage.

"Never mind. Just an old cliché that means about the same as 'living high on the hog', the phrase you just used. So I take it the six-month lock-out period is over?"

"Exactly," she replied. "Trey knew some of the investors would be anxious to pull their money out as soon as the six months were up. The real IPO had performed well and many would want to capitalize on the big gain and opt out, perhaps moving their money to a more predictable, low-risk investment at that point. Of course, getting their money 'out of the fund' was impossible. They just didn't know it at the time."

"I'm not very knowledgeable when it comes to the stock market, Harlei," I began, "but why would they not be able to draw their money out of the Clean Sweep fund, take the profit and invest it in something less risky?"

"Because there never *was* a Clean Sweep fund. His clients were giving him money to invest and he was putting their money in his own coffers, not an IPO fund. That's what a Ponzi scheme entails."

"So, Tiffany and Chase thought he'd sold off all their stock only a couple days before he was killed. But, in actuality, Trey had never invested their money in that exclusive IPO in the first place." Too late, I realized what I'd said.

"You know the Carpenters?" Harlei asked in a distrustful tone.

"Um, yeah. Tiffany is our granddaughter."

"So, you didn't really stop by to inquire about being taken on as new clients of Monroe Investments, did you?" Harlei asked. "I'm guessing you actually wanted to feel me out on what went down before Trey was killed. I'm sure you felt as if I was involved in the scam, too. Am I right?"

"No, of course not." I knew there was no way to get the proverbial cat back in the bag. It'd be like getting toothpaste back into its tube after it's all been squeezed out. "We would never even consider the idea you were involved in the ruse. We actually just dropped by on Chase and Tiffany's behalf. Naturally, they're desperate to have their money returned, just as you are."

Harlei sounded more disappointed than angry. She now knew we were pumping her for information under false pretenses. She shook her head and said, "I need to get back to work packing up my stuff now. You can see yourselves out."

"I'm sorry, Harlei." And I truly did feel remorseful. "We're just trying to help our granddaughter and her husband get their life savings back. We've been given permission to look into the situation by the lead detective on the murder case, Carlos Gutierrez."

Too late I realized I should never have told anyone about our pact with the detective. Rip's glare spoke volumes. I now had to try to dig myself out of another hole I'd dug for myself.

"Actually, that's not true. We just mentioned to him we were interested in the case, and he said if we heard anything that might be pertinent, to let him know. Kind of like our own personal tip hot-line, you see." When it appeared as though

Harlei wasn't interested in our connection with the detective, I changed tack. "We'd like to help you get your money back, too, of course. I was afraid you wouldn't be as open with us if we told you we were investigating the financial end of this terrible hoax while the homicide detectives concentrate on tracking down Trey's killer."

Harlei's green eyes locked with my blue ones, and after a long uncomfortable silence, she said, "All right. I *would* like to get my money back. I guess it would be in my best interest to help you in any way I can."

"Thank you for understanding why we led you on," I said with sincere gratitude. After Harlei nodded in response, I asked, "Do you have any idea about who might've killed your boss?"

"Didn't you just say you were going to leave Trey's death to the detectives while you concentrated on the financial end? At the moment, I'm more concerned about getting my investment money returned than finding out who was pissed off enough about being ripped off to kill Trey."

"Yes, of course."

Harlei and I locked eyes again. She appeared to be waiting for me to offer an explanation for my inquiry. For once, I was at a loss for words. Rip leaned forward in his chair and took over. "That's exactly what we are most concerned about too, Ms. Rycoff. Rapella was just asking your opinion about Trey's killer out of curiosity. Is there anything else you can tell us that might help lead to the location of the funds that seem to have vanished into thin air?"

"Unfortunately, I've told you about all I know. I'm just as baffled as to where the money went as you are. I'd assume it's all in an offshore account in the Caymans, because I overheard one of the SEC agents talking on the phone the day they came in to shut the business down. He said all of the firm's bank accounts that could be traced were emptied and closed out just prior to

Trey's death." Harlei stopped speaking and glanced from Rip to me, as if judging our reactions. Seemingly satisfied, she continued. "And I haven't a clue who might have killed Trey, although I can see why there might've been quite a few folks who wanted to. I'll admit I'm very angry about being defrauded. I feel like the biggest nincompoop alive, because all of this was going on right under my nose the entire time. I was so impressed by Trey's success that I encouraged a number of my friends with money to invest in the Clean Sweep fund along with me. I feel terrible now because those same friends have lost even more money than I have."

"I doubt they hold you personally responsible for their loss," I said. "We hope to help set things right not only for the Carpenters, but also for you *and* your friends. We'll do all we can to see you get your money back, or at least as much of it as possible. I can't believe Trey would do something so vile to his trusted assistant and two of his very closest friends. I think Tiffany and Chase are as hurt by his betrayal as much as they are infuriated over losing their life savings."

"To be honest," Harlei began, "Trey *wasn't* one of their closest friends. Trey made every investor feel as though they were special, and that's why they felt honored that he'd invite them to join the fund. He'd have them over to eat, or take them out on the town, or even invite them to play a round of golf—but never in the company of other investors. They all thought they and the Monroes were the best of buddies. They were all being played. By making clients think they were being given preferential treatment and being let in on an elite investment, they all jumped at the chance to turn their money— sometimes in the hundreds of thousands, or even millions, of dollars—over to Trey. It was a classic Ponzi scheme, not much different from the one Bernie Madoff engaged in for nearly twenty years before being caught. Crazy thing was, at one point,

Madoff thought the gig was up when a SEC auditor asked him for his DTC number."

"The investment business sure uses a lot of acronyms," I said. "What's a DTC number?"

"DTC stands for Deposit Trust Company. The number is used as an ISIN number, which—"

"There you go again," I interrupted Harlei with a chuckle.

"Intended security identification number. It's a unique four-digit number that every RIA must have to operate."

"As in registered investment advisor," I said. It's not that Harlei needed me to tell her what RIA stood for; it's just that I wanted to show her I was paying attention. She'd used the acronym earlier in our conversation, and I wanted to commit it to memory.

"Exactly!" Harlei winked at me, knowing full well why I was repeating what she'd already told us. "So, anyway, Bernie Madoff spat out a random four-digit code, purely off the top of his head because he'd never even bothered to register for a DTC number. He thought the SEC would surely look up the number to verify it, and his goose would not only be cooked, but also booked. Amazingly, no one ever verified the number, which allowed him to go on screwing over his clients for many more years."

"Wow! So how'd he eventually get caught?" I was curious to know.

"I'm sure you remember the stock market crash of 2008?" After Rip and I both nodded, she continued. "The Dow Jones industrial average fell nearly seventy-eight percent on the heels of Congress's rejection of the bank bailout bill. Madoff's clients began to get suspicious when he kept assuring them their portfolios were still going up in value, despite the overall market collapse. He tried to convince them there was no call to sell off their investments. To make a long story short, his greed finally got the best of him."

"As well it should," I said. "Sounds as if he got his just rewards. I reckon the market is driven by two emotions; fear and greed."

"That is exactly right," Harlei concurred. "It's a classic example of FOMO."

I looked at Harlei as a ten-year-old might look at a scientist explaining the theory of relativity. "Since it begins with an 'F', I don't even want to guess what that acronym stands for."

"LOL." Harlei laughed heartily at my remark, the first time since we'd entered the office that she hadn't acted like her new puppy had been flattened by a garbage truck. "It means 'Fear Of Missing Out.'"

"Good to know. And, Harlei, you do realize that it takes the exact same amount of time to say 'LOL' as it does to say 'laugh out loud', don't you? Not all acronyms are an efficient way of conveying a message." *Besides, who actually says "LOL"? Texting it is silly enough!* I wanted to say. Instead, I smiled at her sheepish grin, and said, "I'm curious about something."

"What's that?"

"How could Sandy Monroe not realize her husband was up to no good when he was sucking up to all of his clients, making them each feel as if he and she were their closest friends?"

"He was playing her too, I'm sure. I assume she thought that was the role he had to play to entice potential investors to hire him as their advisor. He was slick. He had me fooled, and I worked closely with him five days a week. I thought I was a pretty good judge of character until this fiasco blew up in my face. Boy, was I wrong!"

"I'm so sorry this happened to you, dear," I said in earnest. "I appreciate your honesty and openness. If you think of anything that might help us find out the truth behind all this, please don't hesitate to give us a call."

"I won't," she replied, as I scribbled our phone number down on a blank post-it note pad she had yet to add to the box she'd been loading when we'd walked into the office. "Thank you so much for caring."

"Of course," I said. "I'm sure everything will work out all right in the end. Keep your chin up, dear."

We left Monroe Investment's modest office and returned to the truck. We had a lot to think about now, and I knew where I thought we should start. What I had in mind wouldn't be easy, but I had a strategy laid out to possibly pull it off. "Possibly" being the operative word. Getting Rip onboard with my plan might be another story altogether.

THIRTEEN

"I want to hide a voice recorder in the Monroes' house and see if we can catch Sandy and/or Manuel making incriminating statements about Trey's death."

Rip shook his head. "We need to concentrate on determining where the funds from the stock sales went, like we told Harlei."

"We will. But if we can get an idea of who killed Trey, it would make it much easier to locate the money." When Rip made no rebuttal, I asked, "So what do you think about hiding a voice recorder in the Monroes' house?"

"Not your best idea, Rapella." Rip's response to my suggestion had actually been more encouraging than I'd thought it'd be. I'd expected an emphatic "No frigging way, José" from him. But then he followed up with, "Are you trying to get us all thrown in jail? Or worse yet, killed?"

"No," I said meekly. "Of course not."

"Then why would you ever even *think* of doing something so risky? There are so many hazardous holes in that idea that it doesn't even warrant consideration. It'd be an incredibly foolish endeavor."

"Do you agree with me that Sandy Monroe and the house manager, Manuel de la Cruz, are the two most likely suspects?" I asked Rip as we sat across from each other at the kitchen table in the Caboose.

"Not really. I suspect one of his clients didn't take kindly to being ripped off. Either way, it doesn't make your little ploy a wise thing to try and pull off."

"Hear me out, honey," I added the term of endearment to help soften Rip up, even though it was like softening up an iron anvil with a can of *Sterno*. I remember using cans of the ethanol gel to heat up a fondue pot in the seventies, when that fad was all the rage. The thought made me crave a fresh strawberry dipped in hot chocolate. I cast the notion aside and said, "I saw a listening device on Amazon that's so tiny you can hide it in the keyhole of a doorknob."

"Swell." Rip's tone was that of a man who'd just been told he needed to create a weapon of mass destruction using a five-gallon bucket, a tube sock, and a bottle of nail polish remover, and then ignite it with a single matchstick. And he had five minutes to get the job done. Rip was no MacGyver by any stretch of the imagination. The task of disassembling a doorknob to embed a listening device inside it before reinstalling the knob was not exactly in his wheelhouse. "And just how do you plan to get the device inside the door——?"

"Oh, don't be silly." I'd cut him off. "You and I both know it'd take you four-and-a-half days to figure out how to embed the device in a doorknob. I was thinking more of attaching it to something in their home with two-sided tape. We can look for the most logical place to catch the two conversing between themselves or engaging in a telling phone call. I don't know if they were in on the murder together, independently, or——"

"Neither? Don't forget they might not have had anything whatsoever to do with Trey's death," Rip finished the sentence for me, using the driest tone I'd ever heard. The tenor of his voice was so dry the remark should have turned to dust in his mouth. "Do I need to remind you that what you're suggesting is illegal?"

"Actually, it's not," I countered. "I looked it up before even considering the idea. New Mexico is a 'one-party consent' state. I'm the one party who'll consent to it."

"Wrong. It means you can record a conversation as long as you are a party to the conversation, which you wouldn't be. Not to mention, if you *did* happen to hear a confession, or an incriminating conversation, there's no way we could take the evidence to Carlos without incriminating ourselves. For that matter, the evidence wouldn't even be admissible in court."

"I know." I tried to keep my impatience from showing. "I realize all of that. And I understand now that recording a conversation I'm not a part of is illegal. But it might give us an idea what part either one of them played in the crime. Then we could find another way to get them to turn themselves in, or at least repeat their confession in another place and time in such a way we *could* take the evidence to the detective. I still think Sandy and Manuel might have been in on the murder together. Did you see the way Sandy looked at Manuel when she introduced us to him? She had the same expression on her face as you do when I set a juicy sizzling T-bone in front of you. She literally looked like she wanted to eat the man up! Personally, I think if we took any incriminating evidence we garnered from the listening device to Carlos, he'd be impressed with our ingenuity."

"And I think he'd arrest us for illegal eavesdropping, and we'd serve more time than either Mrs. Monroe or her house manager." Rip was adamant.

"It's only illegal if we get caught," I said. An absurd statement to make, I soon realized.

Rip looked at me as if I just admitted to wiretapping the

phone in the Oval Office. "Are you saying murdering Trey Monroe is only illegal if the killer gets caught? It's the same difference."

"Okay, I see your point. Still, I can't see Carlos arresting us for trying to assist in the investigation. I truly believe he'd find a way to use the data to arrest the perpetrator, *or perpetrators*, without implicating us. He obviously thinks very highly of you, Rip."

"And I'd like to keep it that way. Carlos might react the way you just suggested," Rip replied, "but not if he's the police officer I think he is. I'd have never gone for a stunt like that when I was a detective, and I don't think Carlos will either. I'm sure he takes the Law Enforcement Oath of Honor seriously. 'On my honor, I will never betray my badge, my integrity, my character or the public trust. I will always...'"

I waved him off and left the room, leaving him to recite the remainder of the oath to himself. Not that I couldn't have heard his voice from anywhere in the trailer, but at least I had the satisfaction of walking away. I didn't want to go behind Rip's back, and I knew he'd never cave in to any pressure I piled on him. But I did know someone who might be able to sway him.

"Pleeeeeease." Tiffany drew out the one-syllable word like it was sixty-five letters long. "Come on, Gramps! I could go over there alone. Grams doesn't even have to get involved. I am perfectly capable of placing the eavesdropping device in a suitable place."

I cringed when she used the word "eavesdropping" after Rip's remark about being arrested for illegal eavesdropping. For some reason, the word made my idea sound more despicable. "Listening device" had a much less contemptible ring to it.

"How are you going to get the device inside the Monroes'

house? Breaking and entering is the same as criminal trespassing, and it's a misdemeanor, an offense that could earn you both jail time and a fine. Add that on to the sentence you'll get for illegal eavesdropping, and you're talking about some serious time."

"I wouldn't have to break into their house, Gramps!" She looked at Rip as if he'd suddenly grown horns. "Sandy would let me in the house without a moment's hesitation. We've been friends for quite a while now, and still are."

"Are you willing to jeopardize that friendship by trying to pull off this ridiculous ploy your grandmother has devised?" Rip asked.

"I think it's an awesome plan." Tiffany turned and nodded at me before returning her attention to her grandfather as he launched another "what if" at her.

"What if it turns out neither Sandy or her house manager had anything to do with Trey's death?"

"That'd be a good thing. But what if it turns out one or both of them did?" Tiffany asked.

"What if Sandy discovers what you've done? Worse yet, what if the police find out what you've done and drag you by your feet, kicking and screaming, to jail? Do you truly think your friendship with Sandy will survive if something like that happens?"

Tiffany giggled at the visual her grandfather had just put in her mind. "If Sandy, good friend or not, did have something to do with the death of her husband, it's not like we'd remain good friends while she's rotting away in a prison cell."

"Better *her* rotting away in prison than you and your grandmother for recording someone's personal conversation without their knowledge or consent." Rip looked smug, knowing he'd brought up a good point, but it didn't faze Tiffany one bit.

"What if the man she hired to run her household killed her husband?" Tiffany lobbed the "what if" back into Rip's court. The metaphorical volley I'd been watching was spellbinding. I'd never seen my granddaughter so determined. "Wouldn't she want to know? Wouldn't *you*, if you were in her shoes? And, on the other hand, what if Sandy was in on the Ponzi scheme her husband carried out? She's nearly as much of a money-grubber as he was. Maybe she was planning to join him in the Cayman Islands where the money is sitting in an offshore account under an assumed name."

Good one, Tiffany! I thought. *You've obviously been giving this situation as much thought as I have. We're clearly on the same wavelength.* That exact scenario had been running through my mind for several days. I kept my thoughts to myself, however, and continued to listen to the barrage of questions Rip and Tiffany fired at each other.

Rip nodded at Tiffany. "I agree that's a plausible scenario. But it's only one of many possibilities. What you're talking about doing is still illegal. Like I asked before, are you willing to risk not only jail time, but also your friendship with Sandy in an effort to get to the truth behind Trey's death?"

"Yes!" Tiffany exclaimed. "I most certainly am! No matter what happened, or who killed Trey, our money is missing, and Sandy's husband is responsible for it. At this stage of the game, it'd be difficult to ever restore the close relationship Sandy and I once shared. And jail time be damned! I'm willing to roll the dice if Grams is."

Tiffany and I exchanged a look of mutual consent. Our unspoken agreement was not lost on Rip, either. He shook his head and said, "I feel like I'm being ganged up on. Looks like it's two against one. I guess you two can do whatever you want, but leave me out of it. Just do me one favor. Please try to be as cautious as possible. If either Sandy or Manuel killed Trey, they have nothing to lose by dropping two more bodies."

"We will," Tiffany and I responded simultaneously.

"And if it ever even looks like your plan might take a bad turn, abort the execution of it. Immediately!"

"We will abort immediately!" Tiffany and I repeated, again in stereo. However, this time our response was much more enthusiastic because we realized we were being given the go-ahead to implement our sneaky course of action. I appeased my sense of justice by telling myself that although my plan might be unlawful, on a legal scale, our offense couldn't hold a candle to murder.

I was excited and a bit apprehensive about carrying the idea out, but I quickly ordered the listening device before Rip could change his mind. I was anxious for the plan to be successful, so I splurged on one of the more costly models. I justified the expenditure with the knowledge I was saving on the shipping cost with my Amazon Prime membership. By enrolling in Amazon Prime months ago, I not only received free shipping, but I could also anticipate the device's delivery in just two days' time. In the meantime, Tiffany and I could work out the details of our scheme.

As I sat back in my chair and took a long gulp of the tequila sunrise that had me hacking up the burning liquid from my windpipe for a full five minutes, I thought to myself, *I hope this isn't a two-hundred dollar purchase I'll live to regret. I could get over the budget-busting expense, but I don't want to live with the notion I got myself, much less my granddaughter, into legal trouble. And if my plot gets Tiffany injured in any way, I'll never forgive myself.*

FOURTEEN

Three days later, as we sipped on our coffee on the back patio, I asked Tiffany, "Are you ready for this?" The listening device had been delivered to Tiffany's address the previous day.

Rip had dropped me off at the Carpenters' at nine that morning. One of our tires on the truck must have picked up a nail, and he was on his way to have it fixed. "It's a slow leak, but it won't remain that way if the issue is ignored much longer," he'd said.

I turned toward Tiffany as she responded to my inquiry. She nodded slowly. "Yes, I'm ready, but I'll admit I'm more nervous than I thought I'd be."

As she attempted to take a sip from her empty cup, she absentmindedly picked imaginary lint off of her blue sweater. If they weren't merely figments of her imagination, they were the tiniest lint balls I'd ever seen. She was obviously uptight, and I was afraid her edginess would be a tell-tale sign that she was harboring ulterior motives for her visit with Sandy Monroe.

"You know, sweetheart," I began, "I don't particularly like the idea of you being involved in this plan, which was my idea in the first place. I really think it'd be best if I handled it alone."

"No!" Tiffany shouted at me from two feet away. "You'll need me to distract her while you place the listening device somewhere in her kitchen where no one will notice."

I sensed there was no swaying her. In actuality, I was relieved she'd insisted on accompanying me. "All right. If you're sure you want to join me, I'd be glad to have your help."

"I am one-hundred percent certain."

"Let me change into something that doesn't have a road map of coffee stains down the front. I'll grab the least dirty shirt from the load of laundry I brought over to do while I'm here. We can head that way in about five minutes if you're ready."

"I'm ready to go when you are, but take your time. I'll finish up my coffee in the meantime."

Honey, I thought as I chuckled to myself, *you finished that cup of Folgers a long time ago. The last three sips you've taken were nothing but air.*

After I donned a red and white floral top, I pulled my brand-new iPhone out of my back pocket. Rip and I had visited the Apple store in the Uptown Mall on Q Street the previous day. We'd decided it was high time we both carried a phone at all times, both for security and convenience. After admiring the blue and black Otterbox cover I'd selected to protect the expensive device, I sent a text to Rip to let him know Tiffany and I were heading over to the Monroes'. It wasn't because I was afraid something nefarious would happen to the two of us; I just knew Rip would be upset with me if I didn't keep him in the loop. That, after all, was the purpose behind purchasing another phone. Besides, he was already disgusted with me for attempting such "Tomfoolery," as he'd put it.

After a ridiculously long wait, I got a response. Rip reminded me of my promise not to do anything risky and advised me again to exercise extreme caution. Don't just throw it to the wind as you usually do. Remember if you place yourself in a perilous position, you're placing your granddaughter in one too.

I was not in the mood for a lecture via text, but I was also aware of the worry I was causing Rip, who'd give his own life for either mine or Tiffany's. I promise we won't do anything crazy or dangerous, I texted back, adding an emoji of a face throwing a kiss at the end of my message.

This time, Rip's response came immediately. He'd obviously typed it hurriedly and let the auto-correct function take over. I've cured cats before. Fittingly, the emoji he added was that of a cat imitating that *Home Alone* kid, with its mouth open and its paws on either side of its face.

I know you've heard that before, but I mean it this time.

"What took you so long?" Tiffany asked when I rejoined her on the back porch.

"I was waiting for a text to come over my phone from your grandfather."

"Oh. Enough said. He does text at a blazing two words per minute, doesn't he?"

As I showed her Rip's last text, I said, "Yes, but at least he has the ability to cure cats."

We both laughed and headed out to the driveway to get into Tiffany's silver Honda Fit. It was an economical little car for her, and cute as a button. With fingers trembling like an Aspen leaf on a breezy day, it took her several tries to get the key in the ignition.

"Want me to drive?" I asked. "There's no reason to be

nervous. This part of the plan will be easy-peasy. It's retrieving the device that might be tricky."

"I'm okay," she replied. "I'm not nervous."

"Then why do you look as uptight as a pigeon flying over a falcon's nest?"

"I don't know. Why are you so calm? And why do you look so giddy, Grams?" She asked in return. "You look like you can't wait to pull off this ploy. I'm beginning to wonder if you and I aren't akin to Dumb and Dumber heading out on a foolhardy mission."

"We'll be fine," I assured her. Her verbiage was almost the same as her grandfather had used, and I didn't want her to know I was wondering the exact same thing. By the time we turned onto Zinfandel Avenue, Tiffany had calmed down. For the first time, I was confident our mission would go off without a hitch.

"Good morning, ladies," Sandy greeted us amicably. She didn't come off as a grieving widow the way Rip had depicted her. "It's so good to see you again, Tiffany. You too, Mrs. Ripple."

"Please, call me Rapella, like all my friends do. Anyone who's a friend of my granddaughter's is a friend of mine."

"Thank you, Rapella."

"Are you doing all right?" Tiffany asked Sandy.

"I suppose. It's been a tough day though, between frequent crying spells and getting a call from the lead detective on my husband's case demanding I drive down to the Albuquerque substation to give a statement."

"That sounds stressful," Tiffany said, as the three of us stood in the Monroes' foyer.

"It is. To tell the truth, girlfriend, I'm more than ready for a drink." As Sandy spoke, she picked her half-finished beverage up off a marble table. The fact it had a couple of green olives pierced by a swizzle stick in it made me wonder if her drink was a martini. "I have no idea why I need to give a statement. You'd think they'd leave the widow of a murder victim alone to grieve in private rather than harass me for a statement."

"Don't worry about it too much," I said. The fact Sandy had used the word "harass" made it apparent Carlos had called her more than once to come to the station. *Why is she putting him off?* I wondered. *If I were her, I'd jump at the chance to do whatever they asked of me, in hopes it would lead them to my husband's killer.* "My husband was in law enforcement his entire career. I've heard him say repeatedly the spouse is always a prime, if not the number one, suspect. It doesn't mean they truly think you killed your husband. It's just standard protocol to check out your alibi and get a written statement from you."

For a moment, I was afraid Sandy had swallowed one of the green olives in her drink and it'd gotten wedged in her windpipe. She opened her mouth to respond and nothing came out. She looked ill all of a sudden. When she could finally speak, she said, "Won't you two join me for a dirty martini in the sitting room? I don't have to be at the police station for another hour, and I could sure use another drink. I polished off the Ciroc last night, so Grey Goose will have to suffice."

"Thank you, but we'll have to take a rain check on the drink," Tiffany replied to her friend, who still appeared to be shook up over my remarks about the spouse being a prime suspect. Did she have reason to worry? It sure seemed to have taken the wind out of her wobbly sails.

On the drive over to Sandia Heights, Tiffany and I had decided the kitchen would be the best room in which to place the device, since it was the hub of most households. Tiffany had assured me the Monroes were no exception. She and Chase had shared many laughs with the Monroes while sipping wine or coffee around Trey and Sandy's kitchen table. So, when Tiffany turned to follow Sandy to the sitting room, I said, "That's why we (cough) decided to come over and (cough) check on you this morning. We thought maybe (cough, cough, cough), you might (hack)—"

Tiffany turned toward me in concern. "Grams, are you okay?"

I winked at her and then turned toward Sandy and coughed like I was trying to expel my left lung.

"Oh, dear," Sandy said as she patted my back. "Are you sure you're alright, Rapella?"

I nodded and coughed several times in quick succession. Sandy stared at me for a few moments as if waiting for me to hack up a hairball, and eventually turned toward her kitchen. "Let me get you some water."

"Thank (cough) you. That'd be (hack, hack) wonderful." I coughed one more time as I motioned for Tiffany to join me in the kitchen with Sandy.

"Oh!" Sandy gasped. She was startled by my presence directly behind her when she'd turned around with the bottle of water she'd taken out of her refrigerator. She'd clearly expected us to wait for her in the foyer. I reached for the bottle and took it back to the square kitchen table, where I pulled out a chair and plopped down into it. Tiffany followed suit, sitting directly across from me. Sandy shrugged and sat down between us.

I sipped on the water, coughing now and then, while Tiffany and Sandy chatted about the fact the murder case seemed to have come to a dead end. A lone tear rolled down Sandy's cheek as she reminisced about the good times the two couples had shared in the past. She sniffled. "It just won't be the same without Trey."

"It sure won't," Tiffany agreed. She reached over and grasped Sandy's hands. It was a compassionate gesture of genuine consolation.

Before long, the two young ladies were engrossed in a lively conversation about the Albuquerque International Balloon Fiesta, an annual festival held in Albuquerque in early October. The fiesta had just taken place less than a month prior, ending about a week before Trey's death, and the two couples had attended the event together. I gulped down the remainder of my water and stood up to dispose of the empty bottle.

"Don't worry about the bottle, Rapella," Sandy said. She was such a nice lady; I could find no reason to dislike or mistrust her. I prayed she wasn't guilty of murdering her husband. "I'll get it later."

"Oh, don't be silly," I said. "I'm already up. You've been so kind to me already. You don't need to wait on me hand and foot. Just point me in the direction of your trash receptacle."

After Sandy turned around to point to the silver can beside the fridge, which I'd already spotted, Tiffany distracted her. "I see you have a bag on your table from Bruiser's Barbeque. That's who Chase had contracted to cater the birthday party we unfortunately had to cancel."

"Oh, yes. I'd forgotten all about the party, actually. It seems like a lifetime ago because the last two weeks have been so chaotic. Did you have a nice birthday, anyway?" Sandy asked.

As Tiffany explained that she'd spent an enjoyable evening with her grandparents and Chase, who'd just been released from jail, I slapped the listening device on the top of the refrigerator, making sure to turn it on beforehand. Sandy, whose back was to me, was involved in the conversation with Tiffany and paying no attention to me. Tiffany shot me an odd look, which I attributed to her thinking I hadn't attached the device securely enough. I reached back up and wiggled it to make sure the small bug was firmly affixed. Though I was taller than the average woman, I couldn't see the device from where I stood. Manuel was only about five-ten and Sandy was several inches shorter than me, so I felt secure in knowing the listening device would go unnoticed. I didn't think either of the two would be dusting off the top of the appliance any time soon. After all, if they were like most folks, out of sight meant out of mind.

As I walked back to the kitchen table, I caught Sandy glancing at the clock on her microwave. I knew she had an appointment to keep with Detective Gutierrez. *Our work is done here anyway*, I thought. "Well, Tiffany, we'd best be going so Sandy isn't late to her appointment."

We thanked Sandy for her hospitality and wished her good luck at the police station. I wanted to comfort her. Oh, who am I kidding? What I really wanted was to watch and judge her reaction to my next remarks. "Don't sweat it, dear. Just put the whole truth and nothing but the truth in your written statement. As long as you answer their questions truthfully, you have nothing to worry about. I've been in an interrogation room myself, and it's not nearly as scary as it sounds."

"Interrogation room?" Sandy asked, with a catch in her voice.

"Yes. I don't want to mislead you. It truly *is* as scary as it sounds. In fact, it's downright terrifying! You get the feeling they're trying to wear you down and make you confess to a crime you didn't commit. But, if you're honest, and just tell them what you know, it'll all be over quickly enough."

I'm sure she did swallow an olive out of her drink at that point, or perhaps her own tongue. Sandy breathed in so sharply, she might have inhaled a loose tooth, or two, as well. She stared at me in silence for an uncomfortably long time before responding, "Um, yeah, okay."

About thirty seconds later, Tiffany and I were walking down the sidewalk to the Monroes' driveway. Tiffany whispered, "That's not going to work, Grams."

"What do you mean, sweetheart?" I was confused by her

remark. I'd been mentally patting myself on the back when her comment made me stop mid-pat.

"I read the owner's manual that came with the listening device this morning and it said it had to be within ten feet of the source of the sound you wanted to record. The refrigerator is too far away. Trust me; they do all their talking sitting around the table, not standing around the fridge."

"Oh, crap!" It *was* a huge kitchen and the refrigerator had to be at least fifteen feet from the table. "I knew I should have read those darn instructions before we left. Why didn't you tell me that on the way over here?"

"Because I thought you *had* read the instructions! You're not exactly a tech geek, Grandma."

I wanted to remind her that this morning was the first time I'd laid eyes on the device, but she was already perturbed. The "grandma" she'd used said it all. I had no other choice but to correct my mistake. "Where would you suggest I put the device?"

"I assumed all along you were going to put it under the kitchen table."

"Well, get us back in their kitchen and I'll move it to underneath the tabletop."

"All right." Tiffany sighed deeply. Twice. She sounded reluctant when she added, "Just follow my lead."

When Sandy answered the door the second time, she wasn't nearly as effusive as she'd been the first go 'round. "Did you ladies forget something?"

"No, Sandy," Tiffany sounded uneasy. "I'm worried about my grandmother. She's coughing again and can barely catch her breath."

"(Hack! Hack!)" I coughed on cue. I tried to look as if once again I was having trouble getting enough air down my windpipe.

Tiffany glanced at me as though afraid I was about to pass

out on Sandy's doorstep. "I don't think we need to call for an ambulance, but could we trouble you for some more water?"

"Oh, yeah, of course." As she said the words, Sandy sounded as if her friend had asked for her last bottle of vodka. She began to close the front door behind her, to leave us waiting on her front porch, but Tiffany pushed it back open and we stepped inside. When Sandy turned to head toward the kitchen, Tiffany and I were directly on her heels. When she handed me a second bottle of water, I immediately sat down at the table and Tiffany kneeled down next to me, pretending to be concerned about my well-being.

Sandy, on the other hand, stood rigidly by her sink. She had her arms folded across her chest. In that position, if she could nod like Barbara Eden on the old sitcom *I Dream of Jeannie* and make the two of us disappear, Tiffany and I would have gone up in a puff of smoke instantly.

I wasn't sure if my cohort had a plan devised to get Sandy out of the kitchen or not. I was trying to concoct one myself when Tiffany turned suddenly toward Sandy, and said, "Did you hear that?"

"Hear what?" Sandy asked.

"I think someone just knocked on your front door."

"I didn't hear it. Why wouldn't they just ring the doorbell? No worries. Manuel will get it."

"Yeah, you're right, Sandy," Tiffany said with a shrug. "Besides, I might have just imagined it."

After a long silence, Sandy nodded and smiled in obvious relief. Tiffany then exclaimed, "There it is again!"

Trying to sound as hoarse as I could muster, I said, "I heard it too that time."

"Damn it! Why hasn't Manuel answered the door?" Sandy asked in a perturbed tone.

"Who knows? Maybe he's busy doing something else,"

Tiffany replied. "Gee, I hope it's not the police. They might be concerned that you're also a target of the person who killed Trey. They may even bust your door in if no one responds to their knocking. It would be a shame if they destroyed that beautiful stained glass mural in your front door."

It occurred to me then my granddaughter should have been an actress rather than a wedding photographer. By the look on Sandy's face, I knew Tiffany's offhand remark had hit home. I suppressed a smile as Sandy said, "I guess I better go see who's at the door. I'll be right back."

After I watched a flustered-looking Sandy scurry out of the kitchen, I jumped up, ran to the fridge, and peeled the listening device off the top.

"What are you looking for?" A masculine voice said behind me. I quickly palmed the device and turned to see Sandy's house manager standing in the kitchen doorway. I glanced at Tiffany, who appeared to be frozen in place. I was caught off-guard but felt I'd recovered quickly enough so as not to raise suspicion. When I didn't reply immediately, Manuel asked, "Can I help you reach something?"

"Oh, no. But thanks! I was feeling around to make sure there wasn't a hinge or something that would cause this bottle to tip over if I set it up there while I used both hands to figure out how to open the lid on the trash can." I held up the water bottle in my other hand as if for confirmation of my statement.

"You just lift the lid up, like basically every other standard trash can." Manuel's tone sounded mocking. I didn't want to know what was going through his mind.

"I see that now. I guess I expected a magnificent home like this to have some fancy-schmancy trash can that took a brain surgeon to figure out."

"Nope. You just lift the lid up," he repeated.

I forced a smile and nodded as I lifted the trash can lid up and deposited the bottle inside. I hadn't appreciated his sarcastic tone. He might look like a Chippendale dancer, but in my opinion, he was denser than a landscaping brick. Otherwise, he would have wondered why I was worried about an empty plastic water bottle, with the lid screwed back on, no less, tumbling over and falling to the floor. It's not like it would have spilled water on the floor, much less shattered or damaged the marble tile in any way. Good thing for him he had the looks and physique of an underwear model, because his brains weren't going to take him very far in life. *Maybe the guy really doesn't know how to operate a smartphone, like Sandy inferred.*

After Manuel exited the kitchen, I sat back down next to Tiffany at the table and had just long enough to affix the bug to the bottom of the tabletop before Sandy reappeared. The adhesive backing on the listening device was still extremely tacky, so I knew it would hold. Sandy looked at Tiffany and said, "There was no one at the door."

"Really? Oh, sorry." Tiffany managed to sound sincere despite the fact her voice was trembling. "I must've heard Manuel walking up the hallway. He just stuck his head in the door for a moment."

"Are you ready, honey?" I asked Tiffany before Sandy could ask what Manuel had wanted. "I think I'll be fine until we get home and I can take some of my prescription cough medicine."

"I'm ready. Thanks again for the water, Sandy," Tiffany said. "I'm going to take Grams home right now. We were going to go shopping, but I think she needs that cough syrup right away. She's really starting to worry me."

Sandy nodded. I'd read more into my granddaughter's last remark than she had, I'm sure. Since we'd first stepped onto the Monroes' front porch, Tiffany had been as tense as a retinology patient who'd been told they'd be receiving an injection in their eyeball.

Sandy reached into her refrigerator, grabbed a third bottle, and handed it to me. "Take this with you. Just in case."

"Thank you, sweetheart. You are so thoughtful," I said, as I followed Sandy and Tiffany down the hallway. And she was. Once again, I found myself hoping she had no involvement in Trey's demise.

Tiffany hugged Sandy and reminded her of her appointment with the detective. "You don't want to be late."

Sandy looked at her watch as we stood in the vestibule near the front door. Scowling, she replied, "Yeah, well, maybe I'll just go down to the station tomorrow instead."

Tiffany would make a good partner in crime-solving, I realized, and I told her so on the way back to her house. Even though our quest to get to the bottom of the missing money and the dead investment manager was a serious matter, I enjoyed getting to spend quality time with my granddaughter. We didn't get together often, and I was loving every minute of it.

FIFTEEN

The following morning, the four of us decided to go to the Cinnamon Cafe on Juan Tabo Boulevard. The restaurant served breakfast and lunch and was just minutes away from the Monroes' home.

"Their breakfast burritos are to die for," Chase said as we walked into the cafe. "That's what I'm getting. And, of course, a cinnamon roll to go."

"Why don't we order four of the rolls to go?" Tiffany suggested, "We'll have them later as a mid-afternoon snack."

"Great idea, Tiff," Rip said. "I've never met a cinnamon roll I didn't like."

A heavenly aroma greeted us as we entered the building. It was pleasantly mild outside, though, so we chose to take advantage of their outdoor seating. I decided if I was going to have to smell the savory scent of cinnamon, I might as well order the Cin-fully delicious French toast, one of the restaurant's specialty items. Rip, apparently deciding to roll the dice on an all-day case of heartburn, ordered a Paseo Pile-up: a combination of hash browns, eggs, bacon, sausage, red or green chile, and cheese.

Tiffany settled on Huevos Rancheros. Considering she never opened her menu, I'd guess she'd had her mind made up before entering the cafe.

Breakfast was delicious and reasonably priced, which surprised me due to its proximity to the high-rent district of Sandia Heights. As we ate, we discussed the listening device Tiffany and I had hidden in the Monroes' house the previous day.

"The instruction manual said the battery was only good for about twenty-four hours, so we decided to pick the recorder up today," Tiffany told Rip and Chase. "That's why I suggested we have breakfast here."

"How are you planning to retrieve the device?" Rip asked. "Ring the doorbell and tell Sandy you need to collect the bug you planted in her kitchen yesterday?"

"Of course not, Gramps," Tiffany said with a laugh. Clearly, she couldn't tell the difference between humor and sarcasm. When she looked at me for an answer, I explained my plan.

"I figured that when people are under duress, depressed, lonely, or sad, they have a tendency to crave comfort food. My guess is Sandy is dealing with all of those emotions right now." I picked a roasted pecan off the top of my French toast and popped it in my mouth, chewed it a few times, and continued. "So I whipped up a batch of oatmeal raisin cookies to drop off at her house. When someone in your household dies, people come crawling out of the woodwork to drop off food at your place. It's just what good folks do, so I didn't think it'd appear odd if we did the same thing. Besides, they don't call me the 'cookie lady' for nothing."

"Yeah, right. I don't recall anyone *ever* calling you the cookie lady," Rip said. He was acting like a jackass for some reason. I decided I wasn't going to stand for it.

"The subcontractors working on the house next to Regina's

gave me that nickname after I baked cookies for them on several occasions," I said in my defense. "It's obvious you got up on the wrong side of the bed, Rip. And that's difficult to do when the bed is up against the wall of the trailer."

Tiffany shifted in her seat. I don't think she liked watching her grandparents bicker. Chase, on the other hand, chuckled at my jab. I knew I liked that boy for some reason. Rip apologized for being disagreeable and asked if there were any leftover oatmeal cookies in his future. I assured him there were, provided he had an immediate self-induced attitude adjustment.

"Seriously, dear," he said. "How's that gonna work? Don't you imagine Sandy will just hold out her hand for the cookies and then close the door in your face?"

"Sandy's not that rude and unappreciative, Gramps," Tiffany said, while chewing on a bite she'd ripped off the end of her tortilla with her teeth.

Oh, to still have teeth you trusted enough to do that, I thought. With my dentures, I'd be lucky if my false teeth weren't still attached to the tortilla when I laid what was left of it back down on my plate. I'd hate to risk grossing out my eating companions.

"For the most part, Sandy was very cordial yesterday," I began, "and I think I've devised a way to retrieve the device without raising suspicion. I'll just need Tiffany to keep her talking in the foyer while I take the cookies to the kitchen and snatch the bug from under the table. I'm counting on Manuel to be elsewhere. He nearly scared ten years off my life yesterday when he walked in as I was trying to rip the device off the fridge to relocate it."

"Yeah," Tiffany said, "and I was no help whatsoever. I was sure the gig was up when I looked up and saw him staring at you."

"You had me wondering if Sandy had a pet cat," I said to Tiffany.

"No, but Manuel has one." She looked puzzled at my remark. "Why were you wondering if Sandy had a cat?"

"Because it appeared as if one had your tongue."

"Ha! I imagine it did. I was speechless, unable to come up with a single thing to say to explain why you were reaching up on top of their refrigerator. You handled it extremely well, though. I was highly impressed."

I glanced sideways at Rip, expecting to see admiration on his face, or at least acknowledgment of the praise I'd received from our granddaughter. Instead, he glanced at Chase, rolled his eyes, and shook his head. I wanted to slap the forkful of sausage right out of his hand. It wasn't like there wasn't enough food in the "pile-up" on his plate to sacrifice a few chunks of ground pork. In regard to his ever-expanding waistline, he probably could stand to have food slapped out of his hand on a regular basis. As could I!

About a half-an-hour later, Chase pulled up in front of the Monroes' house. Tiffany and I exited the back seat, and I removed a decorative plastic plate the size of a turkey platter out of the trunk of the car and rearranged the cookies that had toppled on the ride over. Atop the platter now were tall stacks of cookies that looked as if they might collapse like a house of cards. I'd intentionally piled them high to make for an unstable balance.

When Sandy came to the door, she had a surprised expression on her face. "You two again?"

Tiffany visibly winced at the implication we were wearing out our welcome. I truly hoped we would get some beneficial information on our first try at eavesdropping on Sandy and Manuel, because I didn't particularly want to go through this procedure again. And talking Tiffany into repeating the process might not be an easy task. If, indeed, it was possible at all.

"Yes," Tiffany finally said. "We apologize for the intrusion. Grams decided to make some oatmeal cookies for you. She baked a lot so you could freeze some and thaw them out later when you were hungry for more."

"Oh, that is so sweet of you, Rapella," she said to me. She then turned to Tiffany and continued in what sounded like a persecuted tone. "But I thought you knew we had to swear off sugar several years ago. When Trey was diagnosed as a type II diabetic, I stopped buying anything with sugar in it. Even avoiding sugar wasn't enough, and he started taking insulin injections not long before his death."

Lucky for you, he's dead now, so you can resume eating sugar. I had to bite my tongue to not say what I was thinking.

"Sorry, I forgot about that," Tiffany said.

Before Sandy could respond, I said, "Lucky for you, I used my sugar-free recipe, because I avoid sugar as much as possible, too. My husband is a borderline diabetic, and we both have to watch our weight." As Sandy stared at me, the invisible cat that had Tiffany's tongue yesterday appeared to have Sandy's today. When she finally opened her mouth to speak, I cut her off. "I'll set this on your kitchen table while Tiffany tells you a hilarious joke she told me this morning."

"I can take it to——"

Interrupting Sandy as I continued walking toward her kitchen, I said, "No. It's best I don't try to pass them over to you. I wasn't thinking straight when I piled them so high. One false move and you'll be vacuuming cookie crumbs out of your carpet for days. Go ahead, Tiffany, and tell her that funny joke you told me earlier."

Tiffany shot me a stunned look. I'd thought surely the girl knew one joke. It didn't even have to be humorous. She could act like it tickled her funny bone, even if it didn't seem to amuse her friend. I tell jokes all the time that no one but me finds hysterical.

I rushed to the kitchen in such a hurry, three cookies tumbled off the top of a lopsided pile and fell to the floor. I didn't have time to pick them up, and had I tried, another two dozen might've toppled to the floor as well. I kicked the two cookies I could reach under the sofa in the living room and planned to pick the other one up on my way back to the front of the house.

After setting the large plastic tray on the counter, I snatched the listening device from under the tabletop and shoved it into the front pocket of my jeans. I hurried back to join Tiffany and Sandy, picking up the errant cookie on my way. I shoved it in the other front pocket of my jeans, not wanting to damage the costly device with smooshed cookie crumbs.

As I neared the two young ladies, Sandy had her back to me. Before Tiffany noticed my return, I could hear her saying, "So, a priest, a rabbi, and a monk walk into a bar, and the bartender asks…"

After a pregnant pause on Tiffany's part, Sandy asked, "So, what'd the bartender ask?"

"Dang it! I can't remember the punch line." Tiffany glanced at me, looking like a rat drowning in the sewer, desperate to be rescued. I'd promised her I'd always have her back, so I stepped in to save her.

"A priest, a rabbi, and a monk walk into the bar, and the bartender asks, 'What is this? Some kind of joke?'" I laughed loudly. Neither one of the two younger gals got it, but I thought it was mildly humorous. I decided explaining it to them would only make it sound lamer. Unfortunately, I hadn't gotten to choose a funnier joke because I'd had to find a way to finish the one Tiffany had started.

After a polite, if clearly artificial, chuckle, Sandy said, "Too funny. Thank you so much for your thoughtfulness."

"It was my pleasure," I replied. "We'd better get out of your hair now. You indicated you were going to put off going to the police station until today, so I know you probably need to get on your way to go give your statement. Not to mention, we've got two impatient men waiting for us in the car."

"Pretty slick, Grams," Tiffany whispered as we walked down the sidewalk toward Chase's sports car. "But, please don't ever ask me to tell a joke again. I can hear the funniest joke one minute and forget it the next."

"Welcome to my world. My memory is definitely not what it used to be." Although I still felt as though I was in my prime, I knew she must have thought I was born during the Jurassic Period. She verified that notion with her next remark.

"At your age, Grams, you're probably lucky if you remember to wake up in the morning."

"I beg your pardon." I shook my finger at Tiffany as I opened the back door of the car and climbed in while she boarded from the other side.

Huddled at the Carpenters' kitchen table a short time later, the four of us were listening to the recording device. We heard Manuel's voice asking me what I was looking for and if he could help me reach something. My response came across less nonchalant than I'd thought it had at the time I'd made it. In fact, it sounded uneasy, as if I'd been caught with my hand in the proverbial cookie jar. I hoped it hadn't come across that way to Manuel.

We listened to Tiffany apologize for thinking she'd heard a knock on the Monroes' front door that was likely just Manuel's footsteps in the hallway, and then heard muffled sounds in the background, which would have been Tiffany and me telling

Sandy goodbye at her front door. A few moments later, we heard her holler, "Manuel, dear, I've got to run down to the police station and give a statement before they show up on the doorstep to arrest me."

Dear? Was Sandy just using a common term you might use for anyone you were fond of or, in Rip's case, whose name you couldn't remember? Or was Sandy closer to her house manager than we'd realized?

For the next hour or so, no sounds came from the recording other than the clock over the Monroes' pantry, which could be heard ticking ominously loudly. Meanwhile, the second hand on the Carpenters' wall clock moved eerily slowly. Just as Rip stood up to go look for something more interesting to do, we heard a man's voice.

"Hi there, honey!" Manuel's greeting startled us all. "Have you left the station yet?" There was a short pause. "How'd it go with the detective? Did he take your statement?"

Manuel's voice was loud and clear. He had obviously called Sandy, most likely as he sat at the kitchen table. Rip had quickly retaken his seat, and we were all now glued to the one-sided conversation for its entirety. Manuel's next question made our mouths drop wide open like four baby robins waiting for a bite of whatever their mama had brought to the nest.

"Did he buy it?" There was a long silence while Manuel listened to Sandy's response.

"Really? That's good. Sounds like the investigation is dead in the water."

I gasped. *Not as long as I'm alive,* I almost said to the other three at the table.

"Sure, sweetheart, I know all that."

What do you know, Manuel? Say it out loud! Spill it, pretty boy! I want to know what all you know! My mind was working feverishly as I took in the taped conversation.

"Yeah, I set the trash can out on the curb. And I threw all of Trey's insulin, syringes, and alcohol swabs in it, along with his other medications. Except, of course, for the anxiety medicine. Figured it wouldn't hurt you to have extras now that he won't need them anymore. In fact, I might need to start taking it too." Manuel chuckled at his own brand of sick humor.

I need to check out the medications I took a photo of in Sandy's restroom, I reminded myself. *It's likely the anxiety medication he just mentioned is one of the three I saw lined up on her lavatory.*

"Yes, of course I threw the rest of the KCl out, too."

Note to self: Google "KCl".

"For sure! But I didn't need to fall back on my training as a nurse to give him his insulin injections. It's not like it takes a brain surgeon to jab a needle in the fatty part of an arm, leg, or abdomen."

Good thing, buster, I thought, *because you are clearly no brain surgeon.*

Manuel gave a hearty laugh. "Yes, he was a big wuss. But it turned out to be advantageous, didn't it?"

How can they chuckle about the murder victim's lack of courage at a time like this? I wondered. *How cold and callous can those two people be?*

"Okay, baby. Glad to hear all went well at the police station. That's one less worry, huh? We'll be on our way to the islands soon."

The islands? What islands? Did he really say "islands"?

"I disagree. I think we should wait until the insurance policy pays off. As the saying goes, you can't be too rich or too skinny." His tone indicated he was clearly amused with himself.

You both are already ridiculously skinny, I thought, *and Sandy, at least, is obviously wealthy enough without killing off her husband to collect the life insurance on him. She could have access to the money Trey stole, as well,* I suddenly realized.

"I love you too. See you in a bit."

Holy crap! Sandy is most definitely having a love affair with her hired hand.

We then heard the refrigerator door open and close and the sound of a beer cap being popped off a bottle. Seconds later, Manuel's footsteps could be heard walking out of the kitchen. We all glanced around at each other in amazement.

"Oh. My. God." I was the first to speak. "Those two were in on her husband's death together. It sounds like Sandy planned the murder and her lover carried it out by injecting Trey with a lethal dose of potassium chloride. Trey must have thought Manuel was giving him a routine insulin injection. What Manuel said on this recording is practically a confession of guilt. I think this is all the proof we need to have them both arrested on first-degree murder charges. Don't you, Rip?"

"Yeah, sure," he said morosely. I wondered why he didn't sound more enthusiastic about the damning evidence we'd just listened to. He made it clear with his next comment. "Too bad we can't take it to Carlos, due to the way we illegally acquired the evidence."

"But, but, but…" I stuttered. I couldn't get my thoughts out because I was too shaken by the idea that we now had proof of who Trey's killer was but couldn't do anything with it.

"Well, son of a bitch!" Tiffany exclaimed. She clearly had no trouble putting her thoughts into words. "Because of your bond with the lead detective, can't you just feel him out, Gramps? Maybe you could tell him we overheard him speaking on the phone, without clarifying how exactly we overheard it."

"It *would* be nice to have my reputation completely restored," Chase chimed in. "And, the fact I'd love to get our money back goes without saying."

Rip sighed and turned toward Chase. "I'm not going to lie to Detective Gutierrez, Son, or capitalize on the fact he seems to have a lot of respect for me. That respect would fade like a cheap t-shirt if I did something that sleazy."

"I understand," Chase said.

"Good." Rip gazed deeply into each of our eyes in turn as he'd spoken. I could tell he had mixed emotions about the recording.

When Rip looked at Tiffany's downtrodden expression, he rolled his eyes, sighed again, and caved in like a wet pup tent. "Oh, all right. Let me feel him out. I'll run down to the substation and talk to Carlos personally. I don't want to risk having our phone conversation recorded. It's going to be a delicate enough exchange as it is."

"Oh, thank you, Gramps!" Tiffany stood and planted a noisy kiss on her grandfather's cheek.

"Thank you, Rip," Chase added.

"Thanks, honey." I felt obliged to put my appreciation into words, as well.

After Tiffany, Chase, and I expressed our gratitude, we split up. Rip called Carlos at the police station and invited him to breakfast the following morning. Chase drove to his architectural office to check in. Tiffany called Regina and Milo and gave her parents an update on what'd been going on. And I settled in to learn what other nuggets might have been recorded on the listening device.

While the recording ran, and the sole sound of a ticking clock continued, I finished a cozy mystery I'd been reading and downed two of the wine coolers I'd found in the fridge. Even *they* weren't "Jamaican Me Happy" now. At least they *were* keeping me from being bored out of my gourd from the recording. Except for the clock, it was like listening to a silent movie without the picture screen. Once, when I had nodded off, a lot of loud pounding on the Monroes' front door woke me up. Like Sandy had wondered yesterday, at Tiffany's hoax, I was curious why the visitor on the front porch hadn't just rung the Monroes' doorbell? To my surprise, the knocking continued off and on for the next several hours of the recording.

I turned the device off when I came to the conclusion the remainder of the tape would turn out to be nothing more than a whole lot of door-knocking and tick-tocking. *Does neither Sandy nor Manuel ever answer the door? I'm surprised they opened it when we called on them. And do they never go to the kitchen to grab a snack out of the refrigerator?* I also wondered. *Considering Sandy's apparent overabundance of will-power and her stick-thin physique, I'm guessing those oatmeal raisin cookies I baked are going to go to waste.*

At that point, I had absolutely nothing more to share with Rip when he returned. However, I was hoping he'd have good news to share with us after meeting with the detective the following morning.

By the time we returned to the Chartreuse Caboose later on that evening, I was exhausted. I'd grown tired of listening to the monotonous recording when I was only six or seven hours into it, but felt as if we'd gotten all we needed to implicate Sandy and Manuel in Trey's murder. If Rip was able to get Carlos to listen to the incriminating part of the recording, he could assign some rookie to the task of listening to the rest of it if they thought it necessary. Then the detectives could devise a way to get the pair of killers to confess in a manner that *would* be admissible in court. I'd done my job. The rest was up to the investigating team.

Before I hit the sack that evening, I Googled "KCl" and found out that potassium chloride is an ionic compound, a salt that naturally occurs as a solid that has a powdery and crystalline appearance. Its chemical formula is KCl: it consists of one potassium $(K+)$ ion and one chlorine (Cl) ion. It's a bit complicated for most of us laymen to comprehend. But, as far as Sandy and Manuel were concerned, "KCI" stands for "We poisoned someone to death and are now trying to get rid of the evidence."

I didn't know what the deal was with all of the acronyms, but I did know what Manuel hadn't counted on was RAR, a.k.a. Rapella Ann Ripple.

SIXTEEN

I waited on pins and needles for Rip to get home from his breakfast with Carlos. Rip had been reluctant to meet with Detective Gutierrez at the substation, where they'd be surrounded by other police officers, so had asked Carlos to meet him at IHOP. I asked to be included in the breakfast meeting, but Rip was having none of it because "he knows me too well." I'd be "hopped up," waiting to shoot my mouth off, he'd said, unable to restrain from bragging about the dastardly deed we'd committed. I had not appreciated his play on words or his candor.

To pass the time, I cleaned out several of the undercarriage compartments of the Caboose. Most of the items down there are the same kind of belongings you'd store in any basement. Stuff you know you'll never ever use again (e.g. thirty-year-old golf clubs Rip had used once to set an all-time high-score record at the Rockport Country Club), or look at again (such as our high school yearbooks), and a few things you wished you didn't have to save, but need to, like income tax returns. All the rest is either too sentimental, or you paid too much for the item to pitch it in the nearest dumpster.

The only things I actually tossed were two boxes of quart-sized canning jars I knew I'd never use again and a twelve-roll bundle of toilet tissue that had gotten damp and now displayed blotchy areas of mildew. (Had I been able to foresee the Covid-19 pandemic of 2020, I might've saved the toilet paper rolls regardless of their condition. Even in sub-par condition, I might've been able to unload them for five bucks a roll on eBay.) Both items took up a great deal of space.

Somehow, I was able to rearrange the remaining items in the three storage compartments in such a way so that it looked as if I'd gotten rid of a third of the contents. I was proud of my accomplishment and the time passed swiftly. Before I knew it, Rip was pulling up beside the trailer.

"Well?" I met him at the front door with enthusiasm, hoping he'd gotten Carlos's approval to turn over the recorded evidence.

"It's a no-go," he said. He pulled off his boots and slipped into some slippers. "How about having our evening highballs early? I'm ready for mine now, if you are."

"That's it? That's all you have to say?" I was dumbfounded.

"Umm," Rip looked puzzled. "I meant to say can I *please* have my daily cocktail now?"

"Screw your cocktail!" I exclaimed in exasperation. "What did you say to Carlos? What did he have to say about the evidence we recorded on the listening device? Is he going to—"

Rip held up a hand to stop me mid-question. "We talked about the case, and both of us were frustrated by the lack of evidence. I told him my granddaughter and Sandy were good friends, and it was a shame Tiffany couldn't plant a bug in Sandy's house."

"Seriously?" I asked.

"After I said that, he gave me a look that can only be described as wistful. He said, 'Yeah, it's too bad we couldn't get away with something like that. Believe me, I'm at the point that if it wasn't unethical and illegal, I'd consider stooping low enough to try it.' And that was that."

"Oh." I was crestfallen, and it showed.

"Sorry, honey," he said. "I knew it was a long shot. He's very much a 'by the book' kind of cop, which is a credit to him and his badge. And after he used the words 'stoop low enough', there was no way I was going to tell him you and Tiffany had already stooped that low."

"And gotten what amounts to a confession of murder in the process," I added, in my own defense.

"If nothing else, now you can concentrate on Sandy and Manuel. Perhaps you'll think of a way to get them to trip themselves up. Just promise me you'll keep me in the loop and you won't put yourself in a dangerous position, either with the law or physically. Like I always say, that battle is over, but——"

"But the war has just begun." I finished one of Rip's favorite adages. After a little deliberation, I realized he was right. I had to come up with a new plan.

It was warm for eleven o'clock on a sunny November morning. We enjoyed a cup of coffee in the sling chairs I'd taken out of one of the now more organized storage compartments, along with a small table I'd set up in the shade of the awning. Rip chattered on about the strawberry crepes he'd had for breakfast, and a few other mundane subjects.

I nodded occasionally at his ramblings while musing about what Manuel had said in the recording. He'd told Sandy he'd put all of Trey's insulin and syringes, along with the rest of the potassium chloride, in the trash can at their curb. He'd said it would be picked up in two days, which meant tomorrow was trash pickup day. I'd have bet Manuel's prints were on the bottle of the KCl, and it was possible a print, or partial print, could be lifted off the syringe used to administer the lethal injection. What concerned me the most was that the murder weapon was in the trash can, and the trash inside it would undoubtedly be buried in a landfill by this time the next day. How could I ensure that didn't happen?

The only idea I could come up with was unpleasant, but effective. Go dumpster diving. And arrange to do so preferably when neither Sandy nor her house manager was home. Not only did the idea have numerous built-in land mines, it would also never pass inspection with Rip. He'd said "keep me in the loop," which was ambiguous. Did he mean before I did something, or afterward? Like Rip, I had a favorite adage too. *It is easier to ask for forgiveness than it is to beg for permission.*

As Rip and I were shopping for a few essentials just after one o'clock that afternoon, my phone rang. I knew it had to be Tiffany because she was the only one besides Rip who had my new number.

"Good afternoon, sweetheart."

"Hey, Grams!" She sounded joyful, which did my heart good. "Wanna go shopping with me this afternoon? I was thinking about going to Coronado Center to look for some new shoes, and with winter fast approaching, I thought I'd look for a leather jacket while I was at it."

"That sounds fun. I'd love to join you." I was anxious to spend as much quality time with my granddaughter as I could, because after we headed to Rockdale, Missouri for a visit with

Lexie Starr and Stone Van Patten, I didn't know when I'd see Tiffany again. "Your grandfather and I are picking up a few groceries at Albertsons, but we'll be home in about half an hour. Do you need anything from the store while we're here?"

"I think we're good, but thanks for asking. I'll pick you up in forty-five minutes."

"I'm looking forward to it."

"Me too."

"Before we go to the Coronado Center, we need to do something else first," I told Tiffany after I climbed into her little economy car.

"Sure. What'd you have in mind?"

I reiterated what Rip had told me following his breakfast with Detective Gutierrez. "He told me it was a no-go."

"Well," Tiffany said, "that sucks!"

"Doesn't it though? It's going to make our mission to prove Sandy and Manuel killed Trey a lot tougher. That, in turn, will make finding out where your money is located harder, as well."

"How tough do you think it's going to be?"

"Real tough. Like 'putting pantyhose on while taking a shower' tough."

"Yikes! So, what do you suggest we do next, Grams?"

"I have an idea," I replied, "but I'm not sure how your grandfather is going to feel about it."

"Then, why don't we wait to tell him about it until after we've done it?" Tiffany gave me a mischievous wink. "What's the plan?"

I'd often wondered if my daughter had been switched with someone else's baby at the hospital after she was born, but

Tiffany was living proof Regina was my biological child. My granddaughter had obviously inherited my genes, even if her mother had not.

"On the recording, Manuel mentioned throwing Trey's insulin bottles and syringes in the trash, along with what was left in the bottle of potassium chloride. He said the trash would be picked up tomorrow. So, if today we could somehow locate the syringe with traces of the potassium chloride in it, otherwise known as the 'murder weapon,' we can take it to Detective Gutierrez as proof of Manuel's guilt."

"That's it?" Tiffany sounded disappointed. "That's your plan?"

"You got a better idea?"

"Well, no. But, would something stolen from their trash can be admissible in court?" Tiffany asked.

"I'm not really sure. But it seems to me that something that's been relegated to a trash receptacle on the curb would be considered fair game. That's why if you set a piece of furniture out on the curb, or perhaps a barely used treadmill, it's not considered to be theft if someone pulls up and loads it into their vehicle." As I explained my reasoning, Tiffany nodded in agreement. She appeared dubious, but was clearly able to set her doubts aside in order to pursue the truth behind Trey's death.

"That makes sense, but how are we going to make sure neither Sandy nor Manuel sees us going through their trash?" Tiffany asked.

It was a good question, too; one I didn't have an answer for yet. "Guess we'll just have to play it by ear."

"Hmmm," Tiffany said. "Your 'play it by ear' is not exactly music to *my* ears."

As we were driving down Zinfandel Avenue, we saw Babs Hancock withdrawing a handful of mail from a bank of mailboxes about three houses up the street from their own home. You'd think a fancy neighborhood in the Sandia Heights area would have a nice centralized delivery unit with locking boxes, rather than a bank of mismatched boxes like you'd find on a gravel road out in the country. *But the fact it doesn't have a neighborhood unit with locking boxes might play in our favor,* I thought.

"I've got an idea!" I exclaimed, as I pulled up alongside Babs and lowered Tiffany's window. I leaned across the console to greet the woman. "Good afternoon, Babs. How are you today?"

"Fine," she responded. I sensed she had no clue who we were.

"Tiffany and I are the gals who are trying to get to the bottom of where the money you invested with Monroe Investments went."

"Oh, yes, of course. How are you two doing? Do you have any news on that matter? Has Trey's killer been apprehended?"

"No. And that's exactly why Tiffany and I are over in your neck of the woods today. Have you got a minute or two to talk?" I asked the blue-haired lady, who I was relieved to find clear-minded that afternoon.

"Absolutely. I'll meet you in my driveway." When asked if she wanted a lift, she said, "No thanks. I could use the exercise."

"Great. First, do me a favor," I said. "See if there's any first-class mail in the Monroes' mailbox."

"Whatever for?" Babs acted as if I'd asked her to steal the neighbor's social security check out of their box.

"It will play a part in the mission we're trying to accomplish today in our efforts to get your and the Carpenters' investment money returned." The ploy had hit me as soon as I saw Babs withdrawing her mail from the bank of boxes. "Don't worry. You're going to hand deliver the piece of mail to Sandy, not steal it."

"Oh, all right." Babs looked both directions to make sure no one was watching her before opening a mailbox several boxes down from her own. "Here's a letter from the County Appraiser's office."

"That's perfect," I said. "Stick it in with your own mail and meet us in your driveway."

A few minutes later, as we stood behind the Hancocks' garage, out of sight of anyone in the Monroes' house, I told Babs we were looking for a way to distract Sandy for a few minutes while we looked inside her trash can. However, I didn't tell Babs we hoped to retrieve what we believed to be the murder weapon from the can sitting on the curb. I was hesitant to tell her too much, for fear she'd accidentally say the wrong thing to Sandy, or Manuel, if he opened the front door instead.

"Oh, yes. I saw Manuel roll their trash can out this morning," Babs said.

"This morning?" I asked. "That's odd. He told Sandy he'd already rolled it out when he was speaking to her on the phone yesterday."

"No, I'm sure it was this morning. I was taking a bill to the box to mail, and I waved at him as he rolled it out. I recall wondering why Manuel put the trash out a day early. He normally rolls it out very early on Thursday mornings." Babs seemed confident in her recollection, but I knew how unreliable her memory could be. Not to mention, my days run together all of the time. I often don't know if it's Wednesday or Sunday, and I'm sure she had similar issues to mine when it came to being retired.

I nodded. "The main thing is that we need you to keep Sandy and Manuel occupied for a few minutes so they don't come outside while you're talking to them."

"Of course," she said. "What can I do to help?"

"You can go knock on their door and tell whoever opens it that a piece of their mail turned up in your mailbox. When they reach for the letter from the Appraiser's office, pretend you're light-headed. Tell them you're having one of your dizzy spells. Ask if you can go inside and sit down for a minute or two until it passes. Stall as long as you can to give us time to complete the mission we need to carry out."

"What mission is that?" Babs asked. She appeared lucid enough that I felt safe in explaining what we hoped to accomplish.

"Tiffany and I just need to sort through their trash for the syringe we believe might have been the murder weapon used in Trey's death."

"Oh."

"Are you sure you're up for this, Babs?"

"I think so." Babs didn't look as confident about her acting abilities as she had about her memory of watching Manuel wheel the trash can to the curb. My confidence in her had vanished into thin air, like Dolly does whenever I drag out the vacuum cleaner. "I'll do the best I can. What if Manuel heads outside while Sandy sits with me?"

"Say anything you can think of to stall him. Perhaps ask him if he's related to your friend Anna de la Cruz, who lives down in Truth or Consequences, New Mexico."

"I don't *have* a friend named Anna de la Cruz down in Truth or Consequences." Babs looked perplexed. Her sudden confusion made me even more wary about her ability to pull off her part in the ruse I'd come up with. If she were to mention she was trying to distract them, Tiffany and I might find our gooses cooked. "In fact, I don't know anyone in Truth or Consequences."

"No, I know you don't, but Manuel doesn't! It's just an idea on how to keep him from coming outside. When he says he doesn't believe he's related to your friend, whose name we just made up, ask where his kin are from. If he answers that they're from anywhere but here, ask him how he came to live in Albuquerque. Just keep him talking. Most people enjoy talking about themselves."

"Oh, I see, Rapella. I can definitely keep him tied up answering my silly questions. He's so handsome, I'd like to tie him up in an entirely different manner and then——" Babs stopped talking abruptly. "Oh, pardon me. I must have been thinking out loud."

"No problem. I understand completely." I could imagine her looking through binoculars every Thursday morning as the well-built man rolled the trash can to the curb, salivating over the stud's flexing biceps. The look Tiffany shot me after I winked at Babs was one of repulsion. I'm very adept at reading expressions, and hers clearly read, "Ewww. Gross." When Tiffany got older, she'd understand that a woman didn't quit appreciating a magnificent physique as soon as she became a senior citizen, but would continue to do so until she was pushing up daisies. And, for all I know, even death might not stop us women from welcoming a little eye candy on occasion.

Tiffany and I waited on the porch while Babs ran her own mail inside. She returned a few minutes later with the piece of mail belonging to her neighbors and two pairs of thick latex gloves. "You might ought to wear these."

"Excellent idea!" I replied, suddenly thankful I'd been honest with her about our plan. "I should have thought of that. Sifting through garbage is not my idea of a good time. But in this case, I think it's necessary."

Tiffany and I crossed the street first, ducking behind the Monroes' large trash receptacle to remain out of view of their front door as Babs walked up the driveway to return the "misdelivered" piece of mail. We could hear her voice as she said, "Good morning, neighbor. I hope you're getting along all right. We were so upset to hear the news of Trey's passing. It looks like Cindy misdelivered a piece of your mail. I found it mixed in with mine just now."

"That's odd." Sandy sounded surprised. "Cindy is normally so reliable."

"I found it surprising too," Babs replied. "There must have been a substitute running her route today. Oh, my. I think I'm going to faint."

When we heard the door shut, I raised the lid on the trash can and looked inside. "That bitch!"

"What?" Tiffany was so alarmed by my expletive that she dropped her phone on the ground. Thank goodness for the protective phone covers that let you dribble your phone down the sidewalk like a basketball without shattering its screen. "What is it?"

I pointed into the can. As Tiffany hesitantly looked inside, she said, "Oh. Sorry about that, Grams. I wouldn't take it personally though."

There were only two thirteen-gallon bags stuffed full of trash inside, and across the top of them was an over-sized Ziploc bag full of oatmeal raisin cookies, undoubtedly every single cookie I'd brought over for Sandy.

"Whatever." I picked the bag of cookies off the top of the trash bags and set it aside. Then I grabbed a white trash bag and handed the other one to Tiffany. "Go through it quickly. Just dump the contents in the can as you sort through it."

We both hastily sifted through the contents of the two bags. Thank goodness for the latex gloves Babs gave us, because the bags were full of coffee grounds, leftover spaghetti sauce, used kitty litter, and random garbage. Most of it was sticky, gooey, or just downright disgusting. Tiffany muttered, "Yuck. This is totally revolting."

"Yeah, no shit," I agreed, looking at the litter stuck to the spaghetti sauce on my arm. "And, speaking of that, does Sandy own a cat?"

"No, she doesn't. We went through that before when you thought a cat had my tongue." Tiffany laughed before answering my question. "But Manuel does. It's called a Savannah cat, like the two Justin Bieber owns."

"Who?" I asked. "Is this Justin Bieber a friend of yours?"

"Hardly. Never mind about him. A Savannah cat is an expensive hybrid breed, a beautiful exotic-looking creature that's a cross between a domestic house cat and a serval, which is a wild cat native to Africa," Tiffany explained. "Sandy told me he paid twenty-five thousand for it."

"Twenty-five *thousand*? For a cat? Good grief! There must be gold dust in this litter-covered poop. I had no idea there was an uppity feline breed for the well-to-do. I can't imagine ever paying twenty-five bucks for a pet cat when there are so many at shelters looking for a good home. I wonder how much Sandy is paying Manuel to be her 'house manager'. Like his name, the man's title even sounds snobbish."

As I spoke, I continued to sift through the garbage. "Ouch!" I exclaimed, yanking my right hand out of the trash bag. An open syringe was embedded in the meaty area at the base of my thumb. The latex gloves were great at keeping the funky garbage *off* my hands, but obviously not much good for keeping sharp needles *out* of my hands.

"Oh, no!" Tiffany looked alarmed. "What if that's the murder weapon and there's still potassium chloride in the syringe? You could've been poisoned."

"Don't worry, sweetheart. I doubt there'd be enough in there to affect me, if this is even the actual syringe used to kill Trey.

I'm more concerned that I might have contaminated the evidence."

Just then, a rustling behind a bush next to the Monroes' garage startled both of us. We froze as if we'd just been dunked in a vat of liquid nitrogen.

"You should be more concerned that you are trespassing on private property and going through someone else's trash." The low-timbered voice sounded sarcastic. Tiffany and I looked up to see Manuel step out from behind the azalea bush. He had his cell phone aimed directly at us as he spoke. "And that I have it all recorded on video."

"Oh, well, I, um…" I was tongue-tied, and embarrassed as all get-out. I wondered how he knew we'd likely be going through their trash that day, but was too humiliated to ask. Clearly, he'd wheeled the trash out a day early, knowing we'd come looking for an opportunity to sort through it. I was now positive he'd gathered up the most repulsive things he could find to fill the two trash bags. After all, who pours an entire jar of Ragu in a trash bag and then screws the lid back on the jar? It'd been the first thing I removed from the bag and dropped into the trash can.

"I know you thought you'd successfully palmed the listening device when I caught you trying to attach it to the top of the refrigerator," he said. "But you didn't!"

"Actually, I was removing it to relocate it." I quickly realized it was an idiotic response to make.

"Nevertheless, you aren't quite as good at sleight-of-hand as you thought. I found the device under the tabletop after you left and pretended to be talking to Mrs. Monroe on my phone just to teach you a lesson. I didn't tell her about your little stunt, and I don't plan to. Nor will I mention I found you two digging through our trash."

"Thank you," Tiffany mumbled. "I'd appreciate it if you didn't tell her."

"It's Sandy I'm concerned about, not you, Mrs. Carpenter. I don't want to hurt her even more than she's already hurting from the loss of her beloved husband." Manuel then turned to me. "You can be assured the 'murder weapon' is not in that trash bag, or in the Monroe household. We don't know who killed Trey any more than you do. But I can assure you it wasn't me or Sandy. I mean Mrs. Monroe. The person you should be checking out is that crazy old man across the street, Howard Hancock."

"Why's that?" I asked

"He came to the house the morning of Mr. Monroe's death, about twenty minutes before your husband showed up," he said, now looking straight at Tiffany. While Manuel was distracted, I pulled the syringe out of my hand and stuck it in my back pocket. "Speaking of Chase, have you eliminated your husband as a suspect, Mrs. Carpenter?"

"Of course," she said. Her haughty tone came off as being a little ridiculous as she stood there with what smelled like pork gravy all over her arms. A glob of mashed potatoes hung precariously from her wrist. "Chase would never hurt anyone."

"And neither would I. But that Howard Hancock is freaking nuts! He threatened to kill Trey if he ever laid eyes on him again. He didn't believe me when I told him we hadn't seen Trey and didn't know where he was. Howard even threatened to turn me into the Immigration and Customs Enforcement agency because I've overstayed my visa."

"Really?" I asked. "Do you know if he actually contacted I.C.E.?"

"No," he said. "But I don't really care. Besides, I've already applied for a green card."

Would Manuel apply for permanent residency in the United States if he was planning to flee to the islands? Not likely. Everything he said in that feigned phone conversation was clearly hogwash. I wasn't convinced there wasn't some hanky-panky going on between him and Sandy, however. *If he's telling the truth now, and he appears to be sincere, it sounds like we're barking up the wrong tree. Maybe we should turn our attention to the couple across the street, and bark up the Hancocks' tree instead, as Manuel suggested.*

"I see. Okay, we apologize for not trusting you and Sandy. It's just that Chase and Tiffany have lost their life savings and are desperate to have their money returned."

"I understand, and I don't blame you. I had no idea what kind of despicable game Trey was playing. Frankly, I still find it difficult to believe he'd do such a thing," Manuel said, speaking directly to Tiffany again. Then he turned to me. "There's really no reason to keep that uncapped syringe you stuck in your back pocket. It was an unused syringe out of a new box. I threw the remainder of the box away after Trey passed. There's absolutely no evidence on, or in, that syringe. Left in your pocket, you're liable to end up with it stuck somewhere you'll regret."

I'm sure my face turned as red as the spaghetti sauce dripping off my elbow. I slid the syringe out of my pocket, cautiously, and pitched it into the trash can. Manuel smiled at me—much like the African serval who'd swallowed the baby gazelle—and said, "I'll let Babs know you two are done with your dumpster diving. But, take my word, Mrs. Ripple. Although I don't know why you are doing the job the Albuquerque homicide detectives should be doing, the Hancocks need further investigating. Especially Howard. He's mentally unstable. Babs, on the other hand, is just a nosy old lady."

"She's obviously exhibiting early signs of dementia or Alzheimer's," I said in Babs's defense.

"Or so it would appear," Manuel replied, as if doubtful Babs truly had a mental issue, even though her husband was a screwball.

I ignored his cynicism. "She's still a very congenial person."

"If you say so." Manuel then looked at Tiffany. "I'm curious, Mrs. Carpenter, did that nasty rash ever finally clear up?"

I didn't know what rash he was referring to, but his question clearly embarrassed Tiffany. She must have been too humiliated to answer his question. Instead, she turned and walked away.

I snatched up the bag of oatmeal cookies, determined not to let my kind gesture go to waste. I then gave a curt farewell to Manuel and joined Tiffany beside her car. I wanted to ask her about the rash and how he knew she'd had one, but I didn't want to make her even more uncomfortable. Perhaps she'd discussed the issue with Sandy. Regardless, I let the subject drop. Depending on where the rash had been located, it could conceivably be a very personal topic.

Looking back on our foiled attempt to capture proof of guilt on a listening device, I felt thankful Rip hadn't been able to turn the device over to the authorities. The term "unanswered prayers" wafted through my mind. I'd have been a laughingstock once they'd discovered the trick Manuel had played on us. If I wasn't so mortified by how my plan had turned out, I might have chuckled. Tiffany was so ashamed by her part in the scheme that she said she never wanted to run into Sandy again. "I couldn't face her after that humiliation, Grams."

"I know." It'd been my idea and I felt compelled to apologize. "Although, Manuel did say he wasn't going to tell her about it."

"Yeah, right. Of course he won't." Sarcasm dripped off Tiffany's tongue just as the pork gravy had dripped off her wrist.

"I'm sorry, sweetheart. I was only trying to make sure you and Chase got your money back. Still, I hate to be the cause of you losing a friend."

"That's all right. I think my friendship with Sandy had run its course, anyway. Now let's figure out how we can find out more about the Hancocks' involvement in Trey's death. Why don't we not mention what happened this morning to Gramps? With any luck at all, he'll never even know we didn't spend the entire after-noon shopping." *Yes, Tiffany definitely inherited her spunkiness and perse-verance from her Grams. And clearly a little bit of her evasiveness, as well.*

"Good idea. Now let's go look for some new shoes and that leather jacket you've been wanting. Maybe you can use that prepaid MasterCard we gave you for your birthday."

"That's exactly what I'd planned to do. That is, after we borrow the Hancocks' kitchen sink to wash this garbage off our hands and arms. I'm not getting in Franny with this crap all over me."

"Literally, in my case." With that in mind, I shook litter off my hands like a bird shakes water off its wings. I wanted to be totally free of cat poop before we climbed back into Tiffany's car. I assumed Franny was the name Tiffany had given her Honda Fit. I'd not only named every vehicle I'd ever owned, but I'd also given a nickname to our travel trailer. Once again, I was amazed at how much my granddaughter took after me. I smiled at the thought as we crossed the street.

Babs was waiting for us on her front porch after Tiffany and I had finished cleaning ourselves up in her kitchen. She sat in a wrought iron chair with her hands folded in her lap.

"How'd it go with Sandy?" I asked her. I had no intention of telling Babs how Tiffany's and my part of the deal had panned out. "Did she buy your story that you suddenly felt light-headed?"

"What?" She looked at me as if I was a puzzle she couldn't figure out how to solve. I felt a wave of sorrow pass through my body. "Nobody bought anything from me. I wasn't even trying to sell anyone anything."

"Oh, I see. My mistake. Tiffany and I need to get going now, Babs. Have a nice afternoon." I patted her folded hands as I spoke.

I felt a sense of relief as I crawled back into Franny. It was unlikely Babs would be relaying the dumpster-diving debacle to Howard. She'd probably already forgotten the entire incident. I felt the fewer who knew about it, the better. Like Tiffany, I felt certain it wasn't an incident Manuel could, or would, keep from Sandy. *I hope it doesn't become necessary to visit the Monroe household again*, I thought. *At this point, even I am too humiliated to face Sandy and Manuel again.*

SEVENTEEN

"What'd you and Tiff buy on your shopping spree?" Rip asked when I walked into the trailer. Tiffany had dropped me off at the Route 66 RV Resort after inviting us over for supper in about three hours' time. She'd said she wanted to try out her new chicken casserole recipe on us.

"It wasn't exactly a spree, Rip. I didn't get anything, but Tiffany found a pair of shoes and a jacket to buy with the prepaid MasterCard we gave her. She was really delighted with her purchases, too."

"Good. You couldn't find a single thing you wanted?"

"Not really. Besides, I'm tightening my purse strings."

"If they get any tighter, dear, they might snap." Rip laughed at his own quip.

I found it less amusing, however. It was my conservative nature that allowed us to live the carefree life we were living, seeing the country from our home on wheels. Our retirement fund was adequate, but only if we allocated our money wisely. I knew my next suggestion might take a bite out of that already rigid budget, but I knew there were a few luxuries we allowed ourselves that we could forego for a while, and I was willing to make the sacrifice. I knew Rip would be, too, if it meant helping out his beloved granddaughter.

"I think we should help the kids out if they don't get their investment money returned soon. Tiffany didn't really say as much, but there were several things I could tell she really wanted to buy. She'd study an item longingly and then say, 'I better not.' I'm sure she only bought the shoes and jacket because she had the gift card to pay for them."

"I'm not surprised. Chase said today he might have to look for a second job. He also mentioned the possibility of selling their home and looking for a smaller one in a cheaper neighborhood. That's a real turnaround for them. They were negotiating on a new house in Sandia Heights just two weeks ago." I could tell Rip was troubled by the idea the kids would have to sell their home and downsize because of the injustice Trey Monroe had committed against them.

"I didn't offer our assistance yet," I said, "because I wanted to talk it over with you first. I'm willing to cut back to help them out. What are your thoughts about it?"

"I think we could lend them ten thousand, interest-free, payable at their convenience, only when it won't be a hardship for them," Rip concurred.

"I suppose we could just give the money to them, no strings attached, if you'd prefer."

"No," Rip began, "I don't want to hurt Chase's pride. I know if it were me, I wouldn't want to accept any handouts. I think the interest-free loan is the best idea. He can accept that without looking like a failure in his wife's eyes."

"Good thinking, Rip. You can speak to Chase about it face-to-face tonight when we go over to their house for supper. Tiffany's trying out a new chicken casserole recipe. I'm taking an iced gingerbread cake for dessert."

"Sounds good." Rip nodded. "I'll talk to Chase tonight. And before I forget, Trey's personal assistant at the investment firm called while you and Tiff were gone. She said she had something to run by you."

"Harlei? Did she say what it was about?" I asked, intentionally mentioning her name. I knew from past experience it'd help Rip eventually remember it.

"Yes, but I forgot to put my hearing aids in this morning."

"Rip, dear, you forgot to put your hearing aids in this *year*!" I spoke in a teasing manner, even though his refusal to wear the costly electronic devices was a constant source of irritation for me.

"*Touché!*" Rip replied with a sheepish grin.

"I'll call her and give her my new phone number to call in the future."

"Good idea," Rip replied. "Just in case I've forgotten to put my hearing aids in again the next time she calls."

"You and I both know that's a given! I'll call her back as soon as I change into something more comfortable."

"Change into something more comfortable, huh?" Rip had a mischievous smirk on his face. "Is that a come-hither suggestion?"

"Not hardly. It's a 'get out of my way so I can get something done' suggestion."

"I was afraid of that." Rip walked away laughing. "Since I don't have anything more enjoyable to do, I guess I'll walk up to the campground's office and pay for another week."

"Good afternoon, Harlei," I said into the phone about ten minutes later.

"Good afternoon, Mrs. Ripple. How are you?"

"Please call me Rapella, dear. Rip and I are doing fine. Chase and Tiffany are still upset, of course."

"As am I."

"Rip said you called earlier this afternoon. Unfortunately, the big dummy didn't catch much of what you said because he thinks his hearing aids are like vampires."

"Excuse me?" Harlei said, clearly puzzled by my remark.

"They never see the light of day. They stay tucked away in his toiletry bag so sunlight doesn't render them useless." I laughed and Harlei politely joined in. "So, what is it you wanted to tell me?"

"Actually, I was curious if you had anything new to share with me."

"No." I wasn't about to tell her about the listening device debacle. "I wish I did. Are there any new developments on your end?"

"Not really," Harlei hesitated before continuing. I sensed she was reluctant to give out any personal information about one of the investment company's clients. "I *did* get an interesting phone call this morning. He called me on my personal phone line and said he was going to sue Monroe Investments, and everyone who works for the company, if his money isn't back in his account in the next forty-eight hours. And, as you know, I'm the only other person who worked at Monroe Investments. I'm not supposed to talk about any of the firm's clients. . ."

"No worries," I said when Harlei's voice trailed off. "Mum's the word. So go ahead and explain why the phone call concerned you."

"He was very loud and hostile. I felt threatened by his remarks." There was a distinct catch in Harlei's voice. It was evident she was scared. "I told him I'd been tricked into investing in the Ponzi scheme, too. He didn't seem to care. Just said, 'Well, it was your decision to work for the charlatan.' He just got nastier when I responded that I didn't know Trey was a 'charlatan', and if I had, I wouldn't have accepted the job."

"What was this client's name, if you don't mind me asking?"

"Well, again, this is just between the two of us. All right?"

"Of course." After a lengthy silence, I asked, "So what was the client's name?" I had a sneaking suspicion I already knew the man's name, and she quickly confirmed it.

"His name is Howard Hancock. He's actually a neighbor of the Monroes. Very rich real estate broker who specialized in high-dollar luxury properties before he retired. He was also the biggest investor in Monroe Investment's Clean Sweep IPO fund. Or, the IPO fund that never was, I should say. He also had several million dollars' worth of blue-chip stocks in his portfolio that Trey sold off the day before he was killed."

"Oh, my!" I exclaimed. "I can see why Hancock's bitter."

"I can too, of course. But it wasn't my fault and there's nothing I can do about it. It was what he said before he ended the call that concerned me the most," Harlei said.

"And what was that?" I asked.

"He said, 'That no-account swindler got what he had coming to him and I don't feel bad about it one bit. Like with snakes, the only good crook is a dead crook.'"

"Wow! Those *are* troubling remarks. I'm glad you called to let me know about the phone call from him. I'm still looking into the situation, by the way. I'm determined to get my granddaughter and her husband's money back, and yours, too, along with the money of the other investors who got conned. Even, I suppose, the Hancocks'."

"Thank you. I was hoping you'd say that. I've lost faith in the police department. This morning, I called that lead detective, Carlos Ramirez, I think his name is."

"It's Carlos Gutierrez," I corrected her. "What'd he tell you?"

"He basically dismissed the information I gave him about the

177

Hancocks. He said angry reactions like Howard's are pretty common among people who've been taken to the cleaners by a con artist like Trey. He went on to say it was certainly not an indication of Mr. Hancock being guilty of murder." Harlei sounded discouraged and annoyed at the way Carlos had spoken to her. I couldn't say I blamed her. But I could understand his decision to be upfront with her, rather than just blow smoke up her skirt to appease her. Like Rip had said, Carlos was a "by the book" detective.

"I suppose what Detective Gutierrez told you is true," I began, "but Trey's house manager suggested we should look into not just Howard, but both of the Hancocks. Neither of their alibis could be confirmed. Babs had said she'd purchased some baseball cards from QVC Shopping network that morning, but Carlos told Rip when they contacted the network to obtain confirmation of the purchase, there was no record of a Babs Hancock calling in to buy anything. By the way, do you know if the Monroes' house manager, Mr. de la Cruz, ever attended nursing school?"

"Yes. Actually, Manuel was employed as a P.A. by several different doctors in town, before he suddenly switched career paths and went to work for the Monroes."

"What is a P.A.?" I asked.

"It's a physician's assistant," Harlei replied. Her response explained to me how Manuel might have known about a rash Tiffany had sought medical attention for and why he wouldn't have hesitated to administer Trey's insulin injections. "They can see and treat patients in the place of the doctor, and even make diagnoses and write prescriptions. Most are as capable as a full-fledged M.D., which stands for—"

"Medical doctor," I cut in, not wanting her to think I was a total numbskull. The lady used more acronyms than anyone else I'd ever met.

"And, just F.Y.I.," Harlei said, at least using one that everyone recognized this time. "Manuel is a piece of work. I'd take anything that fellow says with a grain of salt."

"Point taken. I get the impression he and Mrs. Monroe have more than just a working relationship."

"Oh, most definitely." Harlei sounded delighted to have an opportunity to spread gossip. She reminded me of my hairdresser in Rockport, who had loved to pass on every little morsel of scuttlebutt that was shared in her salon. "Even Trey knew the two were involved in an affair. He seemed totally unaffected by the knowledge. In fact, on occasion, he'd even joke about it. He often referred to Manuel as Don Juan, and on occasion he called him his husband-in-law. He and Sandy had the most bizarre marital relationship I've ever seen. I'm pretty certain Sandy first hired Manuel with something entirely different in mind than having him manage their home."

"Sounds like it. It may also explain Manuel's sudden decision to change career paths." My suspicion had been confirmed. Manuel and Sandy were an item. *Were they also co-conspirators?* I asked myself. *I now have to wonder how much of what Manuel said on the recording was nonsense, and how much of it really was the truth. I feel certain it was a mixture of both fact and fiction.*

My thoughts were disrupted when Harlei said, "Thank you so much for returning my call. I feel so much better having talked to you. Being threatened with a lawsuit by Howard Hancock kind of shook me up."

"I wouldn't worry about that aspect of this ordeal too much, dear. I don't know what basis he'd have to sue you. You were as much a victim of Trey's as the Hancocks. He'd likely be advised by his attorney to sue whoever had the deepest pockets, anyway."

"At this point, Monroe Investments doesn't have any pockets whatsoever, and mine have literally been turned inside out."

Well, not literally, dear. Figuratively perhaps, I wanted to say, but decided not to be petty, even though the misuse of the word "literal" was one of my pet peeves. "At least you still have your sense of humor."

"At times, I feel like that's all I have left, and it's waning rapidly."

"Do you have any family you can lean on for a while?" I asked.

"Not really. I was an only child, and my folks both passed away when I was in my early twenties. I have an uncle who lives in Colorado Springs. But Uncle Ronnie's an alcoholic and probably in worse financial shape than I am."

"Do you have any kids?" I asked.

"No. I've been divorced for about seven years. Thomas and I married young and had no children. I always thought I couldn't get pregnant because he had a low sperm count. But he and his new wife have four kids now, three boys and a girl. And guess what? She's got another bun in the oven. She's been spitting babies out like candy from a Pez dispenser since they tied the knot six years ago. They better be thinking about having her tubes tied or they'll soon have enough kids to field a baseball team."

I laughed at her humorous description, and again when she added, "It clearly wasn't Thomas who had the fertility issue, huh?"

"What are you going to do?" I asked Harlei when the laughter stopped.

"I'm not sure." Harlei's mood was much more sober now. I wished I had enough money to help her the way we were going to offer to help Chase and Tiffany. "That's the question that's been running through my mind like a broken record for the last couple of weeks."

"Do you own a home?" I thought about Chase considering

the possibility of selling his and Tiffany's home to get into a cheaper one, with a smaller payment attached to it.

"Yes. I have a four-bedroom split-level in Los Ranchos. I love the place, but it's much bigger than I need."

"Maybe you should consider selling it and down-sizing," I suggested, thinking about what Chase had discussed with Rip. "Rip and I sold our home and the bulk of our belongings when he retired from the Aransas County Sheriff's department in Rockport, Texas. We bought a thirty-foot travel trailer and live in it full-time now. We get to see a lot of the country while avoiding real estate taxes, high utility bills, home insurance, and more. I was concerned at first that I wouldn't like feeling as though I didn't have a place to call home. But now, I realize I'm more than content calling the Chartreuse Caboose my home."

"The what?" Harlei asked. You'd have thought I'd told her we lived in a cave. I decided not to go into detail when there were more important things to discuss.

"Long story."

"I'm not sure I'd feel comfortable pulling a travel trailer around the country."

"I'm not suggesting you buy an RV to live in," I said. "My point is, if you own a home, you always have the option of selling it and using the equity to get by on until you get back on your feet."

"Actually, I have been thinking about selling it for a while now. I might even move away, somewhere the cost of living is lower and I never have to shovel snow." Harlei's mood had brightened, and I was relieved I'd helped turn it around. "Not that we have a ton of snow here in Albuquerque. But we do get some on occasion, particularly here in the foothills area. People also tend to think of Arizona as a place where it rarely snows, but I used to live in Flagstaff and it wasn't uncommon for the snow to drift over the top of the duplex Thomas and I rented."

"That's true," I agreed. "We've been caught in a blizzard more than once as we were passing through Flagstaff. I've seen snow piled up so high in the medians that you couldn't see the traffic on the other side of the street."

"Me, too!" She replied with a laugh. "Thanks again for returning my call, Rapella. You've cheered me up just by talking to me."

"Good. I'm glad, dear. Whatever you decide to do, I wish you the best. Don't hesitate to call again if you have anything new to pass on."

"I won't. You'll be the first person I call! Keep me posted on how your personal investigation is going, too."

"I will," I replied. "You can count on it. Hang in there, dear. Keep your chin up."

I ended the call after giving Harlei my new phone number. I didn't know if I should eliminate Sandy Monroe and Manuel de la Cruz from my suspect list or not. After all, they both had two potential motives to eliminate Trey: lust for each other and the lust for money. Manuel had sounded so sincere when he denied having any part in the murder, and had convincingly argued Sandy's innocence, as well. The fact they were engaged in an affair, one the victim had already been aware of, no less, might make the pair immoral, but it didn't make them killers. One thing was for certain, though. Howard Hancock now occupied the top spot on my suspect list.

EIGHTEEN

Early the next morning, I was sitting outside under the awning, sipping on a cup of strong Columbian coffee, when Rip exited the trailer. "Good morning, sunshine. Why are you up and around so early?"

"I don't know. Guess I just couldn't sleep very well."

"Something bothering you?"

"Not really." I knew I couldn't fool him. My emotions were written all over my face like it was a billboard on I-40. "Just worried about the kids and wondering if this murder case is ever going to be solved."

"You don't need to worry about either, honey," he said. "The kids agreed to take us up on the loan offer, and eventually, the perpetrator in Trey's death will be brought up on murder charges. It might take a little longer than usual, but I'm sure Carlos won't let the case go cold. He seems committed to bringing the killer to justice."

"I know." *I am too*, I could've said. I smiled as Rip leaned over to kiss me on the forehead. "I was just thinking."

"Did it make your head hurt?" Rip laughed at his own joke,

hoping his attempt at levity would lighten the dark mood I was in. It worked.

"You dork!" I laughed out loud. Just then Tiffany pulled up next to the Caboose and got out of her car. "Have a seat, sweetheart. I'll get you a cup of coffee."

"Thanks, Grams."

A few minutes later, all three of us were sitting in lawn chairs, drinking coffee, and soaking up the sunshine on a beautiful November morning. I returned to the subject of the Hancocks to discuss an idea that'd been percolating in my head. "I thought we should go pay another visit to Babs and Howard."

"What for?" Rip asked.

"Because I assured Babs we'd look into the situation and try to find out where their money went. I don't think her husband will rest until it's located, and I'm sure that's putting a lot of stress on Babs's shoulders." I really wasn't very optimistic about getting a lot of useful information out of Babs, but was hoping we could find out more about her husband. Perhaps one of the pair would divulge some nugget that would help us determine if Howard could've been behind Trey's death. If nothing else, we might be able to judge his reactions and character a little better if we could engage him in conversation. I didn't want to approach the unpredictable man alone, however. I'd always believed there was safety in numbers, whether it involved human beings or a large herd of zebras on the Serengeti.

"So, Rapella, what can you tell Babs at this point that will help lift the stress off her shoulders?" Rip wore a dubious expression. I'd wondered if Tiffany had shared information about our dumpster-diving disgrace with Chase, who would have surely passed it onto Rip. I was relieved that Rip seemed oblivious of the entire ordeal when he added, "We don't know any more than we did when we last talked to her."

"I know, but at least I can tell her we haven't given up. I was hoping maybe she'd seen or heard something that might be help-ful. The way her mind works at this stage of her progressive memory loss, recollections could come to the forefront at any given time."

"I guess talking with the Hancocks sounds harmless enough." Rip shrugged. I could sense he thought it would be a futile effort, but knew I wouldn't give up the idea easily. If those were his thoughts, time would prove he was correct on both counts. I real-ized the idea of safety in numbers seemed to be his philosophy, too, when he said, "But I'd prefer you take Tiffany with you. Do you mind tagging along, Tiff?"

"Not at all, Gramps!" Tiffany exclaimed. "I agree it'd be safer for Grams if I went along."

I hoped Rip didn't catch the apprehensive look Tiffany shot my way. She clearly believed the visit would be anything but safe.

When Tiffany pulled Franny up along the curb in front of the Hancocks' house, we saw Howard yanking plants with white blos-soms out of a flower bed on the east side of his house.

"What's he doing?" Tiffany asked. "Those flowers are beautiful."

"Yeah, they are, or at least were."

"What kind of flower is that?"

"They're devil's trumpets, a plant that's known to be a potent hallucinogenic," I said.

"Reckon he got some of it in his system somehow?" Tiffany asked. "He's acting a little deranged."

"I doubt he got any in his system, but I agree Howard's not playing with a full set of brain cells."

"Look at him!" She pointed at the man, who seemed to be

moving his lips and foaming at the mouth. "Now he's yelling at himself."

"I think he's cussing out the plants in the flower bed. Poor guy!" I said, feeling sorry for Mr. Hancock.

"Poor Babs!" Tiffany said, in contradiction to my emotions. "She has to live with the temperamental nut job. Let's see if we can get her to invite us in before he notices we're here."

Too late! Just then, he looked up. "Hey! What are you two broads doing on my property?"

"Well, technically, we aren't on your property." Without thinking, I reacted angrily to his remark. Tiffany gasped at my retort. "We are still in the street, which is one thing you *don't* own. And furthermore, we aren't broads. We are ladies."

"What do you *ladies* want?" His emphasis on the word "ladies" did not go unnoticed, but I refused to rise to the bait this time. "We brought you and Babs a batch of homemade cookies." I opened the back door and picked up the bag I'd put on the floorboard of Franny's back seat the previous day. Fortunately, I'd forgotten to get them out of her car when we'd arrived home.

I held the cookies up for Howard to see. I hoped it'd prove to him we had come in peace. His voice softened ever so slightly as he said, "Babs is inside. Ring the bell."

Howard then turned around and angrily ripped a bonsai-looking plant, known as a desert rose, out of the ground. I whispered to Tiffany, "He's lucky that species of rose plants doesn't have any thorns."

"I'm not sure he would have noticed if they did," Tiffany countered. "What are you going to do with that bag of cookies?"

"Give them to Babs like I told Howard."

"Ewww. Gross." She was clearly disgusted. "They were in the garbage can."

"So?" I flicked off a piece of apple peeling clinging to the

Ziploc bag. "They'll never know the difference. The fact Sandy had the presence of mind to put them in an airtight bag before she pitched them has kept them fresh and clean. They'll be just fine."

I put my finger to my lips and pointed to the doorbell to remind Tiffany Babs could see and hear us through her Ring doorbell app. She nodded, and when we reached the front porch, she pushed the button.

"Oh, good!" Babs rubbed her hands together in delight after she opened the front door and eyed the big bag of home-cooked treats. I was instantly glad I'd left them in Tiffany's car. At least now they wouldn't go to waste. Babs ushered us inside and placed the bag on her kitchen table. "Oatmeal cookies are my favorite. Although I could've sworn you promised to bring me a coconut cream pie when you called yesterday, Henrietta."

Tiffany caught my eye and shrugged. I raised my eyebrows in response, before replying to our host. "I'm sorry, Babs. I must've forgotten."

"You always were the forgetful type, Henri. But don't fret. It's fine, dear. After all, oatmeal cookies are my favorite."

"I knew that, silly." I smiled and patted her blue-veined hand with gnarly fingers that were bent in all different directions. *Arthritis*, I thought. *I hope it's not as painful as it looks.*

"Of course you did. What was I thinking? I'm so glad you brought Clarabelle with you. I haven't seen my favorite niece in ages." Babs leaned over and kissed Tiffany's cheek. She then turned her head and held her cheek out in anticipation of a reciprocal gesture. Tiffany looked horrified, but I gave her a stern look until she leaned over and returned a quick peck to Babs's cheek, which was heavily caked with a wrinkle-concealing foundation.

"It's good to see you, too, Aunt Babs," Tiffany said.

"Babs?" The elderly woman asked in surprise. "When did

you stop calling me Aunt Barbara? You were always the only one who didn't call me by my nickname."

"I just wanted to test you, Aunt Barbara. I should have known you were too sharp not to catch it." Tiffany was a quick thinker and handled the situation perfectly. We didn't want to upset Babs or embarrass her, so with unspoken mutual agreement, we'd decided to just go along with her mistaken identification.

It was obvious we weren't going to get any beneficial information out of Babs, so there was no sense bringing up our quest to find out where their investment money went. She clearly wasn't having a very coherent day if she didn't even realize who we were.

"You were probably busy doing something, so we won't linger. We just wanted to drop off the cookies."

"For our birthday?" Babs asked.

"Um, yes, of course," I said, confused by her use of the word "our". Maybe Babs and Howard shared a birthday today, I reasoned. "You know we wouldn't forget you on your birthday."

"I know you wouldn't. How on earth could you?"

"We'll get going now, Babs." I stood up and motioned to Tiffany to do the same.

"No! You just got here!" Babs said emphatically. We both sat down immediately. "You have to stay and visit for a little while, at least. Our birthday only rolls around once a year, you know."

"Of course. I guess we can visit a few minutes longer." Babs appeared pleased by my remark, and Tiffany and I had nothing else pressing to do.

At that point, Babs got up and walked to her kitchen sink. She washed her hands so long and thoroughly that you'd have thought they were covered in axle grease. She walked back to the table, looked at the bag of baked goods, and said, "Oh, good! Oatmeal cookies! They're my favorite!"

"I knew that," I said. "That's why I baked them for you for your birthday. How old are you now? I forgot."

"Don't be ridiculous, Henri! You and I both turned forty today," Babs said with an impish grin. "But you're still older than I am. I'll always be the youngest child in our family, even if only by seven minutes."

I chuckled along with her. "I was just kidding, of course."

"I know," she said. "You always were the jokester of the bunch. That's why you became a writer and I went into nursing."

So, if memory served her right, so to speak, Babs had been a nurse. "Did you ever work with Manuel de la Cruz, who was also a nurse before becoming the Monroes' house manager?"

I'd hoped asking her a specific question might trigger her mind to focus on the subject at hand. I was relieved the attempt seemed to be effective, at least temporarily.

"Yes. On two occasions, actually. We both worked for Dr. Phillips, who was a physiatrist—"

"What's a physiatrist?" Tiffany cut in. "I've never heard of that term."

"It's a physician who specializes in pain management, which is what Dr. Phillips did," Babs explained. "Manuel and I both worked for Dr. Patel, as well, but I had moved on before Manuel started. Patel was an endocrinologist who specialized in diabetic care and thyroid disorders. That training certainly came in handy for me recently."

"How's that?" I asked.

"Well, the other day, Trey—"

Just then Howard walked into the kitchen. He looked anxious as he interrupted his wife. "What'd I tell you, Babs?"

"I don't remember, Howie." Babs seemed to shrink into herself at his chastising tone. It was almost as though she was afraid of disobeying him.

"I told you not to discuss the Monroes or the money they

scammed us out of. It only gets you rattled and upset, and it makes you more forgetful. Let me worry about all that. You know I'll take care of it, and it's not good for you to dwell on the situation."

"Yes, dear," she said, as compliant as a scolded child. "I won't mention it again."

"That's my girl. You know I'm only trying to protect you, as I always have."

"I know, Howie." Babs looked down at her hands, which were folded in her lap. She began to knead the palm of her right hand with her left hand, as if it ached.

"What were you ladies talking about before I came inside?" He spoke in a deep voice as he glared straight at me. His comment was clearly not idle chatter. His demeanor demanded an answer.

"We were discussing Babs's birthday today." I hoped my response would appease him. Instead, he shook his head in denial.

"Babs's birthday is August eighteenth."

"Oh, my mistake," I said.

Howard noticed my discomfort and actually winked at me. It was such a 180-degree turn that I felt as though I'd been flung off a rapidly spinning carnival ride. In a much softer tone, he said, "Every day's her birthday, if you know what I mean."

"I understand." And I did understand. I was glad she thought of every day as a reason to celebrate something, rather than something to be depressed about. I thought I should seize the opportunity, while Howard seemed to be in a more pleasant mood. "You appeared to be laboring hard in the garden and probably worked up an appetite. Why don't you join us for a cookie or two?"

I really didn't think there was a chance in Hades he'd accept my offer and join us at the table, but he did. He reached into the bag and withdrew four cookies. I glanced at "Clarabelle" as he took a big bite out of one. She looked a little green around the gills. I'm afraid if she'd actually eaten any of them, she'd have *literally* been tossing her cookies right about then. And, in this example, the word was used correctly.

Babs took a cookie out of the bag and then passed the bag to me. "Would you ladies like one? My sister, Henrietta, dropped them off for me this morning."

Howard rolled his eyes with a loud sigh. He turned toward Tiffany and me. "She gets confused a lot these days."

"We just ate," I replied to Babs after nodding at Howard. Tiffany gave me an appreciative smile. I could tell she thought I was going to insist she eat one of the "rescued from the dumpster" cookies.

Howard was being affable for the most part, and I decided if I didn't broach the subject soon about Trey and the missing money, our opportunity would disappear like a twenty-dollar bill in a Las Vegas casino.

"So, Howard," I began, "it doesn't look like there have been any new developments on the murder case or Ponzi scheme situation."

Suddenly, Howard slammed his fist down into the middle of a cookie, killing it instantly. The dead cookie lay still on the table, busted into a hundred pieces. So taken aback by his sudden fit of fury, I gasped and Tiffany jumped back from the table. Babs didn't even flinch. Howard hissed, "That no good slimy @&*!#. If he wasn't already dead, I'd slap him into next week, and then I'd slap him back into this one."

"Don't mind him," Babs said. In a moment of pure clarity, she added, "He's just upset because he thought of Trey and Sandy as if they were his own kids. He thought he and I meant something special to them. That's why he thought Trey let him in on such a good deal. That IPO fund was really supposed to skyrocket in value. Turns out there wasn't an IPO fund at all. We were just a bunch of silly old fools investing in a pipe dream."

I glanced at Howard, who seemed as stunned by Babs's remarks as Tiffany and I were. When he could finally speak, he said, "Now, now, Babs. You told me you wouldn't speak of Trey and the missing money again."

"Yes, dear." Babs resumed trying to work a sore spot out of her right palm.

'When she didn't get the details right regarding her where-abouts when Trey was killed, the investigators got all excited and I had to do a lot of explaining. I truly believed UPS would be delivering a box of baseball cards in the near future." Howard spoke directly to Tiffany and me. "She's right though, ladies. I thought very highly of Trey. I still can't believe he would do something like that to us."

"He did the exact same thing to us," Tiffany said. "We thought Trey and Sandy were two of our dearest friends. Instead, he was just setting us up to be taken advantage of. In fact, his personal assistant, Harlei Rycoff, told us he did the same thing to all of his clients. Made them all think they were special friends of his and his wife's, and only because of his fondness for them, he let them in on the Clean Sweep phenomena, a surefire money-maker. The stock *did* skyrocket. Too bad none of the money we both gave Trey was actually invested in it."

"That's what angers me the most," Howard said. "I am upset with myself for falling for his scheme to begin with. I thought I was wiser than that. I guess that little punk was smarter than all of us. I don't understand how Ms. Rycoff didn't know what was going on. After all, as his personal assistant, she took care of all of the paperwork for him."

"Trey was clever. Harlei said he cooked the books and gave her the fictitious statements to send out to all the investors," I said in Harlei's defense. "She trusted him completely. So he used her loyalty to him against her, and talked her into investing in the fund, too. I'd hazard to guess she could ill-afford to lose her investment money even more than you."

"Probably," Howard said with a sigh. "Trey was a crafty devil. I'll give him that. He got his just rewards in the end, though, didn't he? I couldn't be happier about it."

"I suppose," I said. Tiffany just stared at Howard in disbelief. His cold and callous attitude was bone-chilling.

"Babs needs to rest now, ladies. You should be going. Conversations about that con artist get her upset." Howard spoke in a no-nonsense voice. I'd hazard to guess it was he, not his wife, who was angered by talk of the Ponzi scheme and its creator. We could be discussing a huge meteor about to collide with Earth for all Babs appeared to be taking in from our exchange with her husband at that point. Howard said he was happy about Trey's death, but what he did next did not seem like what a "happy" guy would do. He banged his chair back against the wall, startling all three of us women. He walked out of the room, slamming the door behind him. As he strode away, however, I spotted a lone tear tracking down his cheek.

Is he crying over the loss of his money? I wondered. *Or, perhaps the loss of a neighbor he'd considered a close personal friend? Instead, was it that friend's betrayal that had prompted the tear?*

"Babs," I said after he'd departed. "We do need to be going, as Howard suggested. But before we do, do you know where your husband was the morning Trey was killed?"

"No," she replied, "but that morning I saw Trey arguing with another man in his front yard. I could tell by all of the finger-pointing, it was a contentious exchange."

"Really?" I asked. "What'd the other man look like? Did you recognize him?"

"No. From where I was sitting on my front porch, he looked a lot like Trey. They could've been twins, like us. It was a short discussion. Trey stomped over and pulled his car out of the garage. The stranger he'd been squabbling with got in a white vehicle parked at the curb and followed Trey."

"What else did you see?" I asked, wanting to get as much information out of Babs as I could while she was so clear-minded. Unfortunately, my window of opportunity was about to slam shut.

"Just the white car."

"Was it a man or woman driving it?" Tiffany asked.

"Couldn't tell," Babs replied.

I turned to Tiffany. "Chase has a white car, and he was at Trey's house that morning. They are both dark-haired and of average height and weight."

"That describes Manuel, too," Tiffany said, with a huff. Her tone was defensive, but I might have come off as accusatory. "As Babs mentioned before, Sandy owns a white Lincoln Navigator that Manuel drives all the time. We have proof from the Hancocks' Ring doorbell app that Chase didn't follow anyone."

"I realize that, sweetheart. I wasn't accusing Chase of killing Trey." I then turned my attention back to Babs, who was swatting at something I couldn't detect, perhaps an imaginary gnat. "Do you recall what kind of car the white vehicle was, Babs?"

"What white vehicle are you talking about, Henrietta?"

"Never mind, Babs. It doesn't matter." I shared a knowing look with Tiffany. "I think we better be heading out, Clarabelle. We have a lot of errands to run today."

"Okay." Tiffany had a poignant expression on her face. I felt sadness flood through me, too. "It was great to see you, Aunt Barbara."

"It was great to see you two, as well. Don't be strangers. Thanks for stopping by on our birthday, Henri."

"Nothing could have kept me away on our special day," I replied.

As we got up to leave, Babs added, "And thanks again for the coconut cream pie."

Tiffany and I were both on the verge of tears as we exited the Hancock home. A sadder disease than Alzheimer's is difficult to imagine.

NINETEEN

s we pulled away from the curb on Zinfandel Avenue, I looked into Tiffany's eyes. She appeared troubled and sullen. I felt compelled to apologize. "When I mentioned that Chase had a similar build as Trey and a white vehicle a couple of minutes ago, I wasn't implying I thought there was a snowball's chance in hell he was involved in Trey's death, sweetheart. I was merely wondering if Babs saw his vehicle but was confused about the timing. Chase had been there, just later than Babs might've remembered."

"That's quite possible," Tiffany conceded. "When we were sorting through the videos on her Ring doorbell app, we looked at all of them from that morning. We saw no sign of Trey arguing with another man in his front yard."

"That's true," I responded.

"It was probably a memory of an actual event, but the scene Babs was describing probably occurred on an earlier date."

"Absolutely!" I agreed. "That's the most logical scenario. Besides, can we trust anything Babs says at this point?"

"I doubt it. My question is, where was Howard at the time

of Trey's death? Has anyone been able to confirm he was in San Antonio taking photos of a client's ranch property?" Tiffany asked. "He clearly has a very volatile temper. And why is he so determined that Babs not discuss Trey, or anything to do with his death or the missing money? Does she know something he's afraid she'll reveal, either when she's coherent or when she's not? Or do you believe his excuse of being concerned she might give the wrong details to someone and cause another stir?"

"I wondered the same thing. It *is* true the detectives discovered a fallacy in her alibi when they couldn't verify she'd purchased baseball cards off the QVC channel. And I'm sure that took some explaining to the authorities on Howard's part."

"You and I are hardly authorities, though."

"That's true," I replied. "I also question whether he could've convinced her to do something to Trey, knowing she wouldn't recall doing it or any of the details later on."

"Uh-huh." Tiffany uttered.

I looked at her to judge her reaction. She appeared to be deep in thought, so I continued. "Babs said she spent her career in nursing. I believe her when she said she worked for a diabetic specialist. She seemed very rational when she talked about it and gave so many details. Is it possible he convinced her to give Trey an insulin injection, or at least what she believed was an insulin injection? Instead, he could've loaded the syringe with a fatal dose of the potassium chloride. It's too bad he had to enter the room at that precise moment, or we might've learned something incriminating."

"I agree. She had just remarked that her training as a nurse had come in handy recently. Perhaps Manuel was otherwise engaged and Sandy asked her neighbor, someone she knew who had a nursing background, to give her husband his insulin injection. Apparently, Trey was too big of a chicken to give himself the shots. Funny, 'cause he always acted like he was such a tough guy."

I chuckled at Tiffany's comment. "It might have been a crime of opportunity on Sandy's part. She might've wanted all the money from the sale of his clients' portfolios for herself, and decided to put the deadly KCl compound in the syringe rather than his usual insulin. She then could've let Babs do the dirty work for her."

"That's an interesting theory, Grams," Tiffany said. "She could've figured it might come down to a 'she said, she said' situation. Who would the authorities be more apt to believe—her or her mentally impaired neighbor, Babs Hancock?"

"Exactly!" I exclaimed in agreement. "It bears thinking about."

"Yep. It sure does." Soon Tiffany was in heavy traffic, so I kept quiet for the rest of the drive and mused to myself. My suspect list was getting more complicated with each passing day. I felt like, in all good conscience, I couldn't eliminate anyone from the list. It was as though we were back to square one. I couldn't even let myself look past my grandson-in-law, although I'd never tell another living soul that. The airport was not so far away that he couldn't have injected Trey and then come back to his victim's house to ring the doorbell and ask to speak to him. Perhaps by doing so, he was trying to establish an alibi. I didn't know how quickly potassium chloride could kill a person, but it stood to reason that the time could be altered by adjusting the size of the dose you injected.

I still felt as though I was overlooking something or someone. *Who was that individual with the Asian name Detective Gutierrez mentioned had given an alibi they hadn't been able to verify?* I asked myself. *If that is still the case, how can we find out more about him? I recall Carlos saying the man was not much of a physical threat but had powerful friends and acquaintances.*

I was going to call Carlos myself when I returned home. I'd scribbled his number down on a post-it note I'd stuck to the refrigerator door. Tiffany could show me how to add him to the contact list in my new phone. So far, my contact list contained four names: Rip, Tiffany, Harlei Rycoff, and my daughter, Regina. I had to wonder how long it'd be before I began receiving twenty unwanted telemarketer calls every day. I could already visualize myself screaming into the phone, "How many times do I have to tell you I don't want to buy an extended service agreement on a car I sold six years ago?"

"His name is Chen Ho," Detective Gutierrez said. I could tell my call had caught him at a bad time. "I have a meeting to attend in a few short moments. All I can tell you is Mr. Ho is a bail bondsman on the south side of town. His alibi has not been verified, but we have found no evidence tying him to Mr. Monroe's death, either. He came to the station and gave a written statement two days after Mr. Monroe's death, and nothing in it raised any red flags. We haven't officially removed him from our persons of interest list yet. However, we haven't had a reason to contact him since he gave his statement two weeks ago, either. I don't recommend you or Rip meet with him. You need to exercise great caution while nosing around in this investigation. Whoever killed Trey would not hesitate to add another notch or two to his gun belt. And if you tell anyone I gave you permission to look into the case on your own time, I'll deny I ever did anything of the sort, Rapella. Just saying."

Carlos laughed, but his words sounded more like a warning than a joke. I felt compelled to set his concerns to rest.

"Oh, you needn't worry, Carlos. We would never mention to anyone that you told us we could look into the case, nor would we consider doing anything that might jam you up. Our objective is to snoop around for intriguing clues to pass on to you, not put ourselves in the middle of a dangerous situation."

"Good," he replied. "Chen Ho may not look like much of a threat, Rapella, but some of his clientele over the years have been pretty unsavory and capable of about anything. And a few of them probably owe him a favor, or two. A favor, and/or money."

That's exactly what I was thinking, and why I'm quickly developing an interest in the bail bondsman, I could've said. Instead, I thanked him for the information. "I'll let you get to your meeting now. Thanks for taking my call."

After ending the call with the detective, I immediately called Harlei. At this point, she seemed to have tossed any client confidentiality concerns out the window, and I figured she'd have even more information about Chen Ho that might be beneficial in my investigation.

"Mr. Ho is a bail bondsman," Harlei said, repeating what Carlos had just told me. "He inherited a ton of money from his parents a few years ago and just recently went through treatment for prostate cancer. He appears to be in remission now. He was one of the biggest investors in the IPO, second only to the Hancocks. He called me on the morning of Trey's death, along with many of the firm's other clients after they'd brought up their accounts online and noticed a zero balance."

"How'd he take it when he found out his account had a zero balance?" I asked.

"Pretty much like all the rest of the investors; surprised, but confident the computer glitch would correct itself and their money would soon show back up in their accounts. At that point, it wasn't yet known by any of us that most of the stock in those accounts had been sold off and none of the clients' money had ever been invested in the IPO fund in the first place. We were all convinced we'd eventually get our money back, along with perhaps a hefty profit. Early on, I was the only one who was concerned that we might have been scammed by Trey. I couldn't imagine him doing something so evil, though, so I kept the suspicion to myself."

"How'd you eventually find out Trey *had* scammed everyone?" I asked.

"It was actually Chen Ho who called me a second time that morning, about an hour after his first call, and asked about the value of his shares in the IPO fund. The six-month lock-out period had just expired, and he wanted to make some adjustments in his portfolio, using the proceeds from his position in the IPO. When I looked it up on the computer, his account balance remained at zero and I could find no record of him ever owning a share of the Clean Sweep fund. I still thought it was just a computer anomaly and told him so. After we hung up, I researched every account held by Trey's clients. All the accounts showed low, or zero, balances, and none showed any investment in the IPO fund. That's when I knew for sure we'd all been taken to the cleaners, in one 'clean sweep', so to speak."

I was amused by her play on words, but couldn't imagine how stunned Harlei must have been to discover her boss was a villain. "Oh, my! That must have been shocking. How did Mr. Ho react to the news that there was no proof he'd ever invested the money in the IPO fund?"

"He was quiet, reserved at the time, but like all of us, he still believed it was just a mistake that would work itself out. Funny thing is, Mr. Ho called again this morning and he was still calm and collected, but frightening at the same time."

"How so? What'd he say this morning?"

"He had an odd reaction, actually. He said, 'My wife is

hysterical, but I'm not worried about it. I promised her I'd get our money back one way or another.' Mr. Ho was so intense. His expression was terrifying."

"I thought you were on the phone with him," I said.

"Yeah, I was," Harlei said. "I was referring to the way Mr. Ho expressed himself. The expression 'one way or another' is worrisome."

"I doubt he meant it as a direct threat to you, Harlei."

"I hope not, but it sure sounded that way. I remember questioning my wisdom in telling him the missing money was still unaccounted for. Afterward, I wished I'd told him the police were working on the case, and the money should be returned to its rightful owners soon."

"You mean you wished you'd lied through your teeth?" I asked with a chuckle.

"Exactly! I figured what he didn't know wouldn't hurt me."

"I agree. Ho's response did sound intimidating, and that's disturbing." There was actually more than just one aspect of her remarks I found troubling, but I didn't mention my concerns. Harlei was stressed out enough already.

"Is it possible he confronted Trey, and they argued? Could he have killed Trey and taken all of the money from the sell-off of the accounts, if Trey had the cash with him as he was preparing to fly to the Cayman Islands?" I asked.

"Most likely, he'd already wired the money directly into an offshore account there. That'd be an awful lot of money to carry around in cash, if it's even remotely possible. Do you know how big a suitcase it'd take to carry nine million dollars in one-hundred-dollar bills, which is the highest amount printed in paper currency?" Harlei thought for a few moments and added, "That's something like ninety thousand bills."

"Good point!" I wasn't in finances like she was, so the calculating I did in my head took a little longer. Like she'd said, Trey must have had the money deposited directly into an offshore account he'd opened on the Caribbean island, which was a popular tax haven. Their secrecy laws protecting account holders made it an ideal place to abscond to. "Nine million dollars? Wow! Do you think it's possible Chen Ho might have made some sort of a pact with one of his seedier acquaintances? Ho might've arranged for a former client of his to kill Trey with the promise of a share of the money. A share of nine million dollars makes for a powerful incentive."

"Anything's possible, I guess," Harlei said. She didn't sound convinced, though. "I suppose it could've also been a deal where a debt the killer owed Mr. Ho was written off in exchange for the debtor performing the hit on Trey. Chen was a polite guy, and a laid-back kind of gentleman, especially for a man who spent his entire career as a bail bondsman. It's hard for me to imagine him being behind Trey's death. But he did make the threat about promising his wife he'd get their money back one way or another, and he does have a lot of unlawful acquaintances. His wife, Fenfang, is a whole different ball of wax."

"How's that?"

"She's younger, but very assertive, to an almost overbearing level. Fenfang definitely wears the pants in that family." As Harlei spoke, I wondered if we were barking up the wrong Ho tree. Maybe it was the wife we should think about investigating. "She's determined to see their son, Gung, grow up to be a successful Chinese American stand-out. She wants him to be a prominent neurosurgeon. At fourteen, Gung is already taking college courses at night, after attending high school during the day. Their son is on track to be enrolled in medical school by the time he's eighteen. It sounds a little harsh of her to expect so much of the boy, but Gung's just as determined as she is that he be a world-renowned physician."

"Wow!" I said. "For a teenage boy, he sure sounds gung-ho."

Harlei laughed loudly at my play on words. "You always manage to make me laugh, even during my darkest moments."

"Sorry. I couldn't resist the pun. It makes me wonder if she didn't saddle her son with 'Gung Ho' so he'd feel obligated to live up to his name."

"You know, now that I think about it, you might be correct. I can see her doing such a thing. I've gotten to know the pair fairly well over the last few years of working with them and handling their investment portfolio. Still, I suspect if either of them is behind the murder, it'd be Chen. He was always willing to do her bidding, almost as if he was afraid not to."

Harlei sounded as if she was trying to convince herself Chen Ho could be behind the killing of her former boss. Whether she was succeeding or not, I couldn't tell. The idea he would do whatever his wife asked made me unwilling to overlook her as the instigator, even if her husband was the perpetrator. The couple could be co-conspirators in the crime. I had a lot of questions I wanted to ask Mr. Ho, but wasn't sure a face-to-face meeting with him was advisable. Harlei validated that concern with her next remarks. She seemed to be on the same wavelength as Carlos when it came to the bail bondsman.

"I know you and your husband are looking into this case, but I wouldn't advise contacting Mr. Ho in person. He's a wisp of a fellow, but he hangs out with thugs who are more than happy to settle a score for him. The fierceness of his voice when we spoke on the phone still has me shook up. Just be careful, Rapella. Okay?"

"I will be. Thanks for the warning, dear."

"On another front," Harlei said. It was clear her mood had changed on a dime once again. "I have listed my house with a guy named David Colmer. He's an independent broker with Remax Realty and has a great reputation as a *gung-ho* agent."

"Awesome!" I said with a laugh. "I'm not going to be able to get that phrase out of my head now."

"Me neither. Obviously," she replied with a chuckle.

"I'm glad you have a plan and are moving ahead. Have you decided where you want to move once your house is sold?"

"No, but it will be somewhere away from here. Someplace remote, where it's warm and the cost of living is reasonable. I grew up in Rochester, New York, on the east side of Lake Ontario. The lake-effect snow there was forecast in feet, not inches. I remember being thrilled when we heard we were having a snow day, and then wishing I was in school when we had to spend the bulk of the day shoveling snow. I don't ever want to even own a snow shovel again, much less have to use one."

"Good for you, Harlei. Keep me posted on both the sale of your home, and if you hear any news about Trey or the missing money."

"Will do," she replied. "You do the same. And don't forget to keep your chin up."

"Hey! That's my line!" I teased.

"Not if I use it first," she countered.

We hung up laughing, which is always a good way to end a conversation. Laughter is good for the soul. It releases feel-good endorphins. Crying, on the other hand, just messes up your makeup.

TWENTY

"Rapella, I need to get a refill on my medication," Rip said that evening as we were sitting outside under the awning enjoying our cocktails. Our primary physician, Dr. Herron, had prescribed a drug to combat Rip's borderline diabetes at his last checkup in October, while we were in our hometown of Rockport, Texas.

I, on the other hand, had been declared fit as a fiddle and told to keep on doing whatever it was I was doing to stay in such good shape. I'd gained ten pounds since my last annual appointment, but lost seven of it in the weeks leading up to my appointment. That's how badly I wanted to avoid the lecture I knew Dr. Herron would bestow on me about my weight gain. The three-pound difference from my last visit with her fell within the margin of error, so she didn't harp on it. Sometimes I thought it'd be easier to just get a new doctor. This time I'd look for one that didn't run marathons. And, preferably, one that bordered on chubby.

"All right, honey," I replied. "I'll call your prescription into

Walgreens tomorrow morning. We can pick it up on our way over to Tiffany and Chase's."

"Thanks." Rip picked up a new issue of *Farm and Ranch Living* magazine to thumb through. He had never lived on a farm or a ranch and never professed to want to own one of either, but he thoroughly enjoyed the monthly publication. I found it odd. On the other hand, I enjoyed *Good Housekeeping* magazine, and I didn't find any great enjoyment in keeping house. I only completed those tasks so Rip and I didn't have to live in squalor.

As Rip flipped through the pages, I thought about what else we might need to pick up at Walgreens. I had taken the last Extra-Strength Tylenol a couple of days prior for a sore back. I'd somehow managed to strain a muscle while hanging a coat up in the closet. We were also running short on fiber supplements, which we both needed if we wanted to stay regular these days. Another bottle of Tums for our occasional bouts of heartburn was needed, as well. A tube of Icy Hot and a bottle of Centrum Silver multivitamins completed the mental list I was preparing. My pharmacy list was a brutal reminder there was really nothing golden about the "golden years". When one reaches the age they can injure themselves by hanging up a coat, it's time to have their body bubble-wrapped. If only that was a feasible option.

Thinking about the over-the-counter medications we needed to pick up reminded me of the photo I'd taken in Sandy's restroom. I'd forgotten all about it until that moment. I'd snapped the picture with the phone Rip now exclusively carried. I'd noticed it on the kitchen table as I was fixing our drinks.

"I've got to run inside," I told Rip as I set my tequila sunrise on the table between our chairs. "Need anything?"

"I could use a refill while you're inside," he said hopefully.

"So could I, but neither one of us is going to get our wish fulfilled," I said. "We promised Dr. Herron we'd limit our alcohol to one drink per day. Alcohol is one of the worst things for your borderline diabetes, and I don't need the calories either."

"All right," he said, feigning discontent. Maybe "feigning" is not the correct word. He desperately wanted that refill but knew he couldn't have it if he wanted to maintain his health. Maintain it as much as possible, anyway. "I thought it was worth a shot."

I came back outside a minute or two later with Rip's phone and brought up the photo I'd taken of the three side-by-side medicine bottles. I used my fingers to enlarge the photos in order to read the labels. Each bottle contained ninety pills of the same pain medication, and yet all three were filled just days apart. One bottle was prescribed by the Dr. Phillips Babs had mentioned and was filled at the local CVS Pharmacy. The second bottle was prescribed by a Dr. Patel and filled at Wal-Mart, and the third bottle was prescribed by a Dr. Martin and filled at the Walgreens we planned to go to the following morning. I showed the photo to Rip and pointed out the inconsistencies.

He nodded. "Sounds like Sandy Monroe has an opioid addiction."

"Sure does."

When Rip's attention turned back to his magazine, I Googled the three doctors who'd prescribed the pain medication for Sandy. Doctors Patel and Martin both had practices in the Albuquerque metropolitan area. Dr. Phillips, however, who Babs had mentioned working for at the same time as Manuel, was not listed. I couldn't find a physiatrist by that name listed in all of New Mexico. After further research, I found an obituary for a Dr. Wayne Phillips, who had practiced pain management in the Sandia Heights area. *How could a doctor who died three years ago still be writing prescriptions?* I didn't know the answer, but I had an idea about how that phenomenon might have occurred. *I need to call Harlei again tomorrow. Maybe she can shed some light on this mystery.*

"If I can't have a refill on my drink, can I have a couple of those leftover oatmeal raisin cookies to make up for it?" Rip asked with a forlorn expression. "I won't tell Dr. Herron if you don't."

"Oh, all right." I was in a charitable mood. After all, Rip had been surprisingly generous about letting me do some personal investigating into who had killed Trey and what had happened to his clients' investment money, even though I knew he wasn't particularly in favor of my interference in the case. He'd even helped out to some extent. I wasn't fooling myself, however. I knew his willingness to contribute to the cause could be attributed to his granddaughter, not me.

"Good morning, Harlei! This is Rapella Ripple again," I said. "I don't want to be a nuisance, but thought I'd check in with you today and see how you're getting along. I was concerned about how down you seemed to be yesterday."

"I'm okay, I guess. You could never be a nuisance, Rapella."

"Thanks, but you don't sound okay to me. Why so glum, chum?" I wanted to cheer her up but didn't know how. My question sounded silly, even to my own ears. "I know everything seems terribly depressing right now. But, trust me, it'll work itself out one of these days. We all just need to be patient. You'll be happy to hear I feel like my own personal investigation into the case is making progress."

"Oh? Tell me what you've learned."

I had piqued Harlei's interest. I thought if I came across as optimistic and hopeful, her mood would lighten. My strategy appeared to be successful.

"I don't know that I've actually learned anything, but I have another tidbit that's got me intrigued. I'm hoping you can supply me with a little more information."

"I'll help in any way I can."

Harlei sounded hopeful. If nothing else, she seemed invested in our conversation, rather than just making short, polite responses.

"You told me the other day that Manuel worked as a P.A. for several physicians. Do you recall their names, by any chance?"

"The last physician he worked for was a physiatrist named Dr. Phillips, who died shortly after Manuel went to work for the Monroes. Before that, he worked for Dr. Patel, but only for a few months. I can't think of the first doctor's name at the moment, but it'll come to me."

"Does Dr. Martin ring a bell?" I asked.

"Yes! That's it!" she replied. "It was Dr. Paul Martin, who was an orthopedic surgeon. I heard through the grapevine he fired Manuel for stealing pain pill sample packs from the office supply room. Martin threatened to press charges, which Manuel, in turn, threatened to appeal on the grounds he'd taken them to give to a patient. In the end, I think the charges were dropped, but Manuel was let go a couple of weeks later. He was also let go by Dr. Patel, but I never heard what preempted that firing."

"That's very interesting, Harlei, and fits in with my current theory," I said. "I'm guessing Manuel also stole some prescription pads from all three of those doctors before he left. Do you know what was behind Manuel's decision to leave the nursing field and go to work for the Monroes?"

"Remember yesterday I told you I thought Sandy's motivation for hiring him as a house manager was more than to just have someone to keep their home and activities in order?"

"Yes," I replied. "I assumed you were referring to the fringe benefits that came with the position. You know, because they shared a mutual sexual attraction to each other."

"That might've figured into the decision. But they first met when Manuel was Dr. Phillip's physician's assistant. Manuel treated Sandy for pain management involving a neck injury she sustained in a car accident. Even at the time, I had the feeling he was feeding her opioid addiction. I saw her several times during that period, and she never appeared to be hampered by a neck injury."

"Maybe that was because she was higher than a kite and the pills were masking the pain." I didn't want to overlook the possibility she had a legitimate injury and was in desperate need of relief.

"Maybe," Harlei conceded, "but Manuel quit nursing and went to work for Sandy and Trey soon afterward."

I told Harlei about the photo I'd taken of the three medicine bottles in Sandy's restroom, and my theory that Manuel was using stolen prescription pads from the physicians he'd worked for to write prescriptions for her pain pills.

"Wow!" Harlei exclaimed. "You are one sneaky and determined lady, aren't you? That is so awesome, Rapella!"

"Thank you." I was glad she couldn't see me blushing and smiling on the other end of the phone. I knew I had a smug expression on my face. "Do you think there's a chance Manuel could've used her dependency to blackmail her?"

"In what way?"

"Perhaps he told her if she wanted her access to the pain pills to continue, she had to find a way to eliminate her husband so they could collect his insurance money, and——"

"He didn't have any life insurance," Harlei cut in. "I know it was a sore subject with Sandy, too, who thought he should cover himself in case something happened. She didn't want to be left out in the cold. I got the impression Trey didn't want to be worth more to his wife dead than alive."

"That might have led directly to his downfall in the end, after all. If she knew about the Ponzi scheme——and it seems to me she'd have had to know——she might have devised a plan to cabbage onto all the money he'd stolen from his clients. I wonder if it would've been possible for Sandy to have purchased a life insurance policy on him that he never even knew about."

"Yes, she could have," Harlei replied. "You can purchase a policy on anyone as long as you can prove their death would negatively affect your financial situation. Clearly, his death would affect her finances adversely."

"Then I wouldn't blame her if she did just that."

"Me neither," Harlei agreed. "My ex, Thomas, carried a policy on himself naming me as the beneficiary for three years after our divorce was finalized. He had to switch beneficiaries once he remarried, naturally."

"That was nice of him."

"It was in the divorce decree, so it wasn't by choice. Still, it was an amicable divorce, and we've remained friends. I even get along well with his new wife."

"The Pez dispenser?" I asked with a chuckle.

"Yep!" Harlei laughed at my reference to what she'd told me about the woman previously. "So, I take it you believe Sandy knew about the Ponzi scheme or found out about it somehow? She could have even talked him into implementing it, I suppose."

"That's a definite possibility. I don't know how she couldn't have known. She obviously enjoys living the good life, but she had to know all the money to purchase things like expensive vacations, a Lincoln Navigator, a huge mansion—and to hire a house manager, for goodness sake—was coming from some-where other than Trey's salary as the owner of Monroe Invest-ments. Along with whatever was left from his clients' Clean Sweep IPO money, the proceeds from all of the blue-chip stocks he sold off from his clients' portfolios made up for a comfortable cache of moola in their joint account. With that carrot dangling in front of their faces, Sandy and/or Manuel could've injected Trey with the potassium chloride. I'm sure they felt certain he'd assume it was just his routine insulin injection."

"You know, that theory sounds very plausible," Harlei said. "The only thing I find difficult to believe is that Trey would deposit the funds in a *joint* account with Sandy. He knew she was having an affair with Manuel. I don't believe he trusted either one of them, certainly not in the way he trusted me as his personal assistant. He even asked me one day if I knew of a good divorce lawyer."

"Really?"

"Yes. But when I brought in a list of highly regarded divorce attorneys I'd researched and compiled for him, he told me he'd changed his mind. Now I tend to believe he'd decided at that point to flee the country with the money he had stolen from his clients. He was probably going to let the chips fall where they may."

"What did you mean by letting the chips fall where they may?" I asked.

"Sandy never worked as far as I'm aware, and without Trey's steady income, she wouldn't be able to afford her lavish lifestyle for very long. She'd just be left with a boy toy who is several years her junior. Manuel's interest in her would undoubtedly fade fast once she could no longer support him. A life of luxury would be a thing of the past for both Sandy and Manuel, which Trey probably thought of as well-deserved karma."

"I see your point, Harlei. A divorce at that point would serve no purpose, especially once Trey had made his mind up to flee to Grand Cayman with the money."

"Exactly!" Harlei replied. "His Clean Sweep scheme was already underway, so I'm not sure that wasn't what he'd had in mind from the very beginning."

"Makes sense to me. Did you bring your theory up with Detective Gutierrez?"

"Of course," she responded. "For whatever good it did. I've heard nothing from anyone about it since."

"Having lived most of my life with a law enforcement officer, I can assure you it doesn't mean they aren't hard at work on the case. They have a tendency to keep their activities and findings close to the vest."

"That's good to know. I'm glad you're still looking into the situation, too. Unlike the homicide detectives, at least you keep me in the loop."

"And I always will," I replied. "Contact me if you hear anything else on your end."

"Absolutely! Oh, one more thing. When I talked to Detective Gutierrez, he said the medical examiner amended the time of death on Trey's death certificate."

"Really? To when?" I asked.

"From eleven-thirty to twelve-fifteen. I think it had to do with a video recording of him on a security camera as he was entering the airport's parking garage or something. That might be a factor to consider as you continue your investigation."

"Yes, it will be." It also made me think I might have to put my grandson-in-law back on my suspect list. The Hancocks' doorbell video showed Chase leaving Trey's home at eleven-thirty-six. If Trey in fact died at twelve-fifteen, Chase might have had time to drive to the airport and inject Trey with the potassium chloride.

Before I ended the call, we exchanged small talk about her house and how she was handling it all emotionally. "Goodbye for now, dear. And as always, keep your chin up!"

TWENTY-ONE

After a breakfast of fresh cantaloupe slices and an English muffin, Rip and I drove over to the Carpenters' house. Rip had promised Chase he'd help him with a shrub- and tree-trimming project, so I planned to spend the day with Tiffany.

"I know the thought of facing Sandy and Manuel again is cringe-worthy, but I need to make another trip over to the Monroes," I told her after the men had gone outside. I didn't mention my determination to get to the truth was more overpowering than my earlier humiliation at getting caught going through Sandy and Manuel's trash. "And I'd like you to go with me."

Tiffany's response came in the form of a groan. Her subsequent reply of, "Why? Why me?" brought flashbacks from when Nancy Kerrigan had just been whacked in the knee with a police baton, and a video of her reaction was played over and over and over again on television. Naturally, I felt bad for the ice skater, but the whining grew tiresome the hundredth time we saw the video replayed on the boob tube.

"It would make no sense for me to pay a visit by myself, sweetheart. After all, you're her friend."

"You mean *was* her friend. I think that friend 'ship' has sailed. What am I supposed to say when she asks why you and I were digging through her trash?" Tiffany sounded as if she'd rather go out on a date with a cannibalistic serial killer than accompany me. "I know Manuel said he wasn't going to tell her, but I believe that as much as I believe the pharmaceutical industry will ever let a cure for cancer be approved. She'll know we're up to something just by looking at how tense I am."

"Maybe you're right. I probably should tackle this one on my own." Judging by her edginess, it might not be a good idea to have her join me after all. Her uneasiness would throw up red flags like nobody's business. I was clever. I could surely devise a reason to stop by that didn't require Tiffany's presence.

"What are you planning to visit her about?" Tiffany asked.

"I'm just curious how much Sandy is controlled by her opioid addiction. At first a person controls their addiction, no matter what it is they're hooked on. But at some point, the worm turns, and not in a good way. After that, the addiction controls the individual. It controls their every waking thought and action. The only thing they care about at that stage is their next fix. It makes otherwise lawful people do incredibly stupid things. Nothing is beyond their capability if it comes to feeding that ever-present craving."

"You been on the Internet again, haven't you, Grams?" Tiffany asked with a smile. "Were you Googling this morning before you came over?"

"Yes, and I was Googling *on* the drive over, as well." I chucked. "But not about drug addiction. I've known all about that subject from your grandfather's career in law enforcement. No town, even one the size of Rockport, is free of illegal drug use. Opioid addiction is affecting people of all walks of life now: teachers, doctors, housewives, even nuns, I'd bet. Who's to say

Mother Teresa wasn't popping hydrocodone tablets between her saintly acts of charity and selfless sacrifice?"

"Grams, you're terrible!" Tiffany exclaimed after laughing hysterically.

"I'm only joking about Mother Teresa, who truly was a saint. My point is, no one is immune to the scourge of opioid addiction. But I wasn't Googling that subject on the ride over. I was actually doing some research on ostriches."

"Did you say ostriches? As in the bird?"

"Yes. As in the bird. We passed a farm on the way over that had two ostriches, or perhaps their smaller cousins, emus, in a field. They made me curious."

"Curious about big birds?" Tiffany asked, mystified by my intrigue.

"Yes. Birds! That's exactly my point! Ostriches are birds. Why did God give them wings if they can't fly?"

"I don't know," she said. "I'm sure you do, though. *Now,* anyway."

"Ostriches and emus use their wings to help them balance when they run, especially if they make a sudden change of direction. They also use them, along with their tail feathers, for displays during courtship. Wanna know why they bury their heads in the sand?"

"No, not really." Tiffany shook her head as she giggled. "But thanks for asking."

I laughed along. "Just so you know, they don't really bury their heads in the sand. It's just a myth."

"I knew you were going to tell me whether I wanted to know or not." Tiffany chuckled at her teasing remark. "But it's good to know in case it ever comes up in a game of trivia. So, Grams, how can some squirrels fly without having wings?"

"I don't know," I said. "But you can bet I will before the sun sets tonight. For now, I better get on the road if I want to pay

Sandy a visit while your grandpa and Chase are busy trimming bushes and trees."

"What excuse are you going to give for stopping by?" Tiffany asked. "You surely aren't going to take more cookies, are you?"

"Oh, hell no. For one thing, I don't have time to bake. Secondly, I'm still ticked off that she pitched the first batch in the trash. I'm hoping to come up with a reason for the house call by the time I get there. I do have one question, sweetheart. In your opinion, do you think Trey knew about his wife's addiction to pain pills?"

"If I had to guess, I'd say no. One day not long before he died, the four of us had gone out to dinner. Sandy looked totally out of it. Trey asked if something was wrong and she replied that her neck had been bothering her again. After suggesting she go back to see the pain management doctor, Trey said, 'If nothing else, maybe Dr. Phillips can prescribe something for the pain.'"

"Yeah, that sounds like he didn't know."

"Exactly," Tiffany said. "If he knew, he'd never have made such a remark. My guess is that Dr. Phillips, who Manuel was working for when he and Sandy first met, had already passed, which tells me she hadn't gone to a pain management doctor in a long time. Apparently, Manuel had been writing her scripts. Dr. Phillips was gone, but Sandy clearly had never told Trey about his passing, so she could pretend to still be seeing him if the matter came up. That's my guess, anyway."

"Interesting," I replied. I had to wonder why Sandy didn't seem to care if her husband knew she was having an affair with their house manager, but didn't want him to know that very same house manager was feeding her all-consuming pain-pill habit. "I had best be going. I'll catch up with you when I get back."

"All right, Grams. Good luck and drive safely."

As I'd mentioned to Tiffany, I'd been hoping an inspiration would hit me before I arrived at the Monroe homestead. One did, just as I pulled up to the curb in front of their house and saw their trash can. As always, I left the truck on the street. I had a pet peeve about folks parking their oil-leaking vehicles on someone's nice concrete driveway. Our Chevy pickup didn't leak oil yet, but one never knew when it might start. The sudden inspiration turned out to be an effective one.

"What do you want?" When Sandy came to the door to greet me, I felt like an unwanted guest. In fact, I felt akin to a Jehovah's Witness on the doorstep of a committed non-believer. I felt even less welcome when Sandy added, "I'm having a hard day, and I'm not in the mood for company right now."

Especially you, she might as well have added. I would have deserved the remark had she actually made it, but that didn't stop me from wanting to get to the crux of the matter.

"I won't stay. I promise," I assured her. "I just wanted to stop by while I was in the neighborhood to see if you still had that large platter I used when I brought over the oatmeal cookies. I bought several of the platters at a store in Texas, and that was my last one. They're so handy for cookie deliveries."

I hadn't seen the plastic platter when Tiffany and I had scoured through their trash. That's what had given me the idea she might have kept it. Although it sounded chintzy, I hoped to get it back. I strongly believed in recycling. "Waste not, want not" was my mantra. At Sandy's nod, just out of pure orneriness, I asked, "I trust you enjoyed the oatmeal cookies?"

"Oh, yes. Enormously. We're still enjoying them, as a matter of fact." Sandy expressed her appreciation for the cookies, even though she hadn't been able to toss them in the garbage fast enough.

"That's great." I smiled at Sandy as I spoke. She appeared to have no idea Tiffany and I had found the cookies in her trash can, which made me wonder if Manuel had indeed kept his word about not telling Sandy about the dumpster-diving incident. *He told us he didn't want to hurt her any further. Could there have been another reason he didn't want her to know about it?* I wondered. I stared at Sandy until she felt duty-bound to show a little appreciation for my act of kindness, which was anything but random.

"They're delicious." Sandy then went on to elaborate on her fabrication. "I froze half of them for later. Thanks again for your thoughtfulness."

Liar, liar, cookies on fire, I thought. In fact, I did burn one batch because I forgot to set the oven timer. When I took the smoldering cookies out of the oven, they resembled hockey pucks. That mistake had cost me an extra visit to the grocery store to purchase more ingredients. Had I known the replacement batch's fate, I'd have just left the blackened cookies mixed in with the others I'd brought over.

Even though Sandy lied about the cookies, her manner had softened, and she seemed friendlier. She opened the door wide and stepped aside. "Come on inside while I go get the platter."

"Thanks. I'm glad you thought to save it." I wanted to add, *instead of pitching it in the trash with the cookies.* Naturally, I restrained my baser nature and merely smiled.

"Oh, yes. I thought you might want it back."

I thought about my conversation with Tiffany a couple of weeks ago about how best to work out a cramp when your calf tightens up like a banjo string in the middle of the night, and made a show of limping as I entered Sandy's house. She gave me an odd look but kept silent. She turned and walked toward her kitchen. I stayed behind because my unexpected bum leg wouldn't let me follow her as I'd done in past visits.

"What's wrong?" Sandy asked as she returned to the dining room with the platter. She sounded more cautious than concerned as she watched me furiously rubbing my lower left leg, trying to work out the knot in my calf muscle. I made such a production out of it, and I'm sure she'd felt obligated to inquire about my obvious distress.

"I woke up early this morning with a horrific Charlie horse. It was the kind that made me holler out loud and jump out of bed. I nearly gave my husband another heart attack. The cramp took forever to loosen up. Unfortunately, it seems to have tightened up again." I groaned as I finished speaking.

"Perhaps you should've waited to collect the platter," Sandy said. I could detect sarcasm deeply embedded in her thoughtful comment. She probably thought I was a hypochondriac at that point, having had a medical crisis nearly every time I'd walked into her home.

"I reckon I should have. I just didn't expect it to cramp up again." I gamely tried to walk a few steps, but had to bend down to knead the knot loose.

"Wasn't it your left leg?" Sandy asked.

Oh, crap! Was it? I asked myself. *Dang it! I should've paid more attention to what leg I was limping on.* I nodded. "It was, but now the right one's cramping up, too. I don't know what the deal is."

"Maybe you're dehydrated." Manuel's low resonating voice filled the room. It was as if Sandy had rubbed a lamp and he'd appeared out of nowhere. He didn't sound any more concerned than Sandy. He seemed more interested in showing off his medical knowledge. "It's due to changes in the electrolytes in your body, such as sodium and potassium. Dehydration makes your muscles work harder, and the heat from that can make them seize up. Drinking water helps fairly rapidly. I'll go get you some."

"Thank you." I was surprised he offered relief after catching me red-handed trying to implicate him in Trey's death. "You're probably right. I haven't been drinking nearly enough water the last few days because I've been so busy——"

"Dumpster diving?" Manuel cut in.

"Well, yes, that and other things, too." I was flushing in embarrassment, and my response sounded inane, even to my own ears. Was his cutting remark proof he *had* told Sandy about catching Tiffany and me face down in their filthy garbage? I was getting mixed signals.

He gave me a knowing look that embarrassed me even further. "I'll fetch you two bottles of water. You should drink both of them as quickly as you can."

"Thanks. I will. I'm grateful for your medical knowledge." I wanted to say I was fascinated with his familiarity with sodium, and more importantly, potassium.

Manuel walked away without responding. When he returned with the two bottles, I realized if this investigation lasted much longer, I'd owe Sandy an entire case of water bottles. "Why did you give up being a P.A.? It seems like you must have been extremely good at your job."

"I was." Manuel didn't seem to question how I knew what he'd done for a living before becoming a so-called house manager. I'm sure he assumed Tiffany had mentioned it. "But I got a better offer."

He winked at Sandy, who looked away quickly. I doubt she wanted me to know about her affair with the hired hand, a love connection I sensed was more about his usefulness at prescribing medicine than his charm and good looks.

"I see." And I really did see. The better offer was not only monetary, but came with a lot of fringe benefits. "What can I do to ease the pain? I can't seem to work it out by merely rubbing it."

"How bad is it on a scale of one to ten?" Manuel asked.

"It's 'stabbed through the calf with a serrated knife' bad." I'd always hated that sliding scale option on whatever pain I was experiencing, so I always refused to give it a number. "It's the fifth time it's happened in the last week or so."

"Do you have any Tylenol with you?"

"No. But I've tried over-the-counter pain relievers before and they didn't help. I need a prescription for pain medication, but I don't have a doctor here in Albuquerque. I hate to have to fork over money for a visit to an urgent care clinic."

"Well," Manuel began, but stopped abruptly. I think his medical training was kicking in. He glanced at Sandy. After a long pause, she nodded. He returned her nod, and said, "I guess I could write you a prescription. My medical license is still valid. A dozen pills should get you by until you can see your family physician."

I thought twelve pain pills was such a nominal amount Sandy could easily spare that many from her impressive stash. However, to an addict, it was undoubtedly like asking a heroin addict for his last syringe full of China White.

"Oh, goodness, Manuel," I said with exaggerated emotion. "I would be eternally grateful."

Manuel left the room and quickly returned with a prescription pad. After he filled out a prescription and handed it to me, I looked at the physician's name on the top of it. "Oh, is Dr. Phillips still practicing?"

"Um," Manuel muttered. He seemed to be stymied by my simple question. "Uh-huh. But not as much as he used to. He's cut back his hours substantially."

"Oh." I nodded before adding, "Being dead probably slowed him down quite a bit."

Manuel suddenly looked like he'd swallowed a June bug. He coughed as if he was trying to hack the squirming insect back up. After sputtering for a bit, he said, "Perhaps it'd be better if I gave you some pills we have here in the house." He gave Sandy a quick look. "Is that all right, boss?"

"Of course," she replied. She didn't look like it was all right at all. In fact, she looked like he'd asked her to donate one of her kidneys to me. She turned to me as if she felt she owed me an explanation of why there was pain medication in her house. "I still have occasional bouts of pain in my neck from a bad car accident I was involved in a while back. It necessitates me keeping a few pills on hand for when those flare-ups occur."

I'm guessing those flare-ups occur on a regular basis. I knew she truly had sustained a neck injury in a car wreck, but I found it hard to believe she needed to keep three bottles of pills, prescribed by three different doctors and filled at three different pharmacies, on hand for an occasional bout of pain. And I'm no rocket scientist, but I also found it extremely hard to believe a dead doctor had only *cut back* on the hours he practiced medicine.

"I'm sorry to hear about your accident," I told her. "I appreciate you sharing a few of your pain pills with me. Are you sure you can spare them?"

"I can spare a few."

"I imagine three would be all I'd need. If it still hurts this bad tomorrow, I'll break down and go to an urgent care clinic in town. Although it's only an educated guess, I'm betting the cramping will subside by then." It really wasn't an educated guess. My calf didn't hurt today, so there was no reason to believe it'd be an issue tomorrow. I rarely experienced leg cramps, though Rip was bothered by them fairly frequently.

As Manuel left the room to retrieve the pills, I stuffed the prescription he'd written for me in my back pocket. I thought it might come in handy as evidence in the future. When the house manager returned and handed me three pain pills a couple of minutes later, I had to swallow one to prove I needed the medication. Swallowing pills had always been difficult for me. I'm certain Sandy and Manuel thought I resembled a blue heron trying to swallow a twenty-pound tarpon as I struggled to get the pill to go down my throat. I hated taking them and hoped the one I'd taken wouldn't make me feel loopy. I would probably flush the other two when I returned home. But to not take one of the pain pills at that point would make me look like I was being deceptive—which, naturally, was exactly what I was being.

Once I'd finally gotten the pill down, I chased it with an entire bottle of water. I promised to drink the other one as I was driving back to my granddaughter's. That was a falsehood, as well, as just guzzling one full bottle made me feel as though I was being water-boarded. I know health experts suggest we each drink no less than eight eight-ounce glasses of water per day, but if it didn't have coffee, tea, or lemonade mixed in with it, it seemed like an impossible goal to me.

It seemed clear Sandy had an opioid addiction. I had to question how strong a hold the pain medicine had on her.

How far would Sandy go to make sure her habit never went unfed? Had Trey been aware of her addiction? If not, what would she have done to make sure he didn't find out and try to intervene? I wondered. *Tiffany didn't believe he had known, but it wouldn't hurt to call Harlei and get her perspective.*

I realized again just then how lucky I was to have someone like her in my corner in this investigation. Not that I'd gotten off first base when it came to figuring out who killed Trey or where all of his clients' money had gone. But I knew just having someone with an inside track, such as Harlei had, could only be beneficial in my quest to get to the bottom of the challenging case.

As soon as I thanked Sandy and Manuel, I hobbled out to the truck and drove off.

TWENTY-TWO

"Good morning, dear," I greeted Harlei when she answered my call on the second ring. "How are you doing?"

"I'm okay, Rapella. How are you?"

"I'm fine, but you sound like you're down in the dumps again."

"I guess I am. It's not so bad I can't handle it. It just seems like I have a lot to do to get my house sold, my stuff packed, and all that. The thought of what needs to be done can be overwhelming at times." I hated that I was too busy to help Harlei with her packing. Just one extra hand could make all the difference. Maybe once we'd solved the case, I'd offer to assist.

I remembered back to when Rip had retired. Going on the road as full-time RVers meant downsizing and getting rid of most of our possessions. I'd been afraid I'd regret selling our personal mementos and the mountain of insignificant "stuff" we'd accumulated during our years together. Surprisingly, I didn't miss any of it. Instead, I discovered simplifying our life was freeing in many ways.

Harlei brought me out of my reverie when she asked, "Any updates?"

"No, unfortunately not. I'm kind of at a dead end. I feel as though we've first got to determine who the murderer was before we can look into where the money Trey stole is located."

"That's kind of what I figured."

"With that in mind, who would you most suspect of killing Trey? If you had to guess, that is."

"Manuel de la Cruz, without a doubt." She sounded dead-set on her chosen perpetrator. "But I wouldn't count out Sandy, one of the Hancocks, or Chen Ho, either."

Thanks! I thought. *You just mentioned my entire suspect list. It appears your insight is no more useful than mine.* "Okay. I'll keep that in mind."

"I doubt it's of any help, though. Huh?" She giggled, which led me to believe she was just yanking my chain.

"Honestly? No, not really. It's the same list of people I've already been scrutinizing. Can you think of anyone else who might have it in for Trey bad enough to kill him? You know all of his former clients. I don't."

"No, I can't say that I do. All of his clients loved him. He was such a nice, friendly guy, if you didn't take into account he was also a lying, thieving snake-oil salesman."

"I'm afraid that's hard not to take into account, Harlei. Give it some serious thought, and if you can think of anyone, drop a dime on me."

"Drop a dime on you?" She sounded completely baffled by the phrase I'd used. I supposed people in her generation had forgotten about pay phones that'd gone nearly as extinct as the cassette recorder. Even accounting for her age——thirty-seven or –eight, I'd estimate——Harlei appeared to be pitifully unaware of old adages.

"It means call me."

"Oh, yes. Of course." She chuckled, and then grew more

serious. "Say, Rapella, have you heard when they're going to release Trey's body? Trey's once-estranged brother, Arthur, called me late last night and asked if I knew when they'd be having Trey's memorial service and when they might be reading his will. Do you know why they're even holding the body?"

"Rip told me they often hold a body that was involved in a homicide in case a subsequent autopsy needs to be performed. Holding the body is better than burying the victim too soon and having to exhume the body later."

"That makes sense."

"Seems odd that Arthur called you rather than the homicide detectives or someone else in their family," I said. "If Arthur had just called the Albuquerque Police Department, they'd have told him his brother was still chilling on ice in the county morgue."

"In more tactful terms, I'd hope." Harlei laughed before growing more somber again. "I wondered the same thing. I don't recall Trey mentioning Arthur more than a handful of times, and even then, it was merely in passing. I'd gotten the sense they'd had a falling out. In fact, I thought Trey was pretty much estranged from his entire family."

"Hmm. That's interesting." Already my mind was whirring with possibilities. "Do you happen to know if he left anything to anyone other than Sandy?"

"No. To be truthful, Trey never mentioned even having a will. He was young enough he probably felt he had a lot of time before he had to draw up documents like a living will, power of attorney, or a last will and testament. I haven't even *thought* about things like that, but I'm only thirty-one. Trey was just a few years older than me."

"That's true. He was pretty young to have had end-of-life documents drawn up. At thirty-one, you're just a year older than my Tiffany." Harlei was younger than I'd thought. Carlos had guessed she was in her upper thirties, as well. No doubt her stressful job had made her appear older than her actual age.

"Yeah, I thought we were about the same age." She sounded more cheerful now. Just hearing a friendly voice was probably all it took to raise her spirits. "How old were you and Rip when you got your affairs in order?"

"We were twenty," I said, with a bit too much braggadocio, even to my own ears. "Our daughter, Regina, had just turned a year old. We'd made the decision not to have any more children after I nearly died during childbirth. As a police officer, Rip's life was on the line every time he reported for duty. We didn't want to take a chance something would happen to both of us, and we'd leave our only child bereft and orphaned. With that in mind, we named Herb, my brother in West Virginia, as her godfather, and he and his wife, Katy, agreed to officially adopt our daughter if we were both to die during her childhood. They were always wonderful parents to their own children and we knew they would be to Regina, as well. Regina is now their granddaughter, Harper's, godmother. At that same time, we also took care of all of the documents you just mentioned. You should think about it."

"I suppose I should. I don't have much, especially now, but I'd want to make sure my niece and nephew inherit what little I do have." Harlei now sounded as depressed as she had when I'd first called. I'd never seen such a roller coaster of emotions. It hadn't been my intention to raise her spirits just to drop them like a hot fireplace poker.

"Every day is a gift, Harlei. That's why it's called the 'present'. We never know when we're about to inhale our last breath." I realized my gloomy remarks were not apt to cheer her up, so I added, "Not that you have anything to worry about. I imagine you have a nice long life ahead of you. Still, why take the chance?"

"You're right," Harlei agreed. "As soon as I get settled in my new home, I'm going to contact an attorney and get everything in order. Just in case."

"Smart decision. Before I ring off, do you happen to know where this brother of Trey's named Arthur lives?"

"I have no idea. My guess is Arthur's some kind of drifter. But Trey's obituary in the *Albuquerque Journal* did list a hometown for his sister. She lives in Santa Fe, which is about an hour north of here. According to the obit, her name is Lucy, although I never once heard Trey mention her name. "

I thanked her for the information. "I'm going to let you get back to what you were doing before I called. Keep your chin up, take care, and call me if you think of anyone else who might've had it in for Trey."

"I will. You take care, too."

After we ended the call, I thought about what Harlei had just told me. I knew it wasn't unusual for long-lost family members to come out of the woodwork when a relative died. Particularly one who was presumed to have a bit of money they might be able to get their greedy, grubby hands on. Suddenly, both Lucy and Arthur Monroe were on my radar as potential suspects. I'd have to see if Tiffany knew any more about Trey's siblings than Harlei did.

A one-hour road trip wasn't out of the question, so I decided to talk Rip into driving to Santa Fe the following day. We'd never been there, but I'd heard the capital city was a quaint, mid-sized city with less than one-hundred thousand residents. It was rumored to have a lot of New Mexico flavor, plus an abundance of history and culture. It was known to be one of the world's greatest art cities, due to all of its galleries and museums. It would be fun to see the sights, even if nothing else was accomplished. I definitely wanted to pay a visit to the Georgia O'Keefe Museum while we were there.

I was sure Tiffany and Chase would relish the idea of having the day to themselves. I'd heard the old saying about company beginning to smell like decaying fish after three days. I involuntarily took a sniff of my forearm, just to make sure I wasn't starting to reek. We'd no doubt outstayed our welcome already. If not for the fact the kids had yet to get their money returned, we would've already been at the Alexandria Inn in Rockdale, Missouri. But I had made a promise, and I wouldn't leave until their investments were returned, and their investment manager's killer had been brought to justice. I wasn't one to make a promise lightly. If I gave my word, I stuck by it until I'd fulfilled my vow or hell had frozen over.

I hadn't achieved my promise yet, and because we humans, at a population of nearly eight billion people, were slowly burning our planet to a crisp with the greenhouse gas emissions from our vehicles, factories, and power plants, it didn't look like hell would be freezing over any time soon.

TWENTY-THREE

"Is Gramps going to be okay?" Tiffany was worried about her grandfather, which I found endearing. "He called this morning and asked if I'd join you on a drive to Santa Fe. He said you wanted to check out some of the quaint little shops in the town square, but he just wasn't feeling up to par. I'm worried about him."

Tiffany sat in the passenger seat while I drove the Chevy truck north on I-25. Along with the shops in Santa Fe Plaza, we wanted to check out the New Mexico State Capitol building, a.k.a. "the Roundhouse," while we were in town, as well as the Georgia O'Keefe Museum and the Cathedral Basilica of St. Francis of Assisi. If time permitted, we'd also visit the Meow Wolf art exhibit, called the House of Eternal Return. Tiffany told me it was an incredible multidimensional mystery house with secret passages and mesmerizing light and art exhibits. The tour also included great music and a fascinating narrative. She was anxious for me to experience it. For the moment, however, I wanted to ease her mind about her grandfather's "illness."

"Your grandfather is suffering from a disease called 'shopitis'. It tends to flare up whenever I mention browsing through shops. From past experience, the best cure for the condition seems to be six hours of rest while watching a half dozen *Gunsmoke* reruns and polishing off an entire bag of barbecue potato chips. Matt Dillon and Frito Lay seem to be just what the doctor ordered for shopitis. Oddly, the disease occurs much more often in men than women."

Tiffany laughed. "Are you saying I shouldn't lose a lot of sleep worrying about Gramps and his sudden ailment?"

"That's exactly what I'm saying. But, to be honest, I'd prefer to spend the day with you anyway, so I pretended to believe he actually wasn't feeling well. It would behoove you to do the same."

"I will," Tiffany replied. "I didn't have to pretend this morning on the phone because he was very believable. Gramps can be very dramatic when feigning illness, can't he?"

"Yes. And very annoying at times, too." I glanced at her with a grin. "But that's neither here nor there. You and I are going to have a good time. The first place I want to stop is at the Southwest Sun Shop."

"What's that?"

"They sell southwestern attire, accessories, boots, and jewelry. Lots of turquoise and leather, I'd guess."

"Are you looking for something specific, like a new purse or jacket?"

"No," I replied honestly. "I'm looking for the owner, whose name is Lucy Monroe. I had to Google her to find out where we might locate her."

"Lucy Monroe?" Tiffany looked like I'd back-handed her in the teeth. My daughter and her husband, Milo Moore, had spent way too much on their daughter's dazzling smile for me to do such a thing, however. Not that I'd ever consider striking my granddaughter, mind you. I'd slash my own wrists with a sabre saw before harming Tiffany in any way.

"Yes. Lucy is Trey's sister."

Clearly blown away by my remark, Tiffany said, "I know. But how in the world did *you* find out about her?"

"Harlei told me Trey's brother, Arthur, called wanting to know when and where the memorial services were to be held and, of course, when the will would be read. She also said Trey's obituary mentioned his two siblings. Naturally, I found Trey's obit online and read it to verify everything Harlei told me."

"Arthur sounds like a greedy jerk!" Tiffany exclaimed. I was surprised she actually seemed to be defending the man who stole their life savings. "I heard Trey mention his sister and brother exactly once. He hadn't had anything to do with either of them since their folks were killed in a plane crash years ago. I can't believe they'd actually believe Trey left them anything in his will. Actually, I'd be shocked if Trey and Sandy had even drawn one up. They didn't seem to be all that concerned about stuff like that."

"This is exactly what Harlei said." I made a turn on to Alameda, a couple of blocks from the Plaza. "We better start keeping an eye out for a parking spot. I'm not sure we'll find anything on the square."

About a block later, we pulled into an open spot. We could hit several of the places we wanted to visit from there. When we walked into the Southwest Sun Shop a couple of minutes later, we were met with a display of elaborate squash blossom necklaces. They were gorgeous, if impractical, and had price tags that staggered the mind. A sales clerk pounced on us as we entered the building, as if she were a car salesman and we'd just walked onto the showroom floor.

"The squash blossom necklaces, iconic jewelry of the Navajo tribe, are made of sterling silver and large turquoise and coral stones, all centered around the universal symbol called the Naja," the pretty young sales lady explained. "Naja is a Navajo word meaning curved, or crescent-shaped. The centerpiece of the necklaces is called a Naja, which protects against the 'evil eye,' or negative forces."

There was a lot of Native American culture and history in these fascinating and lavish necklaces, and for some reason I wanted one very, very badly. One elaborate necklace in particular spoke to me.

"You should buy it, Grams!" Tiffany was insistent. She'd waited until the blonde-haired clerk had wandered off to wait on another customer to try to persuade me. "When was the last time you bought anything for yourself, simply because you liked it? What was your last non-essential purchase?"

"Let's see," I began. "I bought a new brassiere last summer. It was the cross-your-heart type that was advertised to give you better support and comfort."

"How is a bra a non-essential item?" Tiffany asked.

"Well, for one thing, I already had several perfectly good bras. I absolutely did not need another one, which makes it non-essential. And secondly, it was black, which made it totally frivolous."

"Black?" Tiffany was clearly confused. "How does the color make it a frivolous purchase?"

"White brassieres are functional," I explained. "Black, pink, red, or any bra that's not white, falls into the seductive category. I might as well have been shopping at Victoria's Secret, for goodness sakes. Why, your grandfather would think I was having a mid-life crisis if he ever saw me wearing that black bra."

"Oh, Grams! You are so old-fashioned." Tiffany laughed loudly, causing two nearby shoppers to look our way in curiosity. I'm certain they wondered why I was blushing. "So I take it you've never worn the frivolous bra you bought last summer."

"No, of course not. As soon as I got home, I had buyer's remorse, but was too embarrassed to return it to Wal-Mart."

"Wal-Mart? You were too embarrassed to return a bra you bought at Wal-Mart?" Tiffany started cracking up so raucously that everyone in the store was now staring at us. "I return something to our Wal-Mart almost weekly. If you still have it, give it to me. I'll return it at the Wal-Mart I shop at and get your money back."

"Oh, that'd be so kind of you, dear." I really *would* be happy to get my sixteen bucks back.

"But only if you put the money toward a squash blossom necklace for yourself. If you want, I'll call Gramps and get permission for you to buy it."

I really didn't need permission, but Tiffany insisted I pull out my new phone and text him. The salesclerk reappeared and was all too happy to explain the selling points of the particular necklace that had caught my eye. As she was speaking, a response came through from Rip.

Buy the necklace. It will be my Christmas present to you. Buy matching earrings too if you'd like.

I texted back. It's too expensive. I'm not sure if I'd ever wear it enough to get our money's worth out of it.

Rip responded: I don't care if you never wear it. Tiff just sent me a text too. She told me you loved it and I want you to have it.

What a dear, sweet man I'd married. I realized for the umpteenth time I was a very lucky woman to have found the love of my life so early in my adulthood. In fact, I wasn't even an adult when we'd first met, and we'd married at eighteen when I'd found myself pregnant with Regina. What had seemed like a daunting dilemma at the time had turned out to be the best thing that had ever happened to us. Just telling my pappy about the pregnancy had taken ten years off Rip's life. Or so he'd thought at the time. But Pappy had fallen in love with his granddaughter the moment he laid eyes on her and all was forgiven as far as Rip was concerned.

If you insist. I'd stopped reminiscing long enough to reply to my generous husband's text.

I continued to muse about how blessed I was while I waited for Rip's response. It took a while because, as I told you before, the man texts at glacier-melting speed. By the time his reply arrived on my phone, the clerk was already in possession of my credit card and wrapping up my necklace. Only then did my text tone ring out.

I dog insipid.

Apparently, Rip had not proofread what auto-correct had done to his message. But I got the drift. He'd insisted I buy the necklace, which was a fortunate thing because I'd already done so.

After I signed the credit card receipt, I asked if the owner of the shop was available. The clerk's voice caught as she asked, "Is something wrong? Did I do something that offended you?"

"Heavens no, dear! You were wonderful. In fact, I wanted to tell her what an asset you are to her business. It doesn't hurt for customers to drop a bug in the owner's ear that their employees are top drawer."

"Oh, that'd be awesome," the youthful clerk gushed. "Thank you, ma'am. I'll go find her."

"Grams, you are so bad," Tiffany whispered as the clerk rushed off, with visions of a pay raise dancing through her head, no doubt. She returned a couple of minutes later with a dark-haired woman in her early thirties. She wore a colorful Native American gown that flattered her ample hips. Her gorgeous eyes matched the stones in her turquoise earrings, which dangled so low they touched her shoulders.

I introduced myself and my granddaughter and spoke commendably about her sales lady and the shop. "You have a wonderful selection of merchandise. I had no intention of buying a gift for myself, but..." I held up the fancy bag that held my Christmas present. "I'm leaving with one of your nicest squash blossom necklaces."

"Great!" Lucy replied. "That was really a great deal for you."

Sure it was, I thought. I knew I could have probably gotten it cheaper if I'd shopped around, but that was beside the point. It was mine now, and I adored it.

To stall for time, I selected the closest jacket on a rack and tried it on. "Now I need to look for a jacket to go with my new necklace. What do you think about this one, Tiffany?"

I turned toward my granddaughter and winked so she'd know I was buying time to prolong my conversation with Lucy Monroe. She grimaced. "Not too sure that's your style, Grams."

I hadn't even paid attention to the jacket I'd chosen, but realized now it was made of cowhide. I looked like I had skinned a black and white Holstein and draped its skin over my shoulders. I not only looked ridiculous, but I also looked like I should be arrested for animal abuse. But I left it on and admired it in the mirror even though I had no intention of buying the jacket. I turned back toward Lucy, who was nodding her head in approval. I could envision more dollar signs flitting through her mind. She thought she'd lucked into having a woman akin to Oprah Winfrey wander into her store with more money than she knew what to do with. *You get a car! You get a car! And I get a ridiculously-expensive necklace!* I thought.

"Oh! Did you say your last name was Monroe?" I asked Lucy now, as if the familiarity of her surname had just hit me. "What a coincidence. We have friends by that name who live in Albuquerque, although we haven't seen them in quite a while. Are Trey and Sandy Monroe related to you by any chance?"

"Actually, yes." She deliberated for a moment before asking, "So you haven't heard?"

"Heard what?" I asked innocently.

"Trey, who was my brother, was killed a couple of weeks ago."

"He was killed?" To appear shocked at the news, I dropped my lower jaw as if a surgeon was about to pluck my tonsils out with a pair of needle-nosed pliers. "As in murdered?"

"Yes. I'm afraid so. It was so sad." Despite her comment, Lucy didn't look overcome with sorrow. In fact, she looked as if she'd just told us the pet goldfish she'd bought her son had perished on the way home from the pet shop.

"Wow! We hadn't heard. I'm so sorry for your loss." After offering my condolence, Tiffany repeated my sentiments. I then asked, "Did they catch whoever killed him?"

"Nope." Lucy flashed us an unnerving smile. It was replaced quickly by a look of sorrow that didn't quite look sincere. She should have had the decency to act as if she cared whether or not justice was handed down to the perpetrator of her brother's death. I'd hazard to guess closure had come easily for her. In fact, it'd probably come immediately following her brother, Arthur's, assurance he was going to do whatever it took to see that they were the beneficiaries and sole heirs to their brother's estate.

"It's a shame Trey emptied his clients' accounts and the money is still unaccounted for." I suppose it was a little boorish of me to make such a remark, but her callousness called for it, in my opinion.

"What?" Lucy asked. Now it was *her* lower jaw that dropped so low she could've stuck a whole cantaloupe in her mouth. Her striking teal-colored eyes bore into me like a laser beam. "Hey! I thought you just said you hadn't heard about his death."

Oh crap! I'd spoken without thinking. *Honesty really is the best policy. Especially when you can't remember the lies you told just seconds earlier.* To cover my gaffe, I said, "I *hadn't* heard about his death. I'd just heard he'd screwed his clients out of a lot of money by pretending to have set up an **IPO** fund that never existed. Last we heard, he was fleeing the country with the money from the accounts in his care. I guess someone didn't appreciate being scammed as much as Trey thought they would."

"I guess not. Arthur and I were required to give written statements and have our alibis confirmed after Trey's death. We were told at the time there was an issue involving Trey's investment business, but not that he'd done anything illegal. I wonder if he made off with the money in my trust account, too, and that of my brother, Arthur's."

My blunder hadn't turned out to be as much an issue as I'd feared it would because Lucy was single-mindedly fixated on her own bottom line.

"I'm not sure. What trust account are you referring to?" *That's a future question for Harlei,* I thought. *It's the first I've heard of a trust account.* As it turned out, Lucy would tell me all I needed to know about her parents' trust.

"When our folks were killed in a plane crash, we discovered they'd named Trey, who was twenty at the time, as their executor. Their trust spelled out that he was to invest the money and dole out a thousand to my brother and me each month. As the executor, Trey got twelve-hundred. " Lucy sounded bitter as she pointed out the injustice. It was clear she resented the fact the three didn't receive equal amounts.

"That's not unusual," I replied. "It's customary for the executor to get paid a nominal amount for time and services rendered. Being the executor of a trust is a huge responsibility. It seems only fair that the person in charge of liquidating and handling the distribution of the proceeds of an estate be compensated."

As if I hadn't spoken, Lucy continued. "Trey invested the trust fund money into treasury bonds and high-yield money market accounts so our shares would grow in value. Arthur and I weren't of legal age yet, so the trust stipulated we'd get a grand every month until we reached the age of forty. At that point, we'd receive the bulk of our share of the account. Forty frigging years old!"

"Sounds like your brother did you both a favor." I was wondering why Lucy seemed so upset that Trey had invested their money wisely.

"That's like another eight years for me. We both need our money now. Arthur is basically homeless, and I'm living paycheck to paycheck." With a crimson face, she pointed at the fancy bag I was clutching. "How many fools do you think waltz into my shop willing to pony up that kind of money for a necklace they can buy for much less at any little roadside stand along the highway that's selling Navajo jewelry?"

As you can imagine, it ticked me off to be called a fool by Lucy Monroe, even though I suddenly felt like the biggest chowder-head in the world. I opened up my bag and studied the squash blossom monstrosity I'd just purchased. It didn't seem near as appealing to me now. In fact, it looked rather gaudy.

"Whatever," I simply replied. There were a lot of nasty comebacks racing through my head, but I head to remind myself Tiffany and I had a more important purpose for being in the Southwest Sun Shop than to squabble with its owner. "Have the thousand-dollar payments come in a timely manner since your parents' deaths?"

"Yes. On the first day of every month, even when we've requested to get a payment early now and again."

"Why is Arthur homeless?" I asked.

"Actually, he's kind of a sofa surfer. He goes from one friend or acquaintance's home to another, flopping on their couch for a week or so before moving on. He doesn't believe in being weighed down by material things. He's what you'd call a free spirit."

"He's what I'd call a mooch," I began, "who doesn't believe in working for a living. Instead, he's taking advantage of a lot of people's kind-heartedness. Had he been to see Trey recently?"

"Yeah, about three weeks ago Arthur went to persuade him to fork over some of our money. Arthur said Trey wouldn't even invite him inside to talk, so they argued in Trey's front yard. In fact, Trey ordered Arthur off his property. Arthur may not like to work, but he wouldn't *have* to if Trey would've given us the money we had coming." Lucy's response verified Babs Hancock's observation of seeing two look-alike men arguing in Trey's front yard. *Trey was killed about three weeks ago. Could Arthur have murdered his brother to gain access to his inheritance?* I quit musing about the coincidence to respond to Lucy.

"Arthur wouldn't have had to work for *a while*, I think you meant. It wasn't a bottomless pit of money, I'd bet. Once the money was gone, Arthur would've had to resume his hobby of sofa-surfing, only without the grand a month he used to rely on."

"We'll just have to agree to disagree on that matter." Lucy was getting worked up. Perspiration was beginning to glisten across her forehead. I, on the other hand, was sweating like a bull moose in the rut. It wasn't from anxiety, though. It was from wearing a cowhide over my blue and white checkered blouse and khaki capris. I felt like a beef burrito, wrapped in a leather tortilla. If I'd known what was fixing to happen, I would've taken the damn thing off right then. Instead, I wiped my brow with a tissue I pulled out of my pocket and watched as Lucy was getting more and more incensed. She sprayed spittle all over the Holstein jacket when she shouted, "The way I see it, it was Arthur's money and my money to do with as we saw fit!"

I shrugged and remained silent as Lucy continued to vent. "We've been trying to get Trey to divvy up our trust money in a lump sum because we need it now—not when we're forty. But with the a-hole dead now and the money missing, we'll probably never see another dime."

"I'm sorry you're taking the loss of your brother so hard." That was pure sarcasm, and there was no way Lucy could not recognize it as such. But somehow, some way, she didn't.

"Thank you," she replied as if I'd offered further condolences rather than blunt disdain. "What was that IPO fund thing you were talking about?"

"It was a classic Ponzi scheme," I told her.

"A what?"

"A Ponzi scheme. Like the one Bernie Madoff went to prison for." I sensed my explanation had fallen on deaf, or at least dumb, ears.

"Who?" She asked.

"Bernie Madoff. He cheated his clients out of millions of dollars, and your brother did the exact same thing. Trey's clients thought they were investing in a new tech stock, but instead, they were investing in his future life of luxury on a Caribbean beach."

"Oh." Lucy looked befuddled. "So, he screwed people over and then the frigging a-hole went and got himself killed." It was at that precise moment I realized she wasn't clever enough to concoct or pull off the stunt that killed Trey. I couldn't see Arthur, the 'free spirited' brother, being much brighter. The two of them were more concerned about convincing Trey into turning over their share of the inheritance. You can't talk a dead guy into anything, so I doubted the pair had collaborated on a plan to murder their brother.

For some reason, I felt compelled to defend Trey. "I think you were lucky to have had a brother who handled the trust fund as stipulated by your parents. As the oldest sibling, he was doing exactly what they asked of him. Chances are, your parents thought if Trey handed over the inheritance in a lump sum, you'd both be broke in no time. It'd be another rags-to-riches-to-rags story waiting to happen. The trust fund money would be gone and no longer would you two be able to depend on the thousand-dollar payments on the first of every month. You'd now be having to quadruple the cost of this jewelry you sell, rather than double it. Besides, your parents could not have anticipated Trey would steal your inheritance money, as well as his clients' money, and flee the country."

"*What?*" Lucy looked as if she'd swallowed the aforementioned cantaloupe and it was now lodged in her throat. "I can't believe you'd stick up for that son-of-a-bit—"

Tiffany gave me a panicked look, but I was on a roll. It was like trying to stop a five-hundred-pound snowball from tumbling down a hill. "And furthermore, your brother didn't go and get himself killed. Someone took his life. If you were any kind of sister at all, you'd be more focused on finding justice for Trey than ragging on him for fulfilling his legal obligations."

"Let's go, Grams," Tiffany grabbed my arm and was tugging me toward the door. She'd noticed the furious expression on the shop owner's face and didn't want to stick around to see how Lucy would react to the dressing down I'd just given her.

"Get out of my shop now!" Lucy screamed as Tiffany dragged me out the door. "And stay out!"

As we stepped outside, Tiffany took my elbow and led me down the sidewalk. I expressed to her my belief the two Monroe siblings weren't capable of carrying out a plan to kill their brother. Tiffany agreed, then asked, "Did you remember to grab the necklace you purchased off the counter?"

"Oh, dear!" I looked down just then to see the cowhide coat I still had on. Before I could speak again, two cops walked around the corner.

"Stop! Police! Put your hands up," they ordered in unison.

"What are you talking about?" I asked in alarm. Tiffany's reaction was even more horror-stricken.

"Raise your hands over your head, ma'am," the police officer repeated his demand. Tiffany and I both raised our arms. They motioned for my granddaughter to step aside, and one of the cops walked behind me and cuffed my hands.

"What in the heck do you think you're doing?" I asked, appalled at the turn of events

"Cuffing you." The tallest guy spoke while the shorter one said something into his police radio. "You're under arrest for grand larceny."

TWENTY-FOUR

"This is all a big mistake!" I screamed at the police officer who had just slapped handcuffs on me in the middle of Santa Fe Plaza. Shoppers stopped what they were doing to stare. I noticed several people holding up their cell phones to record the action. A video of the humiliating scene would no doubt be going viral by the time we returned to Albuquerque. I hoped Chase didn't see it on social media and show it to Rip. My husband tended to turn into such a sourpuss whenever I got arrested for something that usually was not my fault to begin with.

"Are you saying you didn't steal the jacket you've got on? It still has the price tag hanging off it, as if you were Minnie Pearl or something." He chuckled, grabbed the tag, and turned it over to gaze at the price. "Good Lord! Who'd pay this much for that ugly thing?"

"Not me, I can tell you that!" I replied defiantly. "I wouldn't pay a dime for this repulsive jacket."

"I think that goes without saying. You decided to steal it instead!" The cop had the audacity to laugh at his own snide remarks. "The shop owner called as we were just down the block. She said you left the store without paying for the coat you were wearing. That's pretty much the definition of 'shoplifting'."

"I did not shoplift this coat!" I hollered. "I can explain."

"Did you leave the store wearing the coat?"

"Well, yes, but——"

"Did you pay for the coat?" The officer was young enough to be my grandson and his disrespectful tone was uncalled for. I'll admit, however, I was actually a bit impressed that he knew who Minnie Pearl was and that she was renowned for wearing hats with price tags hanging off them.

"Well, no, I didn't pay for it, but——"

"Then you stole the coat," he reasoned.

"Please, let me explain. The shop owner is holding something I purchased that's probably worth twice what this coat cost. I guess you could say I left my high-dollar squash blossom necklace in there as collateral."

"Seriously, lady?" The second police officer, who was about fifty years old, sounded impatient.

"Yes, please give me a couple of minutes to explain what happened, and how I ended up outside of the store before I could take off the jacket. I was about to return it and collect my necklace just as you two showed up and made a spectacle of yourselves." *Not to mention embarrassing the stuffing out of me and my granddaughter.*

After I was finally able to give an explanation of the situation, the handcuffs were removed. I returned the coat to the shop, and the sales clerk I'd dealt with earlier reluctantly returned my money for the squash blossom necklace. I had buyer's remorse and knew the feeling of regret at having overpaid for it would only continue to grow if I didn't get my money back right then. Only twenty minutes had passed since I'd purchased the necklace and, fortunately, the salesclerk agreed she could not, in all good conscience, enforce the "All Sales are Final" policy. I handed her a ten-dollar bill as a token of my appreciation, and in lieu of an apology that she'd just lost a hefty commission.

Although I didn't relish being handcuffed in public on the streets of Santa Fe, New Mexico, I was glad it happened, in a way. At least now I wasn't going to be saddled with an expensive necklace I'd rarely ever have an occasion to wear, and even then, I'd be so afraid of losing the costly piece of jewelry I'd probably refuse to take it out of its box. It was an "all's well that ends well" sort of event in my mind. In Tiffany's, not so much.

As we walked away from the Southwest Sun Shop, Tiffany said, "Grams, I'm not feeling well."

"Oh, honey," I said with concern. "I'm so sorry about what happened. Is there anything I can get for you?"

"Yes, there is," she replied. "I think I'm coming down with a sudden case of shopitis. I must have caught it from Gramps this morning."

"Didn't he text you?"

"Yes. It's a 'viral' virus," she replied with a laugh. "But, a couple of enchiladas, with guacamole and chips, and a margarita might be just the cure. There's a little restaurant right up the street called La Plazuela At La Fonda. Chase and I have eaten there several times and it's exceptional."

"Let's go then!" I exclaimed in delight. "Lunch is my treat. Getting arrested, or *nearly* getting arrested, in this case, always makes me hungry."

Tiffany laughed and linked her elbow with mine. We walked arm and arm up the sidewalk. A few minutes later, as we were sipping on our margaritas, dipping tortilla chips into guacamole dip, and waiting for our bean and cheese enchiladas to be brought to our table, I asked, "What's next on our list?"

"Anything but shopping. How about we go to the Georgia O'Keefe Museum after we eat?"

"Sounds like a plan!"

The next several hours with Tiffany were enjoyable. The visit with Lucy Monroe had not gone exactly as I'd anticipated, but at least it had been what I would consider successful. I felt secure in crossing both of Trey's siblings off my suspect list. I hoped they'd eventually get the inheritance their parents intended for them to have. If they both blew their wad in six months, so be it. At least they could never say they didn't get what they had coming to them.

There were a lot of people who'd trusted Trey, who now thought he'd also gotten what he'd had coming to him. Me? I wasn't so sure that Trey *did* deserve what happened to him. There was a notion brewing in my mind that I'd been looking at his death from the wrong angle all along.

———

After I explained to Rip I'd changed my mind on the squash blossom necklace because I'd decided it was just too fancy for my taste, I spent most of the evening thinking about the case that had dominated my every waking hour for nearly three weeks. I went over in my mind everything I'd learned and every interaction I'd had with the suspects on my list.

Suddenly, it became clear. I'd had my doubts about this individual for a long time, but now I was confident enough to take my suspicions to Detective Gutierrez. The following morning, before I spoke to Carlos, I wanted to call Harlei and give her the good news.

———

"How are you doing, Harlei?" I asked. The phone rang seven times before she answered. I'd been just about to hang up because my news was too intriguing to pass along via a voice mail message.

"Pretty fair." Harlei was out of breath as if I'd caught her at a bad time.

"Were you in the middle of something?" I asked. "Should I call back later?"

"No. I've been packing and lugging heavy boxes. I needed a break anyway," Harlei replied pleasantly. "How are you?"

"I'm fine. I've got great news. I've narrowed down my list of suspects in Trey's death to one individual, and I'm ready to take my findings to the police. Detective Gutierrez can take it from there."

"That *is* awesome news!" Harlei exclaimed. "Who killed him, and how'd you figure it out?"

"I spent last evening scrutinizing my list of suspects. I turned over every stone in my mind and considered every possibility. Then I thought back to something Howard Hancock had said to me. Suddenly, everything just clicked. I can't honestly say I'm one-hundred percent positive about my intuition, but I'm confident enough to take it to the detective."

"I guess I'm not totally surprised it was Howard." Harlei sounded contemplative. "Although I'd have bet the farm on Manuel being the person behind Trey's death."

"And you'd have lost that bet!" I responded with a chuckle.

"Does it look like everyone might get their money back?"

"I can't promise, but my gut feeling is that everyone who's been wronged will have their money returned to them in due time. It might take a bit to get everything all straightened out and the money returned from the offshore account it was deposited in. But, regardless, I do feel confident about it."

"Oh, thank goodness! That's awesome news, although I'm afraid getting the money out of Trey's account in the Caymans might prove to be more difficult than you'd think." Harlei sounded as delighted as I'd ever heard her. A lot of weight seemed to have been lifted off her shoulders, and she could finally take a calming breath. It looked as if things were going to work out after all. "Thank you so much, Rapella. I don't know how I'll ever repay you."

"No, *thank you*! You don't owe me a thing. I don't know how I'd have ever figured it out without your help. I'm so grateful for all the information you gave me as I was trying to track down the killer. I just pray my theory holds water when the homicide detectives check into it."

"I'm sure it will. I want to hear all about it."

"I don't have time right now, but I feel really confident about it." I repeated, as I looked at my watch. I knew Carlos went to lunch at eleven-thirty, and it was already eleven-fifteen. "I'm in a hurry, but I'll fill you in on the details later. Talk to you soon."

"All right. I'm looking forward to it," she replied before ending the call.

I wished I wasn't as confident as I'd expressed to Harlei. My heart was at war with what I knew I had to do, but my mind was at peace with the realization I had no other option.

TWENTY-FIVE

Late that afternoon, I placed a phone call. I'd been wondering how to set up a face-to-face meeting with the individual I now knew, without a moment's doubt, was the person behind the murder of Trey Monroe. I decided a straight-on approach was my best bet. After an introduction and a few pleasantries, I said, "I'm so glad you answered. I need to meet with you to talk about Trey Monroe's death."

"I have time right now," the voice on the other end replied hesitantly. "What's going on?"

"Well, actually, I think we should meet in person."

"Oh?" The voice now sounded guarded, and with good reason. "You can't just tell me about it over the phone?"

"I could, but I'd rather meet with you and do it in person."

We discussed the details regarding our meeting, which I wrote down on my notepad. I then made another call before heading out for what would undoubtedly be a tense get-together.

Chase was still at work in his office when Rip, Tiffany, and I left the Carpenters' house about an hour later. Using the GPS function of my new cell phone, which I was getting more familiar with, I was surprised to discover it led us to a lone house at the end of a long dead-end road in Los Ranchos. I hadn't wanted Tiffany to join us, but she had insisted, having been involved in the case from the get-go.

"Jeez," Rip said. "This is out where the hoot owls do the chickens!"

"Rip! Hush!" I admonished him. But not before Tiffany giggled at his remark.

"Relax, Grams," she said. "I'm thirty, not exactly a kid anymore."

The sun was setting as we walked up the sidewalk and approached the door. Despite what I'd been told, I didn't see any indication the house was for sale. There was no real estate sign in the yard or realtor's lockbox on the front door.

"Greetings Rapella," Harlei Rycoff said as she opened the front door and locked eyes with me. She then realized Rip and Tiffany were standing behind me. Harlei looked as if she'd just seen Sasquatch walk across her front lawn and mark his territory on her mailbox post. "Oh, my! I didn't realize you weren't coming alone."

"Were you hoping I would?" I asked.

"Well, no, um, er, but—" Harlei stammered. She couldn't seem to put a sentence together.

"Rip knows I don't see well enough at night to drive safely." *And that I might need back up if this meeting goes haywire,* I could've added. "Tiffany was interested in seeing your home, which you'd told me had been put on the market. Like you, she and Chase are looking to downsize, thanks to Monroe Investments."

"I'm sorry. I'm in…in the…same…same pos—" Harlei began to stammer again.

"Are you in the same position, Harlei?" I asked. "Are you really?"

Without responding to my pointed question, she stepped back to usher us inside. I entered with Rip directly behind me. Tiffany followed in her grandfather's footsteps. None of us ever turned our backs to her.

Once the four of us were standing in Harlei's living room, I said, "I don't really think you're in the same position as Tiffany and Chase, or any of the rest of Monroe Investments' clients. In fact, I think you're the reason the rest of them are in such dire straits."

"I take it you think you know something," Harlei said, "but I can assure you that you have no idea what you're talking about."

"Would you like to place any wagers on that? Would you like to bet that farm you mentioned earlier?" I asked. Rip shot me a cautioning look, and Tiffany seemed to morph into a pillar of salt. It was as though she thought if she stood as still as a statue, she'd be mistaken for an inanimate object in the living room. "Are you truly going to look me in the eye and tell me you weren't the person behind both the Ponzi scheme and Trey's death?"

"Keep your hands where I can see them!" Harlei commanded after a stunned silence that seemed to last for thirty seconds. After some serious contemplation, she had suddenly brandished a gun she'd withdrawn from the pocket of her blue denim jacket. She motioned the three of us into a corner of the windowless dining room. Not that it really mattered. Her house was out in the middle of no-damn-where. Tiffany nearly fainted in fright, but Rip grabbed her and positioned her behind him. I knew he would do anything he could to protect her, and me, as well.

He looked steadily at Harlei, and warned, "You won't get away with this, you know. You're only making the situation harder for yourself. Why don't you lower your weapon before you do something you'll regret?"

Unmoved, Harlei replied, "My plan has gone off without a hitch so far. I see no reason why it won't continue to do so."

"I can," I said. "I'm a hitch you hadn't counted on, and I'm pretty sure there's at least one more you aren't prepared for, as well."

"None of you are going to be around long enough to pose a problem for me," she countered. "The insurance money finally came through today from the policy I had purchased on Trey. I was able to purchase one after proving if he died, I'd have no income coming in and my financial health would suffer greatly. Trey even went to bat for me with the insurance company, even though he probably didn't expect I'd ever cash in on the policy."

"No wonder you knew so much about the subject," I said. "I didn't put two and two together at the time."

"I was hoping you wouldn't. Not that it would've mattered. I'll be on a beach in Panama, with a boatload of money in my offshore account by this time tomorrow. I'll have my toes in the sand and a margarita in my hand. While I'm soaking up the sun on a beach, you three will be on the wrong side of the grass. You should have left well enough alone, Rapella Ripple!"

"Probably so. Unfortunately, turning the other cheek is just not in my DNA." Harlei smiled at my remark. It was probably because I'd used an acronym, which she'd always seemed to enjoy. Her gleeful tone about our not-so-promising future irritated me, however. "How are you going to explain three dead bodies in your house?"

"My house?" Harlei laughed. It was then I realized there was nothing but an old butcher block table and broken-down recliner in the room. "This isn't my house. I knew it was vacant because the split-level I've actually been leasing is just a few blocks over."

"Oh, of course. I should have known you lied about owning a

home. What's your real name, Harlei?" I asked. It was an educated hunch she was living under an assumed name. I'd called the six or seven local Remax offices the previous day, only to find none of them had ever heard of a broker named David Colmer. I soon found out my gut was on target.

Harlei hesitated for a few moments. "Since you won't be around to run your mouth, I might as well tell you my real name is Scarlet Craft."

"Scarlet, huh? As in *The Scarlet Letter*? Unlike the scarlet 'A' Hester Prynne had to wear as punishment for being an adulteress, you should have to wear a scarlet 'C' for being a con artist, and a conniving crook." I knew I was taking a risk by antagonizing her. But for some reason, I couldn't stop poking at her like she was a rattlesnake and I had a big stick.

At the moment, however, I had neither a big stick nor any other kind of weapon. All I had was a big mouth, and I was stalling for time. "Why'd you do it, Scarlet? You owe us an answer to that question before you kill us. After all, I was trying to help you get your money back when I still believed you'd been victimized by your boss, rather than the other way around."

"I don't owe you anything. But I'll answer your question if you answer mine."

"Which is?" I had no bargaining power. She had the gun. I had the big mouth. Someone who's been involved with as many murder cases as I have in the past should know you shouldn't take a big mouth to a gunfight. It only got you shot dead that much quicker. However, the longer I could keep Scarlet talking, the more iron-clad proof of her guilt we'd obtain and the better chance Rip, Tiffany, and I had of surviving.

"How did you figure out it was me?" She appeared genuinely interested in what had tipped me off. "I thought you'd determined it was Howard Hancock who killed Trey."

"And that's what I wanted you to believe. I was intentionally evasive. When I asked you how Chen Ho reacted to the news, you replied that Ho sounded calm and collected, but his expression was terrifying."

"So?" Scarlet asked. "I explained to you I was referring to his verbal expression, not his facial expression."

"Your clarification sounded reasonable, but it was your nervous laugh that gave you away."

"You make me sound like some kind of moron. Well, guess what? I'm not as stupid as you think." Scarlet waved the gun in my direction. She was obviously offended by my remarks.

"No. I'm sure you aren't," I said with a rueful sigh. "And speaking of Chen Ho. You failed to tell me he committed suicide the week after Trey died. When you supposedly spoke to him a second time, he'd been deceased for about ten days. Detective Gutierrez informed me today that Ho's prostate cancer returned and had become terminal. Rather than suffer in agony, he decided to take matters into his own hands. That was all I needed to know to cross him off my suspect list and put you at the top."

"I see." Scarlet seemed upset with herself for not realizing I'd eventually find out about the bail bondsman's death. She'd underestimated my ingenuity, and also my ability to draw information out of Carlos, whether the detective wanted to share it with me or not. As I'd hoped, that talent had come in handy.

"Ho's blood is on your hands, Scarlet. The troublesome issue with his investment money may have pushed him over the edge, even though he was probably better off for killing himself with narcotics than continuing to suffer until the cancer took him."

"Killing himself was his choice, not mine," she replied haughtily, not bothering to comment on the fact she'd lied about speaking to him on the phone.

"Whatever. You also told me you called Detective Gutierrez and ran your theory about Sandy and Manuel past him. He told me you'd done no such thing. At the very beginning, Carlos told me you'd reported to him that you'd never been married. He knew nothing about your marriage to Thomas. At that stage of the game, I knew you were a pathological liar. If you were lying to me about those things, I had to wonder what else you were lying about. I began to realize you were treating me like a mushroom."

"A mushroom?"

"Yes. You were keeping me in the dark and feeding me a lot of bull-poop to keep me going down one wrong path after another. I finally figured out why you wanted me to keep you in the loop. You wanted to make sure I wasn't closing in on *you*, the real killer. In the meantime, you fed me tidbits that made me devote my time and efforts to other potential suspects who had nothing to do with the crimes," I explained.

"Of course," Scarlet replied. "I needed to keep you busy and feeding false leads to the detectives while waiting for the insurance pay-off to come through. I also needed a little time to tie up loose ends so I could skip town. As Michael Corleone said in *The Godfather*, you should keep your friends close and your enemies closer."

I nodded. Even though I ironically found it flattering to be considered her enemy, I realized that thinking Harlei and I were friends while investigating Trey's murder had made me vulnerable. I'd put as much trust in Scarlet as Trey apparently had. She had a way of making a person believe in her and want to help her. I tipped my head to the gun in her hand. "You were well prepared for my visit tonight. I have to assume you had some idea I'd stumbled onto the truth. Am I right?"

"Yes. I had a strong inkling that's why you wanted to meet. Otherwise, you'd have told me what you'd discovered over the phone. Also, when I told you that the time of death on Trey's official death certificate had been changed from eleven-thirty to twelve-fifteen to reflect the information obtained from the autopsy report, you sounded as if you didn't believe me." Scarlet appeared royally ticked off I hadn't taken her word as the gospel truth.

"That's because I'd just spoken with Detective Gutierrez, who told me there was nothing new in the autopsy report. I'll admit that at first, I was afraid he'd merely failed to mention a revised time of death, a factor that could potentially implicate Chase in the murder. Then I realized Carlos would never have forgotten to mention something so critical."

"You also sounded suspicious when you said you'd get back with me soon," Scarlet continued. "Your tone and demeanor seemed off to me. And then when you ended the call without saying 'keep your chin up,' I knew you were on to me. That's why I put this Glock in my coat pocket. I purchased it many years ago from my ex-husband's cousin when I lived in Flagstaff." As she spoke about buying the handgun, she walked up to me and stared into my eyes.

Just then, I felt Rip begin to reach for the gun he'd brought along. I whispered, "Not yet." I heard him sigh before Scarlet waved her Glock and spoke again.

"This has a hollow-point bullet in the chamber with your name on it. It's about time I eliminated you three and got the show on the road. I plan to catch the red-eye to Panama tonight." This time Rip did remove the Smith and Wesson .357 from the back of his waistband. Standing partially behind me, Scarlet had no idea his gun was pointed up toward her chest from just left of my right hip.

I had a sinking feeling the situation was about to go downhill like a nine-year-old descending a snowy slope on a trash can lid.

TWENTY-SIX

"**W**ait! Before you shoot me, tell me about the Ponzi scheme. How much money did Trey manage to swindle his clients out of?" I was desperate to keep her talking, and even more desperate to keep her from firing the gun. The more information she decided to share, the better. "Like I mentioned on the phone this morning, I first started considering you as a possible suspect after a comment Howard Hancock made that got me thinking."

"And what comment was that?"

"He asked how someone who did all of the paperwork in Trey's office, including the stock transactions, could not have known her boss was in the process of carrying out such a brazen crime. You'd have had to been walking around the Monroe Investments Office with your head up your—"

"That might be true, but it doesn't mean Trey couldn't have pocketed all the IPO funds without my knowledge," Scarlet replied, cutting me off. "He'd have had to be a lot cleverer than he actually was, though. He trusted me completely, which was his downfall."

"I thought of that," I said. "I also wondered if you were smart enough to figure out how to pull off such a complicated stunt. After much consideration, I concluded you were plenty smart enough."

"Thank you." Scarlet was obviously quite proud of her actions, and her smugness nauseated me.

After a long pause of trying to wrap my head around her overwhelming callousness, I spoke again. "I realized Trey took care of the entertaining and wooing of investors. He really did believe there actually was a Clean Sweep IPO fund. All you had to do was sell off the remaining blue chip stocks and wire the proceeds to your offshore account in Panama, where you planned to move after you tied up loose ends here in Albuquerque. You know, loose ends, such as killing your boss and collecting life insurance proceeds off his death."

"You don't get it, do you?" Scarlet asked. "I really am smarter than you think I am. There was *never* a Ponzi scheme. There actually was a Clean Sweep IPO fund that Trey convinced most of his clients to invest in. He felt certain it would shoot up in value and make his clients even wealthier than they already were, bolstering his reputation as an investment manager in the process. His instincts were spot-on, and the value of the fund increased ten-fold. Once the six-month lockout period was up, and the clients could legally withdraw their funds, I knew it was time to proceed with the final stage of my plan. Using Trey's signature and credentials, I sold off the entire fund, along with all of the high-dollar investments in Trey's clients' portfolios. I transferred the money into my offshore account in Panama. I had to make it look like Trey was perpetrating a Ponzi scheme, so I shredded all evidence that the actual investments had ever been made."

"Did it ever occur to you someone would check with Clean Sweep to see if Monroe Investments had a piece of the offering when it completed the IPO's lockout-period requirements six months later?" I asked. "You could eliminate the paper trail on your end, but not theirs."

"Of course," she replied defensively. "But I planned to be in Panama by that time, and Harlei Rycoff would no longer exist. This is not my first rodeo, Rapella. I've successfully disappeared into thin air before. Besides, I figured the authorities would be chasing their tails looking for Harlei Rycoff, not Scarlet Craft. No one who knows me as Scarlet Craft ever knew me as Harlei Rycoff, not even Thomas, my ex-husband. So far, the main focus of the investigation has been to solve Trey's murder. Only after that were they going to knuckle down and try to find out where the money he'd stolen was located. Had they been closing in on me earlier than I'd anticipated, I'd have sacrificed the million-dollar insurance payout and fled the country already."

"I'm amazed at how you can so cruelly kill a man in cold blood who gave you a job and trusted you completely," I said. "I'd say you're what they call a sociopath."

Scarlet seemed insulted at being labeled a sociopath, but then, who wouldn't be? She shrugged and said, "I did feel bad about killing Trey. He was a thoughtful, kind-hearted man. And, thanks to his foresight, I am nine million dollars richer today. Ten, if you count the insurance money."

"I guess congratulations are in order." I didn't even try to mask the contempt I felt for her.

"I don't appreciate your sarcasm," Scarlet said. "I didn't *want* to kill him. I *had* to. I had no choice."

"Every mistake you've made was a choice, Scarlet." I could hear Rip whispering to me to stop provoking her. Unfortunately, I was too wound up to think rationally. "And they were all *bad* choices. Killing Trey was not only a horrific crime, but also a terrible error in judgment on your part. If the state of New Mexico hadn't abolished capital punishment in 2009, it would've been a fatal decision, as far as your personal future is concerned, as well."

"They'd have had to catch me first. Besides, I told you I didn't want to kill him, but how could I have pulled off my plan otherwise?" Scarlet asked. "In that same vein, I don't relish the thought of killing the three of you, but it's a necessary evil. You three will fall into the category of collateral damage when it comes to having pulled off my plan."

"Don't get ahead of yourself. You haven't actually pulled it off yet," I replied.

"Well, I guarantee you I will. Once I eliminate you three, I'm out of here. I'm going to be living in the lap of luxury, while you three won't be living at all. I hope this teaches you to mind your own business."

How could I be minding anybody's business, even my own, if I'm dead? I wondered. Scarlet's glib remark made no sense, but I didn't think it was wise to bring it to her attention. Better to be patient and let her go on blathering.

"I did my research, you see. The Republic of Panama is a very pure tax haven. Not only will I not be assessed any taxes, but Panama also has strict banking secrecy laws to protect the privacy of account holders. I'll be in like flint."

"No, you won't! Oomph!" I felt Rip's elbow jab me in the ribs. My patience with Scarlet had worn as thin as a beef patty in a ninety-nine-cent hamburger. Maybe even as thin as Rip's patience with me had worn. "You'll be in like 'Flynn'. If you use clichés, at least use them correctly."

"You got a smart mouth, don't you?" Scarlet asked. "I think it's about time to put you out of my misery."

"I'm sorry. Please wait. I want to hear how you pulled it off before you kill us," I said. Scarlet thought about it a moment and took a few steps back. I sensed she was anxious to boast about her scheming, manipulative skills. "How'd you go about getting rid of the only person standing in your way?"

"You mean Trey?" Scarlet asked.

"No. I meant Santa Claus." I was mocking her, which was not a wise thing to do when there was a hollow-point bullet with my name on it in the chamber of her gun. "Of course, I mean Trey."

"One more wisecrack out of you, and you die. I have nothing to lose at this point. Mouth off again and you're dead. And then you'll never hear the rest of my story. Is that clear?"

"Abundantly!" At that point, I decided my best bet was to be compliant. "I apologize. Please go on with your story."

"I'd already asked Trey for a week off to go on a vacation to Grand Cayman. Trey approved my request, so I used his credit card to purchase a one-way ticket in his name."

"You know, there's a place called Hell on Grand Cayman. It's a group of limestone formations in West Bay. Lucky for you, you don't even have to go to the Cayman Islands to go to—"

"How'd you get Trey's credit card?" Tiffany quickly interrupted me. I was glad to see my granddaughter could still talk coherently, despite her overwhelming fear.

"I didn't need his card. I knew the number by heart. He'd often ask me to make dining reservations for him, and on occasion to purchase gifts for clients. I bought the eTicket online, printed it off, and placed it in a sealed envelope on my desk before leaving the office early on the morning of his death."

"Fascinating." I tried to sound as if I was absorbed in her story to keep her talking. If Rip and Tiffany's expressions were anything to go by, I'd come off as condescending, rather than engrossed in her well-thought-out plot. Luckily, Scarlet didn't appear to notice.

"Trey was a creature of habit. He came to work at precisely ten-forty-five every morning, so I transferred all the office calls to my personal number and headed to the airport at ten-twenty. Naturally, he had yet to discover I'd sold off all of the investment stocks, and I didn't want to give him a chance to boot up his computer. So, at exactly ten-forty-six, I called and told him I was at the airport but had left my plane tickets on my desk. I explained I didn't have time to make the round-trip drive to the office and get back to the airport in time to catch my flight."

"And I'd imagine Trey immediately offered to bring you the tickets you'd 'forgotten'?" Using air quotes was probably unnecessary, but I did it anyway.

"Of course he did. I didn't need them, of course, as it was only part of my plan to get him to the airport. If he'd opened the envelope, he'd have seen the ticket inside was in his name and the gig would've been up. But I knew he'd never do that. He was such an honorable guy; I knew he'd see that as an invasion of my privacy. Naturally, the one-way ticket was only purchased to frame him, and the sealed envelope was to use as a means to get him to the airport parking garage."

"Naturally." I spoke civilly, even though I was irked by how much Scarlet seemed to be enjoying the telling of the murder. She clearly was convinced she'd gotten away with the crime. "Go on."

"Trey met me in the far corner of the long-term parking lot, which was dimly lit. I'd already made sure there were no security cameras in the area. As Trey began to exit his car, I stuck the syringe into his upper arm and injected a huge dose of the potassium chloride. I thought the prick mark would blend right in with all of the other injection sites where Manuel had given him his insulin shots. He died quickly. I was glad he didn't suffer."

"How very decent of you. I'm glad he didn't suffer, too." At least *my* words were sincere. "Did it concern you that your fingerprints might be found on the syringe?"

"Of course not! How many times do I have to tell you I'm

not as stupid as you think I am? I wore latex gloves. His finger-prints were on the syringe, but mine weren't. I put the used syringe in his hand after he died, thinking the authorities might believe the lethal injection was self-inflicted. I thought maybe they'd suspect he'd had a sudden change of heart, feeling remorseful for the pain and suffering his actions would undoubt-edly cause all of his clients. He could've killed himself rather than face the music for his crimes. If the authorities didn't suspect suicide, it would at least look like he was planning to catch a flight to Grand Cayman. The one-way ticket would indi-cate he wasn't planning on returning. Either way, I figured it'd work out perfectly. And it did!"

I almost threw up when Scarlet giggled gleefully at her own cleverness.

"Um," I began, "perfectly for you, maybe. Not so much for your thoughtful, kind boss, who went out of his way so you wouldn't miss the flight to your chosen vacation spot. Like they say, no good deed goes unpunished."

This remark hit Scarlet right in the gut like a balled-up fist. The expression on her face became one of pure evil. She lifted the Glock and pointed it at my forehead. "I warned you about making another smart remark."

I instinctively closed my eyes and then flinched as the loud rapport of a gun went off, nearly deafening me. I was amazed at how painless it was to be shot in the head from such close range. I'd barely felt a thing, other than a piercing pain in my left eardrum.

TWENTY-SEVEN

Scarlet couldn't possibly have missed her target from mere inches away, I thought. *I must already be in heaven.* I felt bad I wasn't able to alert the police for Rip and Tiffany's sake.

"Cuckoo!" Tiffany hollered the code word I'd given Detective Gutierrez to indicate immediate intervention was needed. Her exclamation echoed in my head for an incredibly long time, as though I was lingering in a state between life and death. I'd picked a fitting word for the woman holding us hostage. Cuckoo birds go south for the winter, and this confrontation had just gone the same direction. *I finally pushed my luck too far, and have paid the ultimate price*, I thought. *I should have listened to Rip and Detective Gutierrez and let the police handle the confrontation.* I couldn't believe I was able to persuade the detectives to put a wire on me and let me try and draw a confession out of her. Even dead, if Rip or Tiffany were injured, or worse, I'd never be able to forgive myself.

Mere seconds after the sound of gunfire, the front door crashed down to the tile floor and the Glock Scarlet had been holding landed beside it. She screamed and grasped her hand.

The ring finger on that hand appeared to have sprung a leak, as blood flowed from a wound just above the middle knuckle. It was then I realized it was Scarlet who'd been shot rather than me. If, and when I could hear again, I would have to thank Rip for his quick reaction time and dead-on accuracy. From a very awkward angle, he'd managed to shoot Scarlet's gun right out of her hand with his own.

"Albuquerque Police!" Five Special Weapons and Tactics officers shouted in unison as they rushed into the room, with Detective Gutierrez in their wake. All had their guns drawn and pointed at Scarlet.

"Don't shoot!" Rip hollered. "She's been unarmed and needs a medic."

For the second time in as many days, I heard a cop say, "Raise your hands over your head, ma'am." At least this time they were speaking to someone else.

Scarlet froze and the color leached from her face like a drain plug had been pulled. Clearly in shock, she raised her hands slowly and several drops of blood ran down her right arm and dripped off her elbow. It was apparent she was no longer a threat. Her arms were quickly brought down by one of the well-trained officers so her gunshot wound could be evaluated.

"Incredible shot, sir," the young SWAT member tending to Scarlet remarked to Rip. "It's just a flesh wound."

"Thanks. I've had a little experience with guns," Rip said. "I was in law enforcement my entire career."

"He's one of us," Carlos said. I saw Rip smile in reaction to being included in the "boys in blue" club. He deserved the distinction. He'd undoubtedly saved my life, as well as his and Tiffany's.

After her wound was cleaned and dressed, Scarlet was handcuffed. I felt overwhelming sorrow about the way she'd destroyed her entire future. I was also saddened that an innocent man had to die because of her lust for money. I felt a great deal of relief, too, of course. And, I'll admit, an equally overwhelming sense of self-satisfaction.

Scarlet appeared totally taken aback by the S.W.A.T. team storming the building. She looked directly at me now as she stammered, "How'd they…how did they…how the hell did—"

"How'd they know to come to our rescue?" I supplied the question for her, because I was getting tired of waiting for her to complete it herself. I stared directly into her wide-open eyes. "Guess what, Scarlet? I'm not as stupid as you thought I was, either."

The shaken woman was too stunned to respond. I pulled back my shirt enough to expose the wire Carlos had fitted me with before the three of us had driven down the street into her view. I'd called the detective after speaking with the woman I'd believed to be Harlei Rycoff on the phone earlier that evening and had run my suspicions about her by him. Not totally convinced, he agreed to meet us just up the street with the S.W.A.T. team. There he'd reluctantly fitted me with the wire and given us all instructions, which Rip would later accuse me of not following one iota. I'd thought I showed great restraint, considering how much anger was pent up inside me at the time.

The officers had been monitoring the conversation, and told Rip my last remarks concerned them to the point they felt they had to breach the house whether I used the code word or not. They already had all the confession they needed to arrest Scarlet and make it stick. Carlos might not have been convinced of her guilt before, but he certainly was now. He admitted to experiencing a huge sense of regret when he heard the gunshot, afraid they'd held off breaching the house for too long and one of us had been shot. I'm sure he questioned his wisdom at agreeing to my plan for me to try and get a confession out of her while they waited outside. He was probably also considering what career path he'd take next now that his one in law enforcement was undoubtedly about to come to an end for letting citizens get involved in a murder investigation.

After asking Tiffany, Rip, and me if we were all right, Rip suggested the officer who had tended to Scarlet's wound check out my ears. The right one was still aching, and I couldn't hear much of anything out of either one. The officer asked me a few questions and advised me to stop by the emergency room on our way home.

The lead homicide detective read Scarlet her Miranda Rights and prepared to walk her out of the house to his patrol car. I could clearly read Scarlet's lips as she glared at me and spat out, "I hope *you* go to hell."

To which I replied, "Wishful thinking on your part. You, however, are well on your way. You'll get a lot of time to think about where you're going to end up while you rot away in prison. Sorry, Scarlet, but it looks like there'll be no 'toes in the sand or margaritas in your hand,' the way you'd planned. For your own protection, you'd better keep your head up, rather than just your chin."

Knowing I was getting my licks in while there wasn't a gun threatening my life, Detective Gutierrez winked at me. As he and Scarlet brushed by, he whispered, "Great detective work, Rapella."

I felt my chest swell with pride. I just hoped Tiffany wouldn't suffer from post-traumatic stress disorder after our brush with death, or PTSD for those of you who like acronyms as much as Scarlet seems to. I hadn't anticipated the devious woman would be armed, mainly because it never occurred to me she'd caught on to my suspicions about her. My intention had never been to put Tiffany through a traumatic experience, but rather to see that her and Chase's money was returned. I didn't want the couple to have to give up their home or have a debt to us hanging over their heads. I breathed in a long, slow sigh of contentment. My mission had been accomplished.

During our visit to Duke City Urgent Care on Montgomery Boulevard, we were relieved to learn my right eardrum had not ruptured. I was told I could anticipate some ringing in my ears that would likely fade away in a few days.

Rip rolled his eyes when the perky young nurse suggested he move at least fifteen yards away from me the next time he fired a weapon in my presence. She shook a perfectly manicured fingertip at him. "You could have completely destroyed her hearing in that ear. Keep that in mind in the future, Mr. Ripple."

As dry as unbuttered toast, he replied, "Very well. Now could you remind your patient not to ever again put me in a position where I have to fire a weapon to keep her from getting shot between the eyes?"

The nurse's eyes widened. They shifted to me and then back to Rip. Rather than respond to Rip's question, she said, "Why don't you all relax while I go get Mrs. Ripple's discharge papers?"

When the nurse left the cubicle, I sheepishly looked at my husband. "Thank you, honey, for saving my life. And also for being able to do so without killing Scarlet. I'm beyond appalled at what she's done, but I wouldn't want the three of us to have *her* death on our consciences."

"I had no intention of killing her. I only wanted to gain the upper hand, by, well, shooting the one with which she was holding the Glock. Besides, I could tell the safety was still engaged on her gun. I knew it wouldn't accidentally go off if I shot her in the hand."

"I hadn't thought of that." A shiver went up my spine as I

thought about what could've happened had my husband not been such an astute lawman most of his life.

"But I also knew it'd only take her a second to flick it off and fire the gun, so my intent was to disarm her," Rip explained.

"Which you accomplished perfectly," I replied. "I'm just thankful you were there to protect Tiffany and me."

"I would give my life for either of you." Rip smiled warmly at each of us in turn. "Many years ago, I took an oath to protect and serve. I may be retired now, but I will always live by the Law Enforcement Oath of Honor."

"And over fifty years ago, you made a vow to stand by me until death do us part. I'll be forever grateful *that* oath is still in effect too." I leaned over and kissed Rip on the lips as he sat in a chair next to my hospital gurney.

Tiffany smiled at my show of affection. She then chuckled and said, "I'm just glad we're all still alive so you two can come back to Albuquerque next year for my thirty-first birthday. Chase still owes me a party."

We were all laughing when the nurse stepped back inside the curtained-off cubicle with my discharge instructions in her hand.

TWENTY-EIGHT

As it turned out, all of the investment money was recovered. The life insurance proceeds were recalled, as well. Tiffany and Chase were able to resume negotiations on the new home they desired in Sandia Heights and were talking about starting a family soon. The very idea of a great-grandchild filled my heart with joy.

The rest of the clients of Monroe Investments were pleased to have their funds returned, along with a healthy profit on the IPO they'd all invested in. But it was a bittersweet occasion. They were also hit with a wave of sadness as they realized they'd lost a good friend, a man who hadn't ripped them off after all. Trey Monroe had been the victim of a cold-hearted, calculating, and self-serving woman. As Scarlet told us the first day we met, the market was based on fear and greed. Unfortunately, she proved that to be true. Her actions had been greedy, but remarkably fearless.

The Clean Sweep IPO had undeniably *cleaned* up when it came to profits, which Scarlet had *swept* into her own personal account immediately after the six-month lock-out period ended.

Unfortunately, Trey's admirable foresight had cost him his life. He'd accurately foreseen the IPO performing admirably, but he was unable to foresee the evil that lurked within the heart of his employee.

After Scarlet was booked, Detective Gutierrez contacted the owners of Clean Sweep. The confirmations of both the purchase and sale transactions were the final nails in Scarlet's coffin.

Once Scarlet Craft's true identity became known, a background search indicated she'd previously been employed by a small investments firm in Flagstaff where she served as an RIA, which I now knew stood for Registered Investment Advisor. Scarlet was more of a habitual liar than I'd realized. She was actually thirty-eight, not thirty-one, and had given birth to two children with her ex-husband. Following her divorce from Thomas Craft, she'd pulled off a smaller-scale Ponzi scheme there, netting herself five-hundred thousand dollars.

Scarlet skipped town before she could be apprehended, abandoning her kids, who were now being raised by Thomas and his new wife. Two of the four children she'd attributed to the Pez Dispenser had been born to her. Thomas had been trying to locate Scarlet to collect on unpaid child support for a number of years, but had no idea Scarlet had settled in Albuquerque after assuming a new identity as Harlei Rycoff. She had miraculously managed to escape justice and responsibility for her own offspring.

That explained her remark to me about having successfully disappeared into thin air before. Being well-schooled in the financial industry, she landed the new job with Monroe Investments by pretending to have a valid U4, or Uniform Application for Securities Industry Registration or Transfer, a prerequisite for anyone in the financial services business. Trey made the fatal mistake of not performing a background check or verifying the existence of her U4, which, of course, she would never have been granted had she actually applied for one.

Unfortunately for Scarlet, half-a-million dollars didn't turn out to be the bottomless pit of money she'd anticipated, and greed overtook her once again. Only this time, thanks to me in no small part, justice *would* be served. Scarlet would stand trial in both Flagstaff and Albuquerque and ultimately spend the rest of her life in the Northwest New Mexico Correctional Center in Grants, New Mexico after being convicted of first-degree murder and other charges related to her financial crimes. Like I'd told the woman during our confrontation, she was lucky New Mexico no longer allowed capital punishment.

But for now, it was time for Rip and me to pull up stakes. When our RV site rent was up in three days' time, we'd be heading to Rockdale, Missouri to visit with our good friends Lexie Starr and Stone Van Patten. They were already awaiting the arrival of their first grandchild, as Lexie's daughter, Wendy, and Stone's nephew, Andy, had recently announced they were expecting. We'd attended their wedding just a few short months ago and couldn't be any more delighted for the young couple.

It seems Scarlet Craft's name fit her well. The woman was indeed crafty, but she hadn't counted on a woman like me to come into her life and wreak havoc on her plans. Rotting away in an eight-by-ten cell was not at all what she had planned for her future. But at least one of her wishes would be granted. She'd never again have any need for a snow shovel.

The End

NO BIG RIP

A RIPPLE EFFECT COZY MYSTERY, BOOK 7

"What the hell was that?"

"What was what?" My seventy-year-old husband, Clyde "Rip" Ripple asked. We were inside our thirty-foot travel trailer, eating lunch at a rest area outside St. Joseph, Missouri, on Highway 36. We'd just filled up with fuel and were mere minutes from our destination of the Alexandria Inn in Rockdale.

"I heard a weird noise, like the swoosh of someone making a three-pointer with a basketball. Only louder."

"It's probably just your imagination, Rapella. I didn't hear anything."

"Of course you didn't!" I was aggravated because I knew I'd heard something unusual outside. "Hear that? I just heard another sound."

"Nope. Still didn't hear anything. Eat your lunch. I'm sure it's nothing."

"It's not 'nothing', Rip. It's the sound of five-thousand bucks being flushed down a toilet. Why did we buy top-of-the-line hearing aids for you if you're never going to wear them?"

"I do wear them." *As seldom as possible*, Rip should've added.

His next comment almost got his turkey sandwich slapped out of his hand. "I wear them whenever we go some place I'll want to know what someone's saying."

"Thank you for that endearing sentiment. At least you're honest about not giving a rat's behind about anything I have to say."

"What are we behind on that you have to pay?" Rip asked with an ornery grin. I knew he was trying to lighten the mood with some levity by pretending he'd misheard my remark. I whacked him on the head with my paper plate anyway, which prompted him to apologize. "I'm sorry. My hearing aid remark didn't come out quite the way it sounded in my head before I said it."

"Just promise you'll wear them while we're visiting with Lexie and Stone so you can keep up with the conversation."

"Yes, dear." Rip saluted me and took another big bite of his sandwich. "You have my word."

"Yeah, right. Why do I not feel very confident about you *keeping* your word?"

We finished the sandwiches and gave our tubby tabby, Dolly, a few of her favorite tuna-flavored treats. After straightening up from lunch, we were ready to get back in our Chevy truck to make the short and final leg of our trip. When we stepped out of the RV, we were the only people left in the rest area. Or so we thought.

"Hey there, folks! Looks like you've got a flat!" A low-timbered voice exclaimed. Holding a buck knife in his right hand made it clear the owner of that voice, who had glazed, but strikingly blue, eyes was the cause of the ruined tire. It was also evident the dude was under the influence of some illegal substance.

"Get back inside the trailer!" Rip immediately ordered me to retreat back into the RV.

"Why?" I asked. "I want to——"

"Don't argue with me. Just do it!"

I hadn't heard my husband use that tone with me since I'd gotten arrested at a protest in Rockport a couple of years prior. I quickly backed up the stairs and closed the door behind me. I hurried to the window and peered through a gap in the blinds. I saw a battered old motorcycle leaned up against a fence post. What I saw next scared the bejesus out of me. I watched the apparent owner of the decrepit bike—the knife-wielding dark-haired man, with several missing teeth, about a hundred tattoos, and a wiry build—lunge at Rip with the weapon.

Blood began to spread on the left lower sleeve of Rip's shirt and within seconds Rip brandished his hand gun that he carried in a small holster on his waistband under his left arm. From his years of experience in law enforcement, he'd instinctively sensed a confrontation with the hooligan was imminent when he'd ordered me back inside the trailer. I saw Rip's lips move as he spoke to his attacker. I imagined he was saying something like, "Didn't your mama ever teach you not to take a knife to a gunfight?"

I'd just gotten my very own cell phone while we were visiting my granddaughter, Tiffany, and her husband, Chase Carpenter, in Albuquerque, New Mexico, and was prepared to use it to call 9-1-1. I cracked the glass pane open and asked Rip if I should call the police.

Before Rip could respond, the young man bolted like a gazelle fleeing a hungry lion. He was rolling the dice on not being shot in the back by my husband, who'd been a career lawman in our hometown of Rockport, Texas. Before he'd retired from law enforcement nine years ago, he'd served as sheriff of Aransas County for nearly a decade before calling it quits. We'd pulled up stakes at that time, sold nearly everything we owned, bought the travel trailer, and hit the road as full-time RVers. We'd been roaming the country and enjoying the wanderlust lifestyle ever since, never having an unpleasant incident on the road—until now!

"Are you all right? Do you need to have your forearm stitched up?"

"No," he replied. "It's not that bad. I jerked away just in time."

"Why didn't you stop him when he ran off?"

"The only way I was going to stop him was to shoot him, and I might've done so had I truly felt my life was in danger. I'm certainly not killing some desperate drug addict for slashing a tire and attempting to rob us."

"So that's what I heard earlier," I surmised. "Air coming out of the tire."

"Yeah. That's what you heard," Rip replied dryly. "The only other option was to run the guy down and hold him at gunpoint until the police arrived. With my new hip and recent cardiac surgery, I didn't think there was much chance of my catching a slender young man in his twenties who was probably high on meth."

There was absolutely no chance in hell of you catching him, I thought. *With, or without, the hip replacement and triple-bypass operations, it'd have been like Aesop's "Tortoise and the Hare" fable. Only this time, the rabbit would've left the poor turtle choking on the dust in its wake.*

"Well, I'm glad you didn't shoot him or try to run him down," I said. "But don't you think we should report the incident? It could've ended tragically had you not been carrying your gun. The little thug needs to be caught and taken off the streets. Reporting the crime's not a sign of weakness on your part, you know. We'll have to wait for the American Automobile Association serviceman to come change the tire, anyway."

"I can change it myself. Don't go calling AAA. We could be sitting here on our thumbs for two hours waiting on them."

"I highly doubt it. They get exceptional online reviews for quick arrivals and expert service."

Rip shook his head. He was your typical man: proud, hardheaded, and insanely oblivious to his age and physical condition. He might've just thwarted an armed robbery, but that didn't mean he wouldn't be heaving up his turkey sandwich after the exertion required to change a truck tire.

"I guess the AAA membership is kind of like your hearing aids then, isn't it?" I didn't like letting the punk who'd assaulted my husband get off scot-free, and I liked even less not taking advantage of a service we religiously paid for every September.

"How's that?"

"Necessary to have even if we've no intention of ever using it."

"Not in the mood to bicker, Rapella." Rip was irritable and aggressive, like a wounded dog. I couldn't say I blamed him.

"You're right. I'm sorry, honey. I'll call Lexie and Stone and tell them we'll be a little later than we'd anticipated while you change the tire."

"Good idea. We'll need to replace the spare while we're in Rockdale."

"Of course. I still think we should call Detective Johnston when we get there. A violent attack like that shouldn't go unreported." Wyatt Johnston, a close friend of Lexie and Stone's, and now a friend of ours as well, had served on the Rockdale Police Department for eighteen years. He'd know what to do.

"It's really no big rip."

"It might be no big rip to you," I began, "but it might be to the dude's next victim, who might not be as fortunate as you. His next mark might not be packing and end up robbed and injured, or worse."

"I guess you're right, dear." Rip consented. "I think I *will* give Wyatt a call and see if he'll stop by the inn while he's out on patrol."

"Thank you," I said. "Let me dress your wound before I help you tackle the tire."

"Well, all right." I was surprised Rip consented to letting me assist him. There was either a chink in his armor, or it hurt worse than he was letting on.

I retrieved the first aid kit from the storage compartment under our queen-sized bed, praying the terrifying incident that'd just occurred wasn't a sign of how our visit at Alexandria Inn was going to go. After the recent murder case we'd gotten involved in while visiting Tiffany and Chase in Albuquerque, I was ready for some rest and relaxation. But then, I was ready to win a million dollars in the lottery too, and that wasn't apt to happen any time soon, either.

Available in Paperback and eBook from Your Favorite Bookstore or Online Retailer

ABOUT THE AUTHOR

Jeanne Glidewell, lives with her husband, Bob, and chubby cat, Dolly, in Rockport, Texas, on Salt Lake, just off Copano Bay.

Jeanne and Bob owned and operated a large RV park in Cheyenne, Wyoming, for twelve years. It was that enjoyable period in her life that inspired Jeanne to write a mystery series involving a full-time RVing couple - The Ripple Effect series.

As a 2006 pancreas and kidney transplant recipient, Jeanne is an avid advocate for organ and tissue donation. Please consider the possibility of giving the gift of life by opting to be an organ donor should you no longer need them.

Jeanne is the author of a romance/suspense novel, Soul Survivor, seven novels and one novella in her NY Times best-selling Lexie Starr cozy mystery series, and six novels in her Ripple Effect cozy mystery series. She's currently writing Ripple Effect book seven titled *No Big Rip* and expects to have it released late 2021 or early 2022.

www.JeanneGlidewell.com